D0851816

THE MASSACRE
OF THE INNOCENTS

IL CAVALIER MARINO D'ETA D'ANNI LVI.

Si tua vita, Marine, leues est lapsa per vmbras,
Clarior ex vmbris en tibi vita redit.

THE MASSACRE
OF THE INNOCENTS

GIAMBATTISTA MARINO

TRANSLATED BY ERIK BUTLER

WAKEFIELD PRESS

CAMBRIDGE, MASSACHUSETTS

Originally published posthumously as *La strage degli innocenti*, 1632
This translation © 2015 Wakefield Press

Wakefield Press, P.O. Box 425645,
Cambridge, MA 02142

Opening drawing: André Masson, *Massacre*, 1932/1933.
© 2015 Artists Rights Society (ARS), New York / ADAGP, Paris.

Frontispiece: engraving of Giambattista Marino by F. Valesio, after a work by
Simon Vouet.

This book was set in Garamond Premier Pro
and Helvetica Neue LT Pro by Wakefield Press.
Printed and bound in the United States of America.

ISBN: 978-1-939663-08-5
Available through D.A.P./Distributed Art Publishers
155 Sixth Avenue, 2nd Floor
New York, New York 10013
Tel: (212) 627-1999
Fax: (212) 627-9484

10 9 8 7 6 5 4 3 2 1

CONTENTS

THE GARDEN OF EARTHLY DELIGHTS
AND THE CULT OF THE MARTYRS

The works of Giambattista Marino (1569–1625) have been largely forgotten. Such a fate is especially cruel for a writer deemed "the king of his age" and "the poet of the marvelous" by literary historians.[1] Marino's rhetorical inventiveness, formal innovation, and bold imagery defined the style of an epoch.[2] In Italian, *marinismo* and *seicentismo* (literally, "1600-ism") are interchangeable; another synonym is *concettismo*. Whatever one calls it, his brand of artistry trades in surprises that start at the lexical level and extend from phrase to phrase until they command the work as a whole. Poems offer a profusion of detail otherwise associated with painting; varied and colorful elements combine ingeniously to flatter and confound the senses.

Marino made his name writing love poetry. His sonnets take the finely crafted paradoxes of lyric tradition and transform them into odes to pleasurable torment. The sensuous verses do not have the spiritual air that lends the works of, say, Petrarch an uplifting quality; a disquieting melancholy haunts the passionate pageantry. Times and canons change. For arbiters of taste, our author achieved notoriety with *Adonis* (1623), a hulking monument to baroque fancy the size of a small library. Under the vigorous strokes of Marino's pen, the doomed love between Venus and a beautiful youth yields more than 40,000 lines of sterile eroticism. (Ovid, in contrast, devoted just a third of one book of his *Metamorphoses* to the theme.) Jorge Luis Borges appreciated Marino like few other writers of the last century; even so, he pictured the poet on his deathbed "murmur[ing] inevitable verses which—to tell the truth—have begun to weary him."[3] Because they brim with turbulent vitality, Marino's words orbit the grave even when joyous.

Comparatively speaking, *The Massacre of the Innocents* strikes a delicate if gruesome balance between Marino's successes and excesses. It features the brevity and wit of the sonnets, while at the same time treating a grave subject suited to the epic form. Composed in the meter and rhyme of Ariosto and Tasso and hearkening in theme to Dante's *Inferno*, the poem tells of the villainous King Herod, whose desire for power perverts the most sacred bonds and proves his undoing. *The Massacre of the Innocents* boils to the point of overflowing, yet the author holds his verbal torrents in check. The result is a literary monstrance; though strange to unaccustomed eyes, no one can deny the exquisite workmanship. Perhaps the time has come for Marino's star to rise again; at any rate, the volume at hand offers much to intrigue twenty-first-century readers. *The Massacre of the Innocents* has long been a dead letter, buried deep in antiquarian vaults. Brought forth from darkness, it breathes and bleeds like the Word made suffering, mortal flesh.

I SCANDAL AND SENSATION

Our author's variegated oeuvre grew out of an eventful life. Marino was born in Naples to a family of respectable means and culture. Instead of following in his father's footsteps and pursuing a legal career, he became a poet and an adventurer. As a young man he was arrested at least twice before leaving his native city. On the first occasion, in 1598, he seems to have helped the daughter of a wealthy merchant procure an abortion. The woman died. The second time, two years later, he falsified documents to help a friend charged with murder. By showing that the accused had taken clerical orders, it was hoped he would escape prosecution. The ploy didn't work, and the friend was executed. Marino escaped jail by fleeing to Rome, where he lived from 1600 to 1605. Thanks to positions he obtained with Monsignor Melchiorre Crescenzi, to whom he dedicated his first volume of poetry, and then with Cardinal Pietro Aldobrandini, the nephew of Pope Clement VIII, he gained access to a wider audience. When Clement died, Aldobrandini was transferred to Ravenna, where Marino accompanied him. In 1608, the two friends went to Turin, and Marino found favor at the court of Duke Carlo Emanuele I.

By this time, Marino's first anthology, *Le Rime* (1602), had secured his reputation as a literary light. Just a year after arriving in Turin, our hero was inducted into the Order of Saints Maurice and Lazarus. But because he owed the distinction both to his verse and to his mastery of the courtly arts of blandishment and insult, he faced some trouble. Other men of letters were jealous of the upstart—especially Gaspare Murtola, the duke's secretary. Murtola and Marino had exchanged barbs from the beginning, but when the latter was decorated as a knight, his rival decided on another expedient and tried to shoot him down in the street. Marino emerged unscathed, but a companion was wounded, and the provocative poet wound up behind bars yet again. Fortunately, Carlo Emanuele's indignation subsided quickly. After a brief trip to Ravenna with Aldobrandini, Marino returned to Turin and entered the duke's service—where he took Murtola's place.

The further course of the poet's career in Turin was not entirely smooth, either. Murtola and others had created a cloud of infamy surrounding Marino's person and works. As James V. Mirollo puts it, the poet was "variously described as a heretic, hermaphrodite, sodomist, and pornographer"; possessed of "little learning," Marino was said to have "stolen his best poems from others."[4] The Inquisition saw fit to investigate alleged vices and improprieties, and Marino had difficulty publishing his works. In 1611–1612, he was incarcerated once more—this time for fourteen months. It seems enemies had convinced Carlo Emanuele that a scabrous poem written years earlier, in Naples, was in fact directed at him. Marino is also said to have authored a satire about a hunchback, *La Gobbeide*, mocking the slightly malformed duke. Alternately, he is reported to have landed in jail as the result of another messy situation with a woman.

Whatever happened, Marino prevailed. In 1614, he published two major works: a collection of poems called *The Lyre* and *Sacred Discourses*, which he presented as an "unexpected and fantastic" treatise on theology and the arts.[5] Marino spent the next eight years in Paris at the invitation of Maria de' Medici, the Italian-born Queen and Regent of France. When he first crossed the Alps, Marino may not have anticipated a lengthy stay, but royal patronage proved irresistible. If our poet was a voluptuary of language, he certainly appreciated the pleasures on offer at Europe's leading court.

Real information about his years in France is scant. Autobiographical references in the correspondence are so thoroughly stylized—above all, Marino seeks to recount the amusing misadventures of an innocent abroad—that they shed no real light on actual events. Still, life and letters did not constitute separate spheres for this artist of illusion. His likeness emerges, at least in silhouette, through his works. Here and in Italy, Marino advanced socially by hymning parties who wielded power and influence. *The Temple*, for example, is dedicated to Leonora Galigai, one of the queen's ladies-in-waiting and the wife of Concino Concini, the prominent Marshal d'Ancre; it goes so far as to present the courtiers as demigods worthy of worship. As the architect of this cathedral of words, Marino had built a shrine to himself, too. The many points where life and art intersected constitute what Stephen Greenblatt, in a related context, has aptly denominated "Renaissance self-fashioning." Marino's oeuvre may be read both for internal theme and design and as a series of gestures performed to establish and confirm alliances.

Attention to matters of style could prove imperative for survival, for the early modern court was a perilous place. In 1617, fortune turned against Marino's high-ranking patrons when King Louis, still a boy, sided with French nobles who revolted against the queen and her Italian advisers. Concini was killed by the royal guard, and the Parisian mob tore his body limb from limb. His physically and mentally infirm wife was tried and beheaded for practicing witchcraft. Maria de' Medici, in turn, disappeared into exile at Blois. Marino might have had reason for apprehension, but the outsider status he cultivated benefited him. What is more, he still stood in the service of Carlo Emanuele (at least nominally), and maintaining smooth relations with the Duchy of Savoy was important for France. Finally, Marino had admirers from Rome to Paris. Since he could reasonably be considered merely an eccentric man of letters, he survived the upheaval. Had our hero found himself in the wrong crowd in his native land, he might not have fared so well. In France, the brilliant foreigner could shine without dimming the light of rival poets.

All the same, being dependent on the goodwill of others is never easy—and certainly not for an ambitious individual. Marino wanted his works to appear in suitably grandiose editions, especially *Adonis*. His declining health and homesickness complicated matters. The poet now had an enormous body of writings that just needed finishing touches and favorable circumstances to reach a broader audience, and so he busied himself with completing them all. In 1619, he published *The Gallery*, some six hundred madrigals and sonnets devoted to the visual and plastic arts. The following year, *La Sampogna* appeared. This anthology—whose title loses some of its charm in translation (*The Bagpipe*)—features some of Marino's best poetry. Around the same time, *Adonis* began to go to press, too. Unfortunately, the lavish illustrations the author had foreseen were not included.

In 1623, Marino returned to Italy in triumph, hailed for his poetic genius. But if accolades and honors elevated his spirits, the demands they entailed burdened an ailing man. The poet first stopped in Turin for a month, where he received decorations and gifts from Carlo Emanuele and his family (whom, needless to say, he had honored in his works). Then he set out for Rome. In theory, he might still have had to face charges presented to the Inquisition years earlier. Nothing of the kind occurred, and Pope Gregory XV greeted his arrival. Marino had never stood in higher esteem; he came into possession of a new title when the Accademia degli Umoristi appointed him its chief officer, or "Prince." Alas, he could not rest on his laurels; the new position required pronouncing discourses, representing the society in public, and organizing its internal affairs. And so, the following year, Marino abruptly left for his native city, where the academies competed to bestow comparable honors. Marino was declared chief officer of another guild of poets, the Oziosi, and was again exposed to the rigors of service to the world of letters. He contemplated escaping back to Rome—or perhaps even to France—but his health collapsed at the end of the year. On March 26, 1625, "the only *gran poeta*"[6] of the age died.

II PIETY AND POLITICS

The Massacre of the Innocents went unpublished in Marino's lifetime, but not because it counted as a lesser effort. As early as 1605, the author anticipated that it would soon appear in print. For whatever reason, this did not occur. Marino took up his verse and polished it time and again over the next two decades. Because he pursued many projects while attending to the exacting demands of courtly sociability, it seems he simply did not have the time, or a fitting occasion, to publish the poem. When the author went back to Rome near the end of his life, he read a canto to admirers at a banquet and even considered dedicating the finished work to Urban VIII (who became pope when his predecessor died shortly after Marino's arrival).

In conception and execution, *The Massacre of the Innocents* exemplifies the religious culture of the Counter-Reformation. In the sixteenth century, Protestantism had sought to renew the Christianity of old. Luther and other reformers rejected papal authority, discarded medieval ceremonies, and stressed private faith over public works. Rome responded by returning to basics in its own, rather different way. Paul III authorized the Society of Jesus (Jesuits), whose votaries were to serve as soldiers of God and propagate true religion. The same pope set up the Roman Inquisition and convened the Council of Trent to fortify articles of faith and ritual practices inherited from the Middle Ages. Marino, who owed his first sure steps to patrons in the Church, in fact hewed to orthodoxy—if in an unconventional manner.

Marino's strangely reverent poem unfolds within a stark and simple framework. At the bottom of the pit dwells Satan. As for Dante, the Adversary embodies both impotence and sovereignty. On the one hand, Satan is banished and bound for eternity and can do nothing directly. On the other hand—as the utmost symbol of wickedness and, as it were, its principle of gravity—Satan acts on wayward mortals by exploiting their inherent sinfulness and pulling them toward perdition. In *The Massacre of the Innocents*, the enemy of God and humankind sends deceptive images up to the Earth's surface with the help of malignant spirits. Preying on Herod's weaknesses, he encourages the king to indulge the bloody urges he already nourishes. This negative pole in the cosmic architecture is counterbalanced by the power that resides in the Heavens. Divine messengers descend to warn the Holy Family and guide them in their journey to safety before Herod's diabolical plan engulfs them.

Marino's poem translates the design of the eternal world into narrative form, alternating between scenes of cruelty and clemency. However much terrestrial affairs may be prone to the tumults of evil, a stable order is affirmed. *The Massacre of the Innocents* makes the fixed structure of the universe into a succession of temporal events buckled in eternity and ultimately commanded by God's unfathomable will. Hell, Earth, and Paradise correspond to the classical Aristotelian progression of beginning, middle, and end. Therefore, even though the tale is harrowing, it possesses harmony in terms of theology and poetic organization. To underscore the symmetry, *The Massacre of the Innocents* concludes with a song sung by King David as he contemplates the souls of the murdered children borne aloft. Tragedy yields to an edifying vision as horror on Earth is transfigured into a dance in the skies. In a whirling procession of faith reborn, the soaring sprits of the Innocent bear a standard—marching, as it were, in a Children's Crusade to reclaim the Holy Land on a higher plane.

The conception of kingship in *The Massacre of the Innocents* squares with the cosmic order underlying the poem. The head of state governs the body of subjects. Should he be of sound judgment, everyone prospers; if he does not fare well, malady befalls the people as a whole. For this reason, Herod's unwise policy amounts to homicide and suicide in equal measure. The campaign the ruler orchestrates proves disastrous because his servants execute his commands only too fully. Herod's own son dies in the slaughter. Even as he wishes for his own death, the king rants and raves that he would like nothing more than to kill again and again. Herod's dominion falls apart in tandem with his loss of self-control.[7]

At the same time, Marino gives a nod toward the political thinking of the Renaissance, which formulated age-old problems in new terms. Before the massacre begins, two counselors offer opposing views on the proper course of action. First, a bearded sage urges the hotheaded monarch not to yield to passion. There is no real threat, he argues, for prophecy holds that the child now born will not seek worldly power; he comes only to uplift his people's souls. The elder offers practical considerations, too. Wanton bloodshed can only jeopardize Herod's image—and therefore his authority. The sound advice is followed by the counter-discourse pronounced by an unctuous and smooth-tongued creature of the court. This plotter seeks only his own gain: it matters little to him whether his advice will really benefit the king he is supposed to serve. The second advisor tells Herod that his reign stands secure only for so long as he capitalizes on royal privilege. The Machiavellian advice is music to Herod's ears—a further instigation to yield to his incipient satanic impulses.

The Massacre of the Innocents does not critique institutions as they stand, and everything that Herod does before getting his comeuppance affirms the power invested in him. The problem, in Marino's eyes, is that the ruler abuses his authority.[8] For all the blood he spills, Herod is weak and a slave to his passions. However counterintuitive it may seem at first, defenseless women and children are stronger than the tyrant—and more courageous than any of his henchmen. *The Massacre of the Innocents* valorizes noble suffering. Submission and forbearance trump all else, including the might of kings. Ingeniously, Marino renews the logic of martyrdom that fed Christianity in its earliest and most heroic days. The series of mothers and sons calls to mind the holy image of the *pietà*, Mary cradling Jesus. Events become a symbol of Christ's resurrection: death itself is defeated and transformed into the promise of life everlasting.

In Marino's day, Herod and his victims provided a favorite theme for the pictorial arts, and the dramaturgy of *The Massacre of the Innocents* follows this lead. The author of the *Gallery* expresses the wish that his poem may compare, however crudely, to the works of his contemporary Giuseppe Cesari, *Il Cavaliere d'Arpino*.[9] At the same time, Marino adds a dynamic element that is denied to the static arts of statuary and painting. To underscore Herod's fall into ruin and offer a final, emphatic image, *The Massacre of the Innocents* culminates in the king's wife committing suicide before his very eyes. Yet another *mater dolorosa* joins her child in eternity. It is as if Herod stood witness to his own execution. With the extinction of his line, his life and rule are over.

Everything in Marino's poem is crafted to illustrate the wages of sin and instill the teachings of the Church. The more Herod rages, the brighter the glory of divine judgment shines forth. The truth of Scripture was absolute for Marino and his contemporaries. *The Massacre of the Innocents* deviates from the norm only to circle back and affirm it. An immutable law commands the universe, and Herod's waywardness proves the rule. The tyrant's story offers both a lesson in history and a cautionary tale for later generations, whatever their station may be.

III   RANSOM AND REDEMPTION

Because Marino and his works so fully embodied the virtues and vices of his age, he is now practically unknown outside Italy (where he is still more often read about than read). For the same reason, he deserves to be rediscovered. Literary sensibilities change, but the human condition need not. At any rate, past ills illuminate present afflictions. What could ever be timelier than misrule, violence, death of the blameless, and hope for justice (whether in this world or the next)?

The Massacre of the Innocents depicts evil in order to affirm the good. In this, Marino's poem may be likened to the works of Charles Baudelaire (1821–1867), who wrote over two hundred years later. Baudelaire was another unconventional Catholic committed to provoking scandal and outrage to affirm the faith. And although his literary reputation stands firm today, he met with even worse incomprehension and hostility than Marino. It is easy to see only the debauchery and wickedness portrayed in *Les Fleurs du Mal* and to overlook the pious message conveyed by circuitous means. The same holds for *The Massacre of the Innocents*.

Marino's contemporaries were surely not wrong to think he took joy in describing obscenity and cruelty. His poem, a concatenation of tortured and dying bodies, glows with what Roland Barthes—an expert at teasing out subliminal aspects of literature—called the "pleasure of the text." But even guilty pleasures may be joined to lofty purposes. Marino presents sanguinary human passions as offerings to an inscrutable deity. Even the greediest and most self-absorbed impulses pay interest on what the Bible calls the "ransom for many."[10] If God the Father sacrificed himself as God the Son, then the lives of mortals, however spent, are never wasted.

In this light, Marino's perspective is fittingly expressed by the words of Joseph de Maistre (1752–1821)—the arch-reactionary defender of Church and Crown, whom Baudelaire lauded as a spiritual master. Writing against the revolutionary zeal of his own times with the unsparing logic of the Counter-Reformation to which he was heir, Maistre averred:

> From the maggot up to man, the … law of the violent destruction of living things is unceasingly fulfilled. The entire Earth, perpetually steeped in blood, is nothing but an immense altar on which every living thing must be immolated without end, without restraint, without respite, until the consummation of the world, until the extinction of evil, until the death of death.[11]

Maistre sees chaos and strife, yet he discerns a hidden order. Subtle gradations of competing power mean that the general principle of mutual antagonism does not unfold on a level plane; instead, these battles extend to a point in the Heavens from which they are controlled. "An occult and terrible law demanding human blood"[12] represents the summit where crimson tides crystallize into sublime vaults. Here dwells God Himself.

All mortal suffering repeats a drama wherein the Author of the World deigned to join Creation in the flesh. If humankind, in its corruption, ever sought to destroy the Giver of Life, it is only right that collective atonement be made. Inasmuch as they transcend passions that are earthly and base by celebrating the cleansing "blood of the Lamb," the brutality and wantonness on display in *The Massacre of the Innocents* should be hailed with universal joy.

*   *   *

No authoritative edition of *La strage degli innocenti* exists. The text established by Giovanni Pozzi (Turin: Einuadi, 1960) has served as a point of reference, although I opt for variants on occasion. My thanks to Marc Lowenthal and Judy Feldmann at Wakefield Press, as well as Patricia Gaborik, Gabriele Pedullà, and Bernardo Piciché in Rome. As always, the project would never have been poissible without the support of my family and, most importantly, the encouragement (and patience!) of Kimberly Jannarone. This translation is dedicated to our Herodian cats.

Erik Butler

NOTES

1. The first assessment is that of Francesco de Sanctis, quoted in James V. Mirollo, *The Poet of the Marvelous: Giambattista Marino* (New York: Columbia University Press, 1963), 106.

2. For a discussion of Marino's influence in Italy and across Europe, see Mirollo, *The Poet of the Marvelous*, 209–268.

3. Jorge Luis Borges, *A Personal Anthology*, trans. Anthony Kerrigan (New York: Grove, 1967), 83.

4. Mirollo, *The Poet of the Marvelous*, 25–26.

5. Ibid., 30.

6. Ibid., 89.

7. The ancient authority on Herod's rule is Flavius Josephus (37– ca. 100 CE), a Jewish enemy of Rome who switched sides and wrote an account of his people's revolt (*The Jewish War*), as well as a work on Jewish history and customs (*Jewish Antiquities*). Marino takes names and events from this source, but with little care for fitting his poem to what his predecessor recorded. Josephus does not depict Herod in a favorable light, yet he also does not present him as the monster one sees on the pages of *The Massacre of the Innocents*.

8. The inclusion of a servant named "Albina" in the unfolding of the king's fate seems to be an appreciative gesture made to the House of Alba—the family of Marino's protector, Antonio Álvarez de Toledo y Beaumont, the fifth Duke of Alba and Viceroy of Naples. Cf. the laudatory verses at the beginning of the poem (I, 2).

9. Cf. III, 1–2, 59.

10. Mark 10:45 KJV.

11. Joseph de Maistre, *Saint Petersburg Dialogues, or, Conversations on the Temporal Government of Providence*, trans. Richard A. Lebrun (Kingston: McGill-Queen's University Press, 1993), 216.

12. Ibid., 211.

LA STRAGE
DEGLI INNOCENTI

THE MASSACRE
OF THE INNOCENTS

LIBRO PRIMO

L'iniquo re de le tartaree grotte
Prevedendo 'l suo mal, s'affligge e rode;
Quindi esce fuor da la perpetua notte
Furia crudele a insospettir Erode.
Egli, che nel suo cor stima interrotte
Le quieti al regnar, di ciò non gode,
Ma per opporsi a la crudel fortuna
I satrapi a consiglio alfin raduna.

BOOK ONE

In the caverns of Tartarus, the unjust king
Beholds his ills, grieves, and gnashes his teeth:
A cruel Fury, from dark night emerging,
Appears before Herod to trouble his sleep.
Afraid, in his heart, of the calm realm dispersing,
It torments him that his rule will not keep.
Setting himself against fortune and fate,
He calls his satraps to discuss matters of state.

1   Musa non più d'amor: cantiam lo sdegno
    Del crudo re, che mille infanti afflitti
    (Ahi, che non pote avidità di regno?)
    Fe' del materno sen cader trafitti,
    E voi, reggete voi l'infermo ingegno,
    Nunzii di Cristo et testimonii invitti,
    Che deste fuor de le squarciate gole
    Sangue invece di voce e di parole.

2   Antonio, e tu del grand' Ibero onore,
    Germoglio altier d'imperadori e regi,
    Chi non s'abbaglia al tuo sovran splendore,
    S'al Sole istesso l'Alba tua pareggi?
    O de' più grandi eroi specchio e valore,
    Che d'invitta virtù ti glori e pregi,
    Non dispreggiar, di sacre rime ordito,
    Questo picciol d'onor serto fiorito.

3   Né fregiar di tai fior sì degna fronte
    La mia musa divota arrossir deve,
    Di que' fior che nutrisce il chiaro fonte,
    In cui d'acqua vital vena si beve;
    Fior di cui mai non spoglia il sacro monte
    O di Sirio o di Borea arsura o neve;
    Da cui suggendo alte dolcezze ascose,
    Formano eterno mele api ingegnose.

4   Tu che con tanto pregio e gloria tanta
    Di Partenope bella il fren reggesti;
    Ch'Atene o Roma eroe di te non vanta
    Più degno, onde memoria al mondo resti,
    Sì che lieta, non pur celebra e canta
    La mia Sirena i tuoi famosi gesti,
    Ma di tutto il Tirren l'onda sonora
    Il tuo nome immortal mormora ancora.

1   Muse, let us sing not of love, but outrages:
    The bloodthirsty king (such greed for power!),
    Affliction that struck thousands blameless
    At their mothers' breast one unholy hour.
    Angels of Christ, who witness the ages,
    Relish my words, though the taste be sour.
    From gaping wounds, guide my voice along;
    Bring forth blood and banish sweet song.

2   Antonio, great glory of Spain,
    Proud scion of king and emp'ror,
    Who is not blinded by your might? It is plain,
    It outshines the Sun in its splendor.
    Image of valor; without strain,
    You glory in strength and in grandeur.
    I beg: do not scorn this flowery wreath,
    A holy tribute, the words I bequeath.

3   Nor should my muse blush at the ornament
    Adorning her temples that glow,
    Like a flower from pools, it draws nutriment
    From the well where vivid life grows.
    Flower of the Mount without detriment
    From Sirius, the North Wind, or snow.
    Shunning fields elsewhere, here the bee in flight
    Makes sweet honey, an eternal delight.

4   You, to such glory, renown, and praise,
    Direct the course of Parthenope;
    Neither Athens nor Rome can boast greater days
    Than your deeds record in our mem'ry;
    My siren alone does not hymn your ways,
    You, who are worthy of all men's envy:
    On Tyrrhenian Sea, and beyond its portal,
    Your fame and your name echo immortal.

5 Sotto gli abissi, in mezzo al cor del mondo,
  Nel punto universal de l'universo,
  Dentro la bolgia del più cupo fondo
  Stassi l'antico spirito perverso;
  Con mordaci ritorte un groppo immondo
  Lo stringe di cento aspidi a traverso;
  Di tai legami in sempiterno il cinse
  Il gran campion che'n Paradiso il vinse.

6 Giudice di tormento e re di pianto,
  D'inestinguibil foco ha trono e vesta;
  Vesta, già ricco e luminoso manto,
  Or di fiamme e di tenebre contesta.
  Porta (e sol questo è del suo regno il vanto)
  Di sette corna alta corona in testa;
  Fan d'ogn' intorno al suo diadema regio
  Idre verdi e ceraste orribil fregio.

7 Ne gli occhi, ove mestizia alberga e morte,
  Luce fiammeggia torbida e vermiglia.
  Gli sguardi obliqui e le pupille torte
  Sembran comete, e lampadi le ciglia;
  E da le nari e da le labra smorte
  Caligine e fetor vomita e figlia;
  Iracondi, superbi e disperati
  Tuoni i gemiti son, folgori i fiati.

8 Con la vista pestifera e sanguigna,
  Con l'alito crudel, ch'avampa e fuma,
  La pira accende orribile e maligna,
  Che 'nconsumabilmente altrui consuma.
  Con amaro stridor batte e digrigna
  I denti aspri di rugine e di schiuma;
  E de' membri d'acciaio entro le fiamme
  Fa con l'estremo suo sonar le squamme.

5   At the heart of the world, beneath the abyss,
There at the core of the universe,
Within the bowels of the darkest pit,
Sits and stews the spirit perverse,
Captured and held by a hundred asps,
A foul coil that hisses and slithers.
With such chains forever has bound him
The champion whose might did confound him.

6   The judge of agony, gloomy king of torment,
Has undying fire for throne and gown.
The luxuriant garb once was bright raiment,
Before, to dark flames, he was cast down.
His head bears (the sole honor he can claim)
On its top a seven-pointed crown;
Circling his temples sits the royal diadem:
Green and horrible snakes that strike at him.

7   In his eyes, black death and deep sorrow;
Flickers and flashes of uncertain light;
With slanting gazes, his pupils borrow
The likeness of comets in flight;
Nose and lips heave vomit he cannot swallow,
A foul, stinking gust that blights life.
Wrathful and despairing, his bellows ring loud,
Thundering blasts of the cursèd and proud.

8   Creeping plague scars his face cruel and dire,
Exhaling gory breaths, he blows foul smoke—
Rising from the terrible, wicked pyre
Where souls are devoured and choked.
With bitter screeches he beats and gnashes in ire;
Teeth, sharp with rust, grate and croak;
Rattling iron limbs in the flame,
He twitches the scales of his tail in shame.

9 Tre rigorose vergini vicine
  Sono assistenti a l'infernal tiranno,
  E con sferze di vipre e di spine
  Intente sempre a stimularlo stanno,
  Crespi han di serpi inanellato il crine,
  Ch'orrida intorno al volta ombra lor fanno;
  Scettro ei sostien di ferro, e mentra regna,
  Il suo regno e se stesso aborre e sdegna.

10 Misero, e come il tuo splendor primiero
  Perdesti, o già di luce Angel più bello?
  Eterno avrai dal punitor severo
  A l'ingiusto fallir giusto flagello.
  De' fregi tuoi vagheggiatore altero,
  De l'altrui seggio usurpator rubello,
  Trasformato e caduto in Flegetonte,
  Orgoglioso Narciso, empio Fetonte.

11 Questi da l'ombre morte a l'aria viva,
  Invido pur di nostro stato umano,
  Le luci, onde per dritto in giù s'apriva
  Cavernoso spiraglio, alzò lontano,
  E proprio là ne la famosa riva
  Ove i cristalli suoi rompe il Giordano,
  Cose vide e comprese, onde nel petto,
  Rinovando dolor, crebbe sospetto.

12 Membra l'alta cagion de' gran conflitti,
  Esca, ch'accese in ciel tante faville.
  Volge fra sè gli oracoli e gli editti,
  E di sacri indovini e di Sibille.
  Osserva poi, vaticinati e scritti,
  Mille prodigi inusitati e mille;
  E mentre pensa e teme e si ricorda,
  L'andate cose a le presenti accorda.

9   Three pitiless maidens attend the tyrant.
    These minions of the infernal house
    Ply lashes of vipers; and with torrents
    Of horror, they goad and they rouse.
    On their heads appear scaly serpents,
    Which do their work twisting and writhing about.
    A scepter of iron the king bears. In self-hate
    He ever wallows, for all time stuck in his state.

10   Wretched one, how was your splendor lost,
    Who once were fairest Angel of Light?
    A stern master decreed the great cost:
    Just penance—the crime was not slight.
    Seeking the throne of the one you crossed,
    Against Heaven above you took flight,
    But soon you changed and fell into Phlegethon:
    Like Narcissus, you drowned—perverse Phaethon.

11   Up from the shadows, to the living air,
    Envying the lot even of mankind,
    He lifted his orbs to a fissure where
    The famous river bends and winds.
    Where the Jordan dashes its streams, there
    On the banks, he discerns fateful signs
    And sees what tears him apart.
    Wounded afresh, he eats out his heart.

12   Recalling high matters and battles
    That lighted so many flames in the sky,
    His mind revolves edicts and oracles:
    The old pronouncements did not lie.
    The Sibyl spoke words true, not idle,
    A thousand prodigies already draw nigh.
    Fearfully he reflects on what has been done,
    Weighs past matters against the present one.

13   Vede da Dio mandato in Galilea
Nunzio celeste a verginella umile,
Che la 'nchina e saluta, e come a dea
Le reca i gigli de l'eterno Aprile.
Vede nel ventre de la vecchia Ebrea,
Feconda in sua sterilità senile,
Adorar palpitando il gran concetto,
Prima santo che nato, un pargoletto.

14   Vede d'Atlante i ghiacci adamantini
Sciorsi in rivi di nettare e d'argento,
E verdeggiar di Scizia i gioghi alpini
E i diserti di Libia in un momento.
Vede l'elci e le querce e gli orni e i pini
Sudar di mele, e stillar manna il vento,
Fiorir d'Engaddo a mezzo verno i dumi,
Correr balzamo i fonti e latte i fiumi.

15   Vede de la felice e santa notte
Le tacit' ombre e i tenebrosi orrori
Da le voci del Ciel percosse e rotte,
E vinti da gli angelici splendori.
Vede per selve e per selvagge grotte
Correr bifolci poi, correr pastori,
Portando lieti al gran Messia venuto
De' rozzi doni il semplice tributo.

16   Vede aprir l'uscio a triplicato sole
La reggia oriental, che si disserra;
Scardinata cader vede la mole
Sacra a la bella dea ch'odia la guerra,
Gl'idoli e i simulacri, ove si cole
Sua deità, precipitati a terra,
E la terra tremarne, e scoppiar quanti
V'ha d'illecito amor nefandi amanti.

13   He beholds the celestial messenger sent
By God to Galilee, who bows before
A virgin; the angel's knee is bent,
Offering life that will last forevermore.
He sees the womb of the old Jewess spent,
Holding barrenness for fertile store;
To his horror, he does not err in perception:
A child has been born by God's conception.

14   The glaciers' crystalline perfection
Turns to rivers of silver and nectar;
Scythia's mountains change complexion,
Libyan sands yield fruitful acres;
Oaks and pines drip honeyed affection;
The wind gives manna—bread with no baker;
The springs run with balsam upon green hills,
And rivers with milk soon overfill.

15   In the blessèd night, he sees how shades
And dark horrors are struck down by voices
From the harps the angelic host plays.
Hell lies in ruins; the choir rejoices.
Peasants run and shepherds make their way,
Amidst the bright and joyous noises,
Gaily bearing, to the Messiah who has come,
The gifts their simple labors have won.

16   He beholds the glow on the eastern horizon:
A threefold Sun shines over the land.
The temple of the peaceful goddess, undone,
Crumbles, unable to stand.
The time of idols and effigies has run
Its course; they fall and lie in the sand.
He sees their impious couplings there on the ground,
Signs of ancient perversion scattered all 'round.

17   Vede dal Ciel con peregrino raggio
        Spiccarsi ancor miracolosa stella,
        Che verso Betthelem dritto il viaggio
        Segnando va folgoreggiante e bella;
        E quasi precursor divin messaggio,
        Fidata scorta e luminosa ancella,
        Tragge di là da gli odorati Eoi
        L'inclito stuol de' tre presaghi eroi.

18   Ai nuovi mostri, ai non pensati mali
        L'Aversario del ben gli occhi converte,
        Né, men ch'a morte, a se stesso mortali
        Già le piaghe antivede espresse e certe.
        Scotesi, e per volar dibatte l'ali,
        Che 'n guisa ha pur di due gran vele aperte,
        Ma'l duro fren che l'incatena e fascia
        Da l'eterna prigion partir no 'l lascia.

19   Poiché da' bassi effetti egli raccolse
        L'alto tenor de le cagion superne,
        Tinte di sangue e di venen, travolse,
        Quasi bragia infernal, l'empie lucerne.
        S'ascose il viso entro le branche, e sciolse
        Ruggito che 'ntronò l'atre caverne,
        E de la coda, onde se stesso attorse,
        La cima per furor tutta si morse.

20   Così freme fra sé. Ma d'altra parte
        Stassi intra due, non ben ancor sicuro.
        Studia il gran libro, e de l'antiche carte
        Interpretar s'ingegna il senso oscuro:
        Sa, né sa però come o con qual arte,
        L'alto natal del gran parto futuro,
        D'ogni vil macchia inviolato e bianco,
        Dever uscir di verginello fianco.

17   He views, in the Heavens, a wondrous star
Emerge and project wand'ring light.
To Bethlehem it guides pilgrims from afar,
Pointing the way fair and bright,
It foretells the arrival of a messenger,
The faithful escort of the angel tonight.
It draws in its wake, from sweet-smelling lands,
Three far-sighted kings, whose glory is grand.

18   Among the new marvels, unimagined ill:
The Adversary of Good lifts his eyes
And foresees—fatal as Death to his will—
The blows by which he, too, can die.
Unfolding his wings, he shakes and he thrills;
Like sails extending, they cover the sky.
But the iron chains that secure his jail
Hold him fast, and so his efforts must fail.

19   Since he has learned, from effects down below,
The high reasons in the supernal hall,
Shot through with venom, he throws
His hateful gaze upon every wall.
He buries his face, pulls in his claws,
And fills the dark caverns with bellowing calls.
In impotent rage, he gnaws and he bites,
Chewing his tail's coiled end in his spite.

20   He trembles within, but all the same,
He can do nothing, stuck in confusion.
He consults the great book, hopes it will explain
An event that admits no conclusion.
Soon he learns that he toils in vain:
The miraculous birth is no illusion,
Untouched by mankind's defilement and guilt,
Maiden womb brings life, and no blood is spilt.

21   Onde creder non vuol del gran mistero
      La meraviglia ai chiari ingegni ascosa:
      Come possa il suo fiore avere intero,
      Sì che vergine sia, donna ch'è sposa.
      E poi, che'l vero Dio divenga uom vero,
      Strana gli sembra e non possibil cosa;
      Che lo spirto s'incarni, e che vestita
      Gir di spoglia mortal deggia la vita;

22   Che l'incompreso ed invisibil lume
      Si riveli a pastor mentre che nasce;
      Che l'infinito onnipotente Nume
      Fatto sia prigionier di poche fasce;
      Che latte bea con pueril costume
      Chi di celeste nettare si pasce;
      Che 'n roza stalla, in vil capanna assiso
      Stia chi trono ha di stelle in Paradiso;

23   Che 'l sommo Sol s'offuschi in picciol velo,
      E che 'l Verbo divin balbo vagisca;
      Che del foco il Fattor tremi di gelo,
      E che 'l riso de gli Angeli languisca;
      Che serva sia la Maestà del Cielo,
      E che l'Immensità s'impicciolisca;
      Che la Gloria a soffrir venga gli affanni,
      E che l'Eternità soggiaccia a gli anni.

24   E oltre poi, ch'umiliato e fatto
      Al taglio ubidiente, ancor se stesso
      Del gran Legislator sopponga al patto,
      Dal marmoreo coltello piagato anch'esso;
      E 'l Redentore immaculato, intatto,
      Del marchio sia de' peccatori impresso:
      Questo la mente ancor dubbia gl'involve,
      Né ben de' suoi gran dubbi il nodo ei solve.

21   He refuses to believe such a wonder,
Such great mystery, hidden from reason:
The girl's flower is not rent asunder;
It blossoms pure in virginal season.
Though married, she lies chaste in slumber.
Strange that God make Himself a beacon
By donning flesh and, in humble guise,
Walk among men to open their eyes.

22   He is astounded that light hitherto unseen
Greets shepherds as the Son is born,
That the Deity descend in form so mean
And willingly submit to mortals' scorn,
That he drink milk—an infant unweaned—
Who sips nectar from Heaven's horn,
That the God with a throne in the skies be able
To inhabit a shack, to dwell in a stable.

23   It shocks him the highest Sun should deign
That the Divine Word babble like a child,
That the author of fire flee cold and rain—
For laughter of angels, so gentle and mild,
To gurgle below in an earthly drain.
Now, eternal Glory has been defiled.
He cannot grasp how Heaven's majesty
Should be eclipsed and suffer such travesty.

24   Incredible that He lie humiliated,
Suffer that Himself be cut low.
He is judged, whose will legislated
And carved laws in tablets of stone.
And yet the Redeemer is uncontaminated;
Sins of mortals do not dim his glow.
The Adversary's mind yields to doubt,
He tries, yet he fails, to figure it out.

25   Mentre a machine nove alza l'ingegno,
       L'ombra del fosco cor stampa nel viso;
       Del viso l'ombra in quell'oscuro regno
       È d'interna mestizia espresso aviso,
       Come suol di letizia aperto segno
       Essere in Cielo il lampo, in terra il riso.
       Da queste cure stimolato e stretto,
       Un disperato ohimè svelse dal petto.

26   —Ohimè—muggiando—ohimè—dicea—qual veggio
       D'insoliti portenti alto concorso?
       Che fia questo? Ah l'intendo, ah per mio peggio
       M'avanza ancor l'angelico discorso!
       Che non poss'io torre a natura il seggio,
       E mutare a le stelle ordine e corso,
       Perché tanti del Ciel sinistri auspici
       Divenisser per me lieti e felici?

27   Che può più farmi omai chi la celeste
       Reggia mi tolse e i regni miei lucenti?
       Bastar doveagli almen per sempre in queste
       Confinarmi d'orror case dolenti,
       Abitator d'ombre infelici e meste,
       Tormentator de le perdute genti,
       Ove, per fin di sì malvagia sorte,
       Non m'è concessa pur speme di morte.

28   Volse a le forme sue semplici e prime
       Natura sovra alzar corporea e bassa,
       E de' membri del Ciel capo sublime
       Far di limo terrestre indegna massa.
       I' no 'l soffersi e d'Aquilon le cime
       Salsi, ove d'Angel mai volo non passa.
       E se quindi il mio stuol vinto cadeo,
       Il tentar l'alte imprese è pur trofeo.

25   As he lifts his thoughts to abstraction,
    His heart's shadow clouds his visage,
    What he sees drives him to distraction:
    Satan knows but gloom and its image.
    On Earth erupts a gay reaction,
    And laughter brightens every village.
    Goaded by worry, and sick in his breast,
    Sadly he heaves "Woe is me!" from his chest.

26   "Woe is me!" (he roars) "Woe is me!
    What company is this coming here?
    Who is it? Ah, what an honor, I see:
    A troupe of angels is drawing near!
    Would I could change nature's law—if only
    I might alter the course of the spheres!
    I would be rid of portents I cannot savor—
    Then Heaven itself would announce my favor!

27   "What more can He do, who took away
    The heavenly realms and my kingdom bright?
    It should be enough that I am forever prey
    To terror here in the houses of Night.
    Trapped and grieving in mansions of decay,
    No path leads away from my plight,
    Here—to crown my wicked and horrible lot—
    Even my hope to die is for naught.

28   "To the first things, Nature lent base form.
    The lofty Ideas, which shine sublime,
    With earthly matter she deformed,
    Covering Heaven's beauty in slime.
    In protest, I seized Aquilon's storm,
    Rising where none had dared climb.
    Even if, soon, my host was defeated,
    The attempt was noble, my plan not conceited.

29   Ma che, non sazio ancor, voglia e pretenda
       Gli antichi alberghi miei spopular d'alme;
       Che 'n sè con modo indissolubil prenda,
       Per farmi ira maggior, l'umane salme;
       Che poscia vincitor sotterra scenda
       Ricco di ricche e preziose palme;
       Che, vibrando qua giù le fulgid'armi,
       Ne le miserie ancor venga a turbarmi!

30   Ah, non se' tu la creatura bella,
       Principe già de' fulguranti amori,
       Del matutino ciel la prima stella,
       La prima luce de gli alati cori?
       Che, come suol la candida facella
       Scintillar fra le lampadi minori,
       Così, ricco di lumi almi, celesti,
       Fra la plebe de gli Angeli splendesti.

31   Lasso! ma che mi val fuor di speranza
       A lo stato primier volger la mente,
       Se, con l'amara e misera membranza,
       Raddoppia il ben passato il mal presente?
       Tempo è d'opporsi al fatto, e la possanza
       Del nemico fiaccar troppo insolente:
       Se l'Inferno si lagna, il Ciel non goda;
       Se la forza non val, vaglia la froda.

32   Ma qual forza tem'io? Già non perdei
       Con l'antico candor l'alta natura:
       Armisi il mondo e 'l Ciel: de' cenni miei
       Gli elementi e le stelle avran paura.
       Son qual fui, sia chi può, come potrei,
       Se non curo il Fattor, curar fattura?
       S'armi Dio: che farà? Vo' quella guerra,
       Che non mi lece in Ciel, movergli in terra—.

29   "Is this not bad enough? He pretends
      To strip my ancient dominion of souls!
      Now, to my other woes, He adds
      The calling of dead from my rolls?
      The victor descends and upends
      Me, as if His triumph were not already whole.
      Why does He come, why brandish a sword,
      Why mock me, long vanquished and forever abhorred?

30   "Are you—am I—not the beautiful creature,
      The former prince of the radiant dawn,
      The first star to show its heavenly features,
      The light before which the angels did fawn?
      A fire blazing true flames, not fever,
      Against which the stars glowed pale and wan:
      So rich were you—was I—in the Heavens,
      We seemed bright gold and all others leaden.

31   "But what good does it do, without any hope,
      To turn my mind to my former estate?
      Bitter memory widens the scope
      Of my grief and my present fate.
      It is time to stand up, no longer to mope,
      Confound the foe before it's too late.
      When the Devil suffers, it's no matter to God—
      If force will not serve me, then I'll use fraud.

32   "What force do I fear? I did not lose,
      As I fell, my pride or my noble nature.
      Let Heavens and Earth try to prove
      Their might; yea, let the elements labor
      Against me. Still, it will all be no use:
      I am as I was and will be forever.
      Even should God take up arms—I want war!
      Down here on Earth, I'll even the score."

33   Lodaro i detti e sollevar la fronte
Le tre feroci e rigide sorelle,
E tutte in lui di Stige e d' Acheronte
Rotar le serpi e scosser le facelle.
—Eccoci—disser—preste, eccoci pronte
D'ogni tua voglia essecutrici ancelle:
Sommo signor di questo orribil chiostro,
Tuo fia l'imporre e l'ubidir fia nostro.

34   Provasti in Ciel, ne la magnanim' opra,
Ciò che sa far con le compagne Aletto;
Né, perch'oggi qua giù t'accoglia e copra
Ombroso albergo e ferrugineo tetto,
Men superbir dei tu: ché, se là sopra
Al monarca tonante eri soggetto,
Qui siedi re che libero ed intero
Hai de la terra e de l'abisso impero.

35   Se valer potrà nulla industria o senno,
Virtù d'erbe o di pietre, o suon di carmi,
Inganno, ira ed amor, che spesso fenno
Correr gli uomini al sangue e trattar l'armi,
Tu ci vedrai, sol che ti piaccia, a un cenno
Trar le stelle dal ciel, l'ombre dai marmi,
Per sossovra la terra e il mar profondo,
Crollar, spiantar da le radici il mondo.—

36   Risponde il fiero: —O miei sostegni, o fidi
De la mia speme e del mio regno appoggi,
Ben le vostr'arti e 'l valor vostro io vidi
Chiaro lassù ne gli stellati poggi.
Ma, benché molto in tutte io mi confidi,
Uopo d'una però mi sia sol oggi:
Crudeltà chieggio sola, e sol costei
Può trar di dubbio i gran sospetti miei—.

33   The fearsome sisters praised his speech,
         Waving torches and serpentine whips
         From Styx and Acheron, they screeched:
         "Behold, we have come, ready to fix
         And arrange whatever you seek!
         We follow ev'ry command from your lips.
         Highest lord of this horrid dominion,
         Just let us know your will and opinion.

34   "You undertook a bold venture up in the sky,
         Just as Alecto now does with her sisters.
         If, today, in an obscure house you sigh,
         Beneath a roof which the heat blisters,
         Be prouder here, than there on high,
         Where one bows down before lord and master.
         Here is your throne, where your rule is entire:
         You command both the Earth and Hell's deep gyre.

35   "If neither force nor stealth suit your design,
         We can use herbs, magic, or potions.
         Whether for hate or for love, our craft stirs,
         Rouses, and spurs world-changing motion.
         See (if it please you), how we contrive
         To mix stars and the depths of the ocean
         By summoning shades from marble and brick;
         At its heart, the world will be cut to the quick."

36   The proud one answers: "You, who are true
         To my wishes, who execute my plans,
         Of your black arts I have enough proof,
         For I see where the dark stars stand.
         You have my trust. I ask that you pursue
         your wish and fulfill a single demand.
         I only want cruelty. That will suffice
         To dispel all lingering doubts in a trice."

37   Era costei de le tre dee del male
      Suora ben degna e fera oltra le fere,
      E sen gìa d'or in or battendo l'ale
      A riveder quelle malnate schiere,
      Vaga di rinforzar l'esca immortale
      Al foco onde bollian l'anime nere
      Nel più secreto baratro profondo
      Del sempre tristo e lagrimoso mondo.

38   Ululàro tre volte i cavi spechi,
      Tre volte rimbombar l'ombre profonde,
      E fin ne' gorghi più riposti e ciechi
      Tonar del gran Cocito i sassi e l'onde.
      Udì quel grido, e i suoi dritt'occhi in biechi
      Torse colei da le tartaree sponde,
      E per risposta al formidabil nome
      Fe' sibilar le serpentine chiome.

39   Casa non ha la region di Morte
      Più de la sua terribile ed oscura;
      Stan sempre ai gridi altrui chiuse le porte
      Scabre e di selce adamantina e dura;
      Son di ferro le basi e son di forte
      Diaspro impenetrabile le mura,
      E di sangue macchiate, e tutte sozze
      Son di teste recise e membra mozze.

40   V'ha la Vendetta in su la soglia e 'n mano
      Spada brandisce insanguinata ignuda;
      Havvi lo Sdegno, e col Furor insano
      E la Guerra e la Strage anela e suda;
      Con le minaccie sue fremer lontano
      S'ode la Rabbia impetuosa e cruda;
      E nel mezzo si vide in vista acerba
      La gran falce rotar Morte superba.

37   She who, of the malignant deities,
Had charge—the one fiercer than the others—
Took flight and beat her wings constantly,
To visit the band of her brothers.
She flapped to the immortal entryway
To where black souls boil and smother:
She flew to the pit, the deepest chasm,
Where the world chokes in sorrowful spasm.

38   Three times the shouts in the cavernous hollows
Echoed within the remote and blind
Rocks of Cocytus, among the grottos
Where the baleful river winds.
The prince of the realm heard the bellows,
Contorted his eyes, and raged in his mind.
Answering the fearsome call of his name,
Hissing snakes darted forth from his mane.

39   Nowhere in Death's fearsome lands
Is darker than here or more obscure;
The gates close forever on the damned;
No cries pierce the fortress secure;
The deaf walls heed his ev'ry command,
Unyielding jasper and iron that girds.
Filthy with dirt and discolored by mud,
The castle towers in ruins spattered with blood.

40   Vengeance stands guard; clenched in her palm
A blade flashes of shining steel.
Here dwells blind Rage, the en'my of calm,
And War, revolving Death's wheels.
Explosions of Anger ring out like a bomb,
Its violent crashes echo and peal.
In the midst of the horror, behold a sight:
The grim scythe plies its terrible might.

41   Per le pareti abominandi ordigni,
Onde talor sono i mortali offesi,
De la fiera magion fregi sanguigni,
In vece v'ha di cortinaggi, appesi:
Rote, ceppi, catene, aste, macigni,
Chiodi, spade, securi ed altri arnesi,
Tutti nel sangue orribilmente intrisi
Di fratelli svenati e padri uccisi.

42   In mensa detestabile e funesta
L'ingorde Arpie con la vorace Fame,
E l'inumano Erisitton, di questa
Cibano ad or ad or l'avide brame;
E con Tantolo e Progne i cibi appresta
Atreo feroce e Licaone infame;
Medusa entro 'l suo teschio a la crudele
Porta, in sangue stemprato, a bere il fele.

43   Le spaventose Eumenidi sorelle
Son sempre seco; sempre in man le ferve
Furial face; intorno ha Iezabelle,
Scilla, Circe, Medea ministre e serve.
Son de l'iniqua corte empie donzelle
Le Parche inessorabili e proterve,
Da le cui man fur le sue vesti ordite
Di negre fila di recise vite.

44   Circonda il tetto intorno intorno un bosco,
Ch'ha sol d'infauste piante ombre nocenti;
Ogni herba è peste ed ogni fiore è tosco,
Sospir son l'aure e lacrime i torrenti.
Pascon quivi, per entro a l'aer fosco
Minotauri e Ciclopi, orridi armenti
Di draghi e tigri, e van per tutto a schiere
Sfingi, iene, ceraste, idre e chimere.

41   On the walls of the hateful palace,
Whence all mortal ills issue,
Bloody ornaments, proud and callous,
Hang in place of silk tissue:
Wheels of torture, chains of Atlas,
Nails and manacles suspended for view.
All caked in blood, matted with gore—
Brothers butchered, fathers dead by the score.

42   Before a grim table, at a fatal repast,
The greedy Harpies indulge in a feast;
Gluttonous Erichtho breaks her fast
And gorges like a ravenous beast:
Food for Atreus, Tantalus, Procne, and, last,
Infamous Lycaon—by no means the least.
Medusa brings the company a skull:
Gall and blood fill the vessel full.

43   The Eumenides, her horrifying sisters,
Always attend, a whipcord at hand;
Nearby stands Jezebel, who whispers
To Scylla, Circe, and Medea commands.
Here in the court of the wicked mistress,
The ruthless company of Fates stands;
Grim ornaments, in black thread, they weave:
Shortened lives adorn their garments' sleeves.

44   Around the house looms a dark wood;
In the shadows grow poisonous plants:
Herbs bear infection, flowers drip blood,
Sighs fill the air where all tears are spent.
On strange pastures, on flowers and buds,
Graze minotaurs; the cyclops is content.
Bands of dragons and tigers hunt and prowl
While hydras, hyenas, and chimeras howl.

45   Di Diomede i destrier, di Fereo i cani
       E di Terodamente havvi i leoni,
       Di Busiri gli altari empi e profani,
       Di Silla le severe aspre prigioni,
       I letti di Procuste orrendi e strani,
       Le mense immonde e rie de' Lestrigoni,
       E del crudo Sciron, del fiero Scini
       Gl'infami scogli, i dispietati pini.

46   Quanti mai seppe imaginar flagelli
       L'implacabil Mezenzio o Gerione,
       Ocho, Ezzelino, Falari, e con quelli
       Il sempre formidabile Nerone,
       V'ha tutti: havvi le fiamme, havvi i coltelli
       Di Nabucco ed Accabe e Faraone.
       Tale è l'albergo; e quinci esce veloce
       La quarta Furia a la terribil voce.

47   A costei la sua mente aperse a pena
       L'imperador de la tremenda corte,
       Ch'ella di Dite, in men che non balena,
       Abbandonò le ruginose porte,
       E la faccia del ciel pura e serena
       Tutta macchiando di pallor di morte,
       Sol con la vista avvenenati al suolo
       Fe' piombar gli augelletti a mezzo 'l volo.

48   Tosto che fuor de la vorago oscura
       Venne quel mostro a vomitar l'Inferno,
       Parvero i fiori intorno e la verdura
       Sentir forza di peste, ira di verno.
       Poria col ciglio instupidir Natura,
       Inorridire il bel pianeta eterno,
       Irrigidir le stelle e gli elementi,
       Se non gliel ricoprissero i serpenti.

45   Diomedes's mares and Phereus's hounds,
          Lions of Therodamas are here bred.
          The godless altars of Busiris are found,
          Sulla's harsh prisons, Procrustes's bed.
          Nor is that all. Terrible sights abound:
          Lestrygonians feast on limbs and heads.
          At the edge of the wasteland one sees
          Sciron's rocks, Sinis's blood-soaked trees.

46   As many torments as ever could dream
          Mezentius, Ezzelino, or other
          Imperious tyrant who once did scheme
          Like Nero, their murderous brother—
          All the tortures are here. Knives gleam
          From Ahab, Pharaoh, and Nebuchadnezzar.
          Here from the abyss issues a fearsome noise:
          The fourth Fury curses in a terrible voice.

47   To her the ruler of the awful court
          Hardly disclosed his will. In the blink of an eye,
          Lightning-quick, she leapt and darted forth
          Leaving rusty gates to creak and grind.
          Heaven's pure face her likeness distorted—
          She cast discolored light with the black lines
          Of death. The birds in the sky, at her mere sight,
          Fell down to the ground, struck dead in their fright.

48   As soon as Hell vomited the fiend
          Out from the abyssal depths,
          The flowers that grew and the grass that teemed
          Appeared blasted by plague's foul breath
          Or winter's wrath. Nature would freeze,
          It seemed that the Sun would stop, chill with death.
          The stars themselves would stick in their place,
          If serpents did not hide her horrible face.

49   Già da l'ombrose sue riposte cave
     De la notte compagno, aprendo l'ali,
     Lento e con grato furto il Sonno grave
     Togliea la luce a i pigri occhi mortali;
     E con dolce tirannide e soave,
     Sparse le tempie altrui d'acque letali,
     I tranquilli riposi e lusinghieri
     S'insignorian de' sensi e de' pensieri.

50   Quando le negre piume agili e preste
     Spiega l'Erinni e 'n Betthelem ne viene
     (Ché 'n Betthelem lo scettro, a le moleste
     Cure inviolato, il re crudel sostiene)
     E qual già con facelle empie e funeste
     Di Tebe apparve a le sanguigne cene,
     Ricerca e spia de la magion reale
     Con sollecito piè camere e sale.

51   La reggia allor del buon David reggea,
     Ligio d'Augusto, Erode, uom già canuto,
     Non legittimo re, ma d'Idumea
     Stirpe e del regno occupator temuto.
     Già 'l diadema real de la Giudea
     La progenie di Giuda avea perduto,
     E del giogo servil gli aspri rigori
     Sostenendo, piangea gli antichi onori.

52   Scorso l'albergo tutto, a le secrete
     Ritirate sen va del gran palagio,
     Là dove in placidissima quiete
     Tra molli piume il re posa a grand'agio.
     Non vuole a lui, qual proprio uscì di Lete,
     Mostrarsi il mostro perfido e malvagio,
     Ma dispon cangiar faccia e girle avante
     Fatta pallida imago, ombra vagante.

49 Opening its wings, from hidden caverns,
    Slowly spreading the weight of slumber,
    Night descended with shadowy companions,
    As the senses of mortals grew number;
    Its gentle tyranny extinguished their lanterns,
    Which sweet oblivion encumbered.
    Tranquil, soothing rest soon overwhelmed
    The bodies and minds of those in the realm.

50 When the Erinye folded her filthy wings
    In Bethlehem, she directed her course
    To the ruler, who then lay sleeping
    Without a care in the world at his great court.
    As once she had appeared to the king
    Of Thebes, bearing a funeral torch,
    Thus she crept through the royal house,
    Quietly treading, still as a mouse.

51 The realm of good David was, in that day,
    Governed by Herod, a vassal of Rome—
    King by fraud, already old and gray,
    An Edomite who held the throne.
    The seed of Judah had long fallen prey
    To those who stole the kingdom's crown.
    Now they bore the cruel yoke of slavery,
    Mourning the fall of glorious ancestry.

52 The Fury scours the halls and discovers
    Secret chambers in the vast palace.
    There, slumbering under the covers,
    Lies the king, wicked and callous.
    Hiding her own face, the visage of another
    The monster assumes, to show less menace.
    She puts on an image wan and pale,
    A wandering spirit, ghostly and frail.

53   Ciò che di Furia avea, spoglia in un tratto,
      E di forma mortal si vela e cinge:
      Giusippo a l'aria, al volto, a ciascun'atto
      Quale e quanto ei si fu, simula e finge.
      Al re, dal sonno oppresso e sovrafatto,
      S'accosta e 'l cor con fredda man gli stringe:
      Poi la voce mentita e mentitrice
      Scioglie tra 'l sonno e la vigilia, e dice:

54   —Mal accorto tu dormi, e qual nocchiero
      Che per l'Egeo, di nembi oscuri e densi
      Cinto, a l'onda superba, al vento fiero,
      Obliato il timon, pigro non pensi,
      Te ne stai neghittoso e 'l cor guerriero
      Ne l'ozio immergi e nel riposo i sensi,
      E non curi e non sai ciò che vicino
      Ti minacci di reo forte destino.

55   Sai, che de' regi Ebrei dal ceppo antico,
      Quasi d'arido stel, frutto insperato,
      Ammirabil fanciul, benché mendico,
      Là tra le bestie e 'l fien pur dianzi è nato.
      Del novo germe, a te fatal nemico,
      Troppo amico si mostra il vulgo ingrato,
      Gli applaude, il segue, e già con chiara fama
      Tuo successor, suo regnatore il chiama.

56   O quai machine volge, o quai disegna
      Moti sediziosi; il foco ha in seno,
      Il ferro in man; già d'occultar s'ingegna
      Ne le regie vivande anco il veneno.
      Né v'ha pur un che l'ire a fren ritegna
      Del rio trattato, o che te 'l scopra almeno.
      Or va poi tu, con l'armi e con le leggi
      Popolo sì fellon difendi e reggi.

53   The semblance of dread Fury she sheds quick,
To look the way the king's brother appears:
Every feature is like his. By this trick
Her ruse and fraud are unclear.
The king, burdened by sleep, squints and thinks
The cold limb extended to him is dear.
He clasps in his own the false and lying hand.
Waking and resting, he half understands:

54   "You sleep unknowing, like one who sails
On unsteady sea in a foggy shroud,
Against the waves, while harsh winds wail,
Forgetting the path the rudder has plowed.
You have grown lazy, your valor now fails.
Your senses idle, as if in a cloud,
Why so careless, why do you not fear
The great disaster now drawing near?

55   "Know: the ancient line of Jewish kings,
Brings forth fruit from arid stalk;
A wondrous child, though poor in seeming,
Is born; already, he assembles his flock.
The common herd—to you a hostile thing—
Gathers 'round the babe. It gapes and it gawks.
The people salute and follow the one
By whom, they say, your throne will be undone.

56   "What plans it has conceived, and what designs
It hatches in its fiery heart!
Its hand readies the steel, and minds
Contemplate the poisoner's art.
Nor can anyone, in all mankind,
Put an end to the evil that now starts:
Go forth, take up arms, use all that you can
To rein in the rabble that threatens the land!

57   Quell' io che già per stabilirti in mano
De la verga reale il nobil peso,
Posi in non cale e vita e sangue, in vano
Dunque il sangue e la vita ho sparso e speso?
Per più lieve cagion contro il germano
Proprio e propri tuoi figli hai l'armi preso:
Or giaci, o frate, ad altre cure intento,
Nel maggior uopo irresoluto e lento?

58   Su su perché ti stai? qual ti ritarda
O viltate, o follia? destati desta,
Sorgi misero omai, scuotiti e guarda,
Quale spada ti pende in su la testa.
Sveglia il tuo spirto addormentato, ond'arda
Di regio sdegno, e l'ire e l'armi appresta.
Teco di ferro e sangue, ombra fraterna,
Invisibil m'avrai ministra eterna—.

59   Così gli parla, e poi l'anfesibene
De le schiume di Cerbero nodrita,
Ch'al manco braccio avviluppata tiene,
Venenosa e fischiante, al cor gli irrita;
E gli spira in un soffio entro le vene
Fiamma, ch'aviva ogni virtù sopita.
Ciò fatto entra nel buio e si nasconde
Tra l'ombre più secrete e più profonde.

60   Rompesi il sonno e, di sudor le membra
Sparso, dal letto infausto il re si scaglia,
Che, benché ricco e morbido, gli sembra
Siepe di spine e campo di battaglia.
Ciò che d'aver veduto gli rimembra
E ciò ch'udì ne la memoria intaglia.
Pien d'affanno e d'angoscia a voto sfida,
Imperversa, minaccia ed armi grida.

57   "What, did I put the staff into your hand,
        —The scepter that bears royal weight—
        For nothing at all? Are you not the man?
        For less, against your own brother, in hate,
        Did you take up arms and tear sacred bands;
        Against your children, too—you accepted this fate.
        But now you lie idle and pay no heed,
        Sluggish and dull in the time of need!

58   "Up, up, why do you stay? Why are you so slow?
        Are you coward or fool? Rise up from bed!
        Awaken, hurry! Do you not know
        That a sword hangs over your head?
        Bestir your sleeping spirit, and show
        Yourself worthy. Take up arms, strike dread
        In their hearts! I will stand by your side,
        An unseen shade, a trustworthy guide."

59   Thus did she address him; then she struck
        The snake coiled 'round her left side—
        Amphisbaene, whom Hell's dugs give suck—
        Onto his heart, so venom would glide
        Within; hissing, she whispered that luck
        Would favor his pride, if revived:
        Then to deep recesses hidden in gloom,
        She dashed away, down into the tomb.

60   Sleep's spell broken, up from sweaty dreams,
        The king starts from his deep bed,
        Which, though opulent and soft, yet seems
        To be thorns; a war storms in his head.
        He recalls the vision he has seen,
        What just now he has heard said.
        Breathlessly, he surges in furious alarm,
        Shouts imprecations and calls for arms.

61   Come se larga man pascolo accresce
D'esca a la fiamma, o mantice l'alluma,
Ferve concavo rame, e mentre mesce
Il bollor col vapor, mormora e fuma;
Gonfiasi l'onda insuperbita e cresce
Su 'l giro estremo e si convolve e spuma,
Versasi al fine intorno e nocer tenta
A quel medesmo ardor che la fomenta:

62   Così, confuso e stupido, quand'ode
Novo sollevator sorger nel regno,
Sentesi l'alma il dispietato Erode,
Già di timor gelata, arder di sdegno.
Tarlo d'ingiuria impaziente il rode,
Né trova loco a l'inquieto ingegno,
E de la notte, ov'altri posa e tace,
Quasi guerra importuna, odia la pace.

63   Già per mille profetici presagi
Questo dubbio nel cor gli entrò da prima.
Poi, da che vide i tributarii Magi
Nel suo regno passar da strano clima,
A rodergli i pensier crudi e malvagi
Ritornò di timor tacita lima.
Or, che i sospetti in lui desta e rinova
Il fantasma infernal, posa non trova.

64   Tosto che spunti in oriente il giorno,
Ché l'aria ancora è nubilosa e nera,
Vuol che s'aduni entro 'l real soggiorno
De' consiglieri principi la schiera.
Va de' sergenti e de gli araldi intorno
La sollecita turba messaggiera,
Ed a capi e ministri in ogni banda
Rapporta altrui chi manda e chi commanda.

61   Just as bellows strengthen the fire,
      When a strong gust blows on the flames,
      As branches crack and sputter in ire,
      Belching out smoke; in the same
      Way as sap boils and desires
      To burst forth, no longer contained,
      And spill and drown the burning flare
      That made it bubble and seek the air—

62   So confused and utterly stupefied
      That a rebel appears in his realm,
      Cruel Herod feels the anger rise;
      Cold dread and hot rage overwhelm
      Him; indignation gnaws his insides;
      He cannot man his mind's helm.
      He grows to hate the peace of night
      As much as the war he has feared to fight.

63   Already in a thousand prophecies
      Has he beheld something of the kind;
      But when Three Kings honor the prodigy
      Leaving distant lands behind,
      Then his thoughts turn to cruelty;
      All fear parts from his mind.
      Now that misgiving stirs in his breast,
      The infernal vision will not let him rest.

64   As soon as day, from the East, came to the kingdom,
      Though the air was still dark with clouds,
      He ordered his ministers come before him;
      At court, they assembled and bowed.
      The heralds took note of his ev'ry whim,
      And passed word of what he had vowed.
      Promptly was made known throughout the land
      The full import of the royal command.

65   Di che paventi, Erode? e quale acceso
Hai di sangue nel cor fero desire?
Umana forma il re de' regi ha preso
Non per signoreggiar, ma per servire.
Non a furarti il regno in terra è sceso,
Ma te de' regni suoi brama arrichire.
Vano e folle timor, ch'abbia colui
Che 'l suo ne dona, ad usurpar l'altrui!

66   Già per regnar, per guerraggiar non nasce
Fanciullo ignudo e poverel negletto,
Cui donna imbelle ancor di latte pasce,
In breve culla in pochi panni stretto.
I guerrier son pastor, l'armi son fasce,
Il palagio real rustico tetto,
Pianti le trombe, i suoi destier son due
Pigri animali: un asinello, un bue.

65   What frightens you, O Herod? What stirs
Bloody rage in your soul?
The King of Kings, not to rule but to serve,
Has assumed a human role.
He is not come to take your honor,
But to enrich you, to add to the whole.
You indulge false fears, your concerns are unfounded:
By selfless acts a king was never confounded.

66   A naked babe, he was not born to fight.
He suckles still at the breast of his mother,
Small and needy, just a poor wight;
His cradle has scarcely a cover.
Should shepherds be warriors? Is it right
To see riches in a stable's clutter?
Now, a mewling infant calls to battle,
His only steeds are donkeys and cattle.

LIBRO SECONDO

Al consiglio adunato il re palesa
Ciò ch'a lui di temer porge sospetto.
Urizeo, ch'a buon fin la mente ha intesa,
Tenta l'ira crudel trarli dal petto.
Burucco, ch'a la strage ha l'alma accesa,
A contrario pensier scopre l'affetto.
Giuseppe che, sognando il male intende,
Da Giudea ne l'Egitto il camin prende.

BOOK TWO

His courtiers assembled, the king shares
The reasons that he harbors suspicion.
Urizeus, with good reason for care,
Would dispel the ire dwelling within him.
But Baruch, desiring battle's red glare,
Soon counsels the opposing position.
Warned by a dream, Joseph sees the menace in time.
His family flees for Egypt from Palestine.

1   Aveano al carro d'or, ch'il dì n'apporta,
Rimesso il fren le mattutine ancelle,
E 'n su la soglia de l'aurata porta
Giunto era il Sole e fea sparir le stelle,
E la sua vaga messaggiera e scorta,
Fugando i sogni e queste nubi e quelle,
Per le spiagge spargea lucide, ombrose
De la Terra e del Ciel rugiade e rose:

2   Ed ecco in tanto i senatori uniti
Fur da le guardie in ampia sala ammessi,
Dove, al vivo trapunti e coloriti,
Serici simulacra erano espressi.
Aveano in sè di Marianne orditi
Gl' infausti amori e i tragici successi,
Spoglie di babilonica testura,
Fregi superbi a le superbe mura.

3   De la sala pomposa il bel lavoro
Poco curanti e i bei contesti panni,
Al re s'en giro, ed ingombrar costoro
Del senato real gli aurati scanni
Di mano in man, secondo i gradi loro
E del sangue e de' titoli e de gli anni,
Quai più lontani a lui, quai più vicini:
Satrapi, Farisei, Scribi e Rabini.

4   Su 'l trono principal, del regio arnese
Pompa maggiore e meraviglia prima,
Lo qual del re pacifico e cortese
Edificio mirabile si stima,
Immantenente il fier tiranno ascese,
Gli altri intorno sedenti, ed egli in cima:
Il sedil ch'egli preme, eletto e fino,
Forma ha di core, e 'l core è di rubino.

1   Celestial servants had loosed the reins
Of the carriage of morning's light.
Opening golden gates, the Sun now came
And extinguished the stars of the night.
Gleaming Dawn, his herald, did the same,
Chasing off dreams, clouds, and the like.
From the Earth, dim shadows faded away;
Vivid hues of rose announced the new day.

2   Before long, the senators had arrived,
Admitted by palace guards to the hall.
There, a rich tapestry hung, devised
To bring the semblance of life to the wall.
Mariamne's misfortunes were here contrived,
Her luckless loves and unfortunate fall.
It was work woven by Babylonian hand:
A proud image that suited the pride of the land.

3   To the majestic decor the guests pay no mind,
And they ignore the beautiful picture.
All hasten to join in at the king's side;
They neglect the sumptuous fixtures.
They gather by birth, rank, age, and kind,
—Order foreseen by the Scriptures—
And they take seat according to tribe:
Satraps, Pharisees, rabbis, and scribes.

4   To the throne—such a marvel to behold,
A majestic seat intended for those
Who have been fashioned in King David's mold—
The tyrant made his way. All rose
As he took his place on the chair of gold.
Once arrived, Great Herod struck a stately pose.
As he ascended, he stepped upon stools
Shaped like hearts and gleaming with jewels.

5   Il pavimento ov' ei posa le piante
     Tutto di drappi d'or rigido splende;
     Di varie gemme lucida e stellante
     Ombrella imperial sovra gli pende;
     Ha di ben terso e candido elefante
     Sei gradi intorno, onde s'ascende e scende;
     Stanno due per ciascun de' sei scaglioni,
     Quasi custodi a' fianchi, aurei leoni.

6   Quivi s'asside, e 'l fosco ciglio essangue
     Volge tre volte a l'adunato stuolo,
     Poi gli occhi al ciel solleva, ebri di sangue,
     Indi gli affigge immobilmente al suolo,
     In atto tal che 'n un minaccia e langue
     E porta espresso entro lo sdegno il duolo.
     Non piange no, però che l'ira alquanto,
     Come il vento la pioggia, affrena il pianto.

7   Scote lo scettro, e 'l seggio ove dimora
     Tempestandol col piè, par ch'abbia in ira;
     L'aureo diadema, onde le tempia onora
     Si trae di testa e sospiroso il mira;
     La bianca barba ed ispida, talora
     Dal folto mento a pel a pel si tira;
     Al fin tra' lidi de l'enfiate labbia
     Rompe l'onde del duolo e de la rabbia:

8   —Principi, e qual novello alto spavento
     Turba i riposi a le mie notti oscure?
     Quai fantasmi, quai larve io veggio, io sento?
     Quai mi rodono il cor pungenti cure?
     O nostro stato uman non mai contento,
     O regie signorie non mai sicure.
     Dunque nemica insidiosa frode
     Può nella reggia sua tradire Erode?

5   The floor upon which his feet trampled
        Glistened with colored embroidery;
        Stitched with rich gems and many a sample
        Of exquisite refinement and luxury.
        Above, a parasol; on stairs amply
        Decked in ivory stood slaves in fine livery.
        They came and they went, up and down the flights,
        Before which sat lions, shining and bright.

6   Three times he gazes, face empty of life,
        About the court and the standing crowd.
        He eyes the skies as if wielding a knife,
        Then Great Herod stares at the ground.
        The horrid man too is prey to strife
        In his breast—the king is nervous and proud.
        Like fierce wind that checks the falling of rain,
        He refuses, in anger, to let his tears drain.

7   He shakes his scepter and his foot kicks:
        It seems he has been wronged by the throne.
        He sighs as if the sight made him sick
        And off from his head tears the crown.
        He rips his long beard, hoary and thick,
        And throws bloody chunks to the ground.
        Finally, there bursts, at the shore of his mouth,
        The wave of mourning. He releases a shout:

8   "My lords, what new horror has come
        To unsettle my slumber at night?
        The battles man wages never are won,
        Grave worry claws me and bites.
        Indeed, a ruler's work never is done,
        Nor ever are kingly cares slight!
        Is the realm of Herod secure at all,
        If a traitor—at any moment—can make it fall?

9   Versomi in gran pensier, ch'entro i confini
Di Betthelem l'usurpator temuto
Del nostro regno, in fra' Giudei bambini,
Già tant'anni predetto, or sia venuto.
Vidi regi stranieri e peregrini
Ricco recargli oriental tributo;
Poi senza più tornar, rotta la fede,
Per altro calle acceleraro il piede.

10   E vi giur'io per questo scettro e questo
Capo real, ch'a me, non so s'io fossi,
Là presso l'alba, addormentato o desto,
Giusippo innanzi, il mio fratel, mostrossi.
Con quest' occhi il vid'io languido e mesto:
I noti accenti, al cui tenor mi scossi,
Quest' orecchie ascoltaro; o quai m'espose
De' miei rischi presenti oscure cose!

11   Potei già de l'Arabia e de l'Egitto
Fiaccar l'orgoglio, e 'n disusati modi
Del falso Atemion, d'Arbella invitto
Rintuzzar l'armi e superar le frodi,
Antigono lasciar rotto e sconfitto,
Uccider Pappo e 'l mar vincer di Rodi,
Schernir Pacoro, e vendicar potei
Contro il perfido Ircano i torti miei.

12   Ed or, popolo inerme e con paterno
Zelo amato da me sempre e nodrito,
Un fanciul non so quale, al mio governo,
Me vivo ancor, fia d'acclamare ardito?
Ed io dormo? ed io taccio? e 'l proprio scherno,
Re sprezzato sostegno, e re tradito?
E per vana pietà, ch'ad altrui porto,
Contro me stesso incrudelisco a torto?

9   "Suspicion gnaws deep within me. I fear
That a rebel in Bethlehem has arrived.
A Jewish infant—it was told by a seer
Long ago—will come and seek to deprive
Me of power. Behold those who now draw near:
Strange pilgrims and kings approach their prize.
The old ways are over, there's no more faith.
Men walk a new path, leave me in disgrace.

10   "By the staff I hold, by my royal head,
I swear I do not know, was I waking
Or dreaming when there, in front of my bed,
It seemed my brother stood. I have to take
For true what my own senses have said:
I cannot believe the vision was fake.
A familiar voice spoke in my ear
And told me of risks and dangers to fear!

11   "Proud Egypt I yoked, and I bridled Araby.
My sword humbled Atenion, full of deceit.
Not only did I put an end to his victory—
I left Antigonus crushed in defeat.
Pappus I slew and saw Pacorus flee,
Conquered the waves of the Rhodesian sea;
Hyrcanus paid for wrongs he inflicted.
My might knew no bounds, was unrestricted.

12   "And now my own people—weak and unarmed,
Which should look upon me as a father—
Nourishes an infant who will bring harm
To my state. Where is my strength, my valor?
Still I rest and yield to sleep's charms,
Though I am betrayed and dishonored?
Mercy for others brings danger, not rest,
Like turning a knife against my own breast.

13   Strider per tutto intorno a queste mura
         I nemici vagiti udir già parmi.
         Ahi vagiti non son, né m'assicura
         L'altrui tenera età: sento sfidarmi.
         Strepiti son di guerra e di congiura,
         Son minaccie di morte, accenti d'armi,
         Trombe guerriere, onde vil turba ardita
         La mia pace conturba e la mia vita.

14   Con silenzio però duro e mortale
         Tante voci ammutir farò ben io;
         Voglio in un mar di sangue universale
         L'ancora stabilir del regno mio.
         Siasi innocente o reo, poco mi cale:
         Sia giustizia o rigor, nulla cur'io,
         Purché col sangue e con le stragi e l'onte
         La corona real mi fermi in fronte.

15   So che la mia ruina, ancor lattante,
         Va già crescendo entro le fasce occulta,
         Già pargoleggia e già vagisce infante:
         Ma farò sì che non favelli adulta.
         Veggio l'insidia rea, che ribellante
         Già mi vien contro e tacita m'insulta:
         Ma venga pur quanto si voglia in fretta,
         Che precorsa sarà da la vendetta.

16   Ore non trarrò mai liete e tranquille,
         Tanto che, sparso in larga piazza, ondeggi
         Lago di sangue, e di sanguigne stille
         Ritinta questa porpora rosseggi;
         E la salute mia, quasi per mille
         Occhi per mille piaghe, al fin vagheggi
         Scritta a vermiglio; dentro 'l sangue asperso,
         L'altrui perfidia e 'l mio timor sommerso.

13   "Already the enemy clamors and shrieks!
      Riot surrounds me and lays siege to the walls
      —Not children's voices, tender and weak,
      But threats to a house ready to fall.
      The howls announce war and conspiracy,
      Menace death and the struggle of arms:
      Trumpets of armies; their bellows and blows
      Sound designs on my life, which they mean to cut low.

14   "Harsh and mortal silence will I impose
      On them, to bring the noise to its grave.
      Should even the world's blood gush and flow,
      My ship will ride secure on the waves.
      Innocent or guilty, what do I know?
      Justice means nothing. Why should I save
      Others? If they suffer shipwreck and drown,
      My kingdom is safe, and I keep the crown.

15   "My ruin, I know, is not even teething.
      He lies yet swaddled with his nurse—
      Babbling, mewling, pathetically bleating.
      That is bad enough, but there will be worse,
      Should he reach maturity, evilly breeding
      His seditious and treacherous curse.
      Let me then hurry and make no delay,
      I'll have my vengeance and sweep him away.

16   "No rest, no tranquil hour can ever be mine,
      Until blood washes over the streets,
      Flooding the land with its ruddy brine
      —Bitter lakes whose waters are sweet—
      Until thousands of wounds, gaping like eyes,
      Declare the kingdom's safety complete,
      When crimson, scarlet, and dark vermillion,
      Mark the end of the threats posed by children.

17   Ditemi or voi che qui raccolti insieme,
      O miei fedeli, al commun rischio invoco,
      Avrò fors'io le sovrastanti estreme
      Fiamme del regno mio da curar poco?
      O deggio pur, pria che più cresca, il seme
      Primo ammorzar del già serpente foco?
      E, schivando il mio mal con gl'altrui lutti,
      Per ucciderne un solo, uccider tutti?—

18   Tace ciò detto, ed al suo dir succede
      Tra' circostanti un fremito confuso,
      Qual fa talor' il mar, se Borea il fiede,
      Tra cavi scogli imprigionato e chiuso;
      O qual se, carche d'odorate prede,
      Ronzando in cima a i fior, com'han per uso,
      L'api mormoradrici in su 'l nov' anno
      Ai lor dolci covili in schiera vanno.

19   Di quel parlar, fra gl' altri suoi più cari,
      Urizeo sacerdote il fin attese:
      Uom che per varie terre e varii mari
      Molto errò, molto vide e molto apprese;
      Poi, già canuto, in que' secreti affari
      Per fè, per senno, ai primi gradi ascese;
      E gran bosco di barba irsuto e folto
      Gli adombra il petto, e gli avviluppa il volto.

20   Porta egli il mel ne la favella ed have
      In bocca gli ami e ne la lingua i dardi,
      Volto composto in placid' atto e grave,
      Fronte benigna, occhi modesti e tardi.
      Sciolse in candido stil voce soave,
      Ed, a gli accenti accompagnando i guardi,
      Fuor de le labra in bel sermon sonoro
      Versò fiume di latte e vena d'oro.

17   "Counselors who have loyally assembled here,
      For a shared enterprise you have been called.
      Should I not hold the peace of my realm dear
      And destroy whatever threatens its walls?
      Should I not stamp out the fiery seed,
      Douse the flames of ruin that snake and crawl?
      To defend my rule and secure my condition,
      Should I not wager universal perdition?"

18   He said what he said, then fell into a hush.
      A shudder spread among all standing 'round,
      Like the unquiet sea when it is shut
      Between rocks, and its echoes resound
      —Or like bees buzzing over the brush,
      As they bear off the nectar they've found
        (When, laden with their fragrant spoils, they drone
      And from flowering fields make the way home).

19   The priest Urizeus—first of royal grandees—
      Waited until Herod's speech had ended.
      A man well traveled by land and by sea,
      Much had he seen, still more comprehended.
      His hair was white from the many intrigues
      At court, where his reputation was splendid.
      Pious and wise, with a beard thick and full:
      From face down to chest, a forest of wool.

20   Though smooth of speech, his lips can also shoot
      Arrows when the situation demands.
      In his bearing, he wears an earnest suit,
      But a kind soul guides his thoughts and his hands.
      His visage is noble, his gaze astute.
      Whenever he talks, a smooth voice commands.
      Urizeus steps forth and entreats the king.
      A river flows from his tongue, a golden spring.

21 —Troppo—diss'egli—o Sire, alto periglio
In quel che chiedi a consigliarti io veggio.
Se da te fia discorde il mio consiglio
Cadrotti in ira, e ciò né vo', né deggio;
S'al tuo fermo voler poscia m'appiglio
Contro 'l dritto e 'l dover, fia forse il peggio:
Sarò a la patria, a Dio nemico espresso,
Traditore al mio re, crudo a me stesso.

22 Pur non terrò ciò che sovviemmi ascoso.
I' provai già ne l'età mia più fresca
Ch'immaturo capriccio e frettoloso
Raro adivien ch'a lieto fin riesca.
Né dee, tratto da l'impeto crucioso,
Altri cosa esseguir che poi rincresca,
Perché 'n uom saggio error grave si stima
Pentirsi poscia e non pensarlo in prima.

23 Fia dunque il tuo miglior, di quel sì fero
Desir, che lieve e rapido trascorre,
Con ritegno soave e dolce impero
Di ragion consigliata il fren raccorre.
Che, s'a giogo di legge il collo altero
Non ha libero principe a sopporre,
Dritto è però, che chi la diè l'osservi,
Ond' essempio dal re prendano i servi.

24 Che giova al gran signor popoli e regni
Sotto scettro felice aver soggetti,
Ed esser poi de gli appetiti indegni
Servo infelice, e de' vulgari affetti?
Sfrenati amori, irregolati sdegni
Son colpe sì ne' generosi petti;
Ma crudeltà de l'altrui sangue ardente
Al Monarca del Ciel troppo è spiacente.

21   "Great Sire," he says, "I believe danger lies
In this course. Please grant me, your majesty,
Permission to share advice I think wise.
I would not anger you, yet must speak frankly.
For if I endorsed all that you decide,
I would neglect my duty most rankly.
I would bring shame on my God and my country,
Betray my king, myself—and all and sundry.

22   "I cannot hide my thoughts and reservations.
Already in my younger years, I learned
Deeds performed in a state of vexation
Rarely, if ever, bring desired returns.
On the contrary, some hesitation
Often lets a better course be discerned.
Among the prudent it is thought a mistake
To repent afterward, when all is too late.

23   "It were better, therefore, were you to halt
This desire that now has suddenly flared.
Indeed, you should consider it a fault
To yield to whims and impetuous snares.
A prince can refuse the yoke of the law,
True. For him, even the foul can be fair.
All the same, I consider it unwise
Not to think how one looks in others' eyes.

24   "What good is it that a great master bring
Lands and peoples under order and rule,
If then he hangs on appetite's string,
The slave of emotions, their fool?
Untempered loves and hateful stings
Are found in the gentlest of hearts.
Far worse is it to indulge the thirst for blood:
It displeases the King of Heaven above.

25   E se 'n ogni alma ancor vile e villana,
Che l'obliquo sentier segua de' sensi,
Biasmo esser suol, di questa rabbia insana
Aver gli spirti oltre misura accensi,
O quanto meno in anima sovrana
Cotale affetto e 'n regio cor conviensi:
O quanto ei dee de l'empie voglie il freno
A crudel precipizio allentar meno.

26   Che sì come lassù lucida e pura
Sempre è del Ciel la region sublime,
Né mai basso vapor né nebbia oscura
Vela il suo chiaro o 'l suo sereno imprime;
E come Olimpo in parte alta e secura
Sovra i folgori e i nembi erge le cime,
Così petto reale e nobil mente
Mai turbo o tuon di vil furor non sente.

27   Fu, per spavento altrui, più d'una legge
Con asprezza e rigor dettata e fatta
Che poi nell'essequir, da chi ben regge,
Con molle mano e placida si tratta.
Convien chi buon destier frena e corregge,
Ch'accenni di ferir, più che non batta:
E qualor Giove i fulmini disserra
Molti atterisce sì, ma pochi atterra.

28   Tolga il Ciel, ch'al mio re d'opra sì brutta
L'essecrabile eccesso io persuada;
Che la dolce mia patria orfana e tutta
Del suo pregio maggior sfiorata, cada;
Che sì nobil città vota e destrutta
Abbia a restar da cittadina spada,
Povera signoria, vil scettro indegno,
Duce senza guerrier, re senza regno.

25   "If, in a soul—however common or base—
Which follows the rude senses' course,
It counts as a defect whenever rage
Gives rise to immoderate force,
How much less should your kingly grace
Perform actions so cruel and so coarse?
To the extent he stands above his inferiors,
A king should show his restraint is superior.

26   "Just as the highest part of the firmament
Always shines bright, lucid, and pure,
Nor ever does vapor or murky element
Discolor its splendid azure,
As Mount Olympus occupies eminent
Peaks, where it stands safe and secure
—Thus should royal breast and noble mind
Leave uncouth murmurs of the rabble behind.

27   "To act as deterrent, more than one law
Provides penalties harsh and rigorous,
But then, in practice, the sting is withdrawn
That the judge seem kind and generous.
It behooves the rider to correct the flaws
Of his steed to make it more vigorous.
In the same way, when Jove rains down lightning,
It strikes but few, yet to all it is frightening.

28   "The terrible excess of such enterprise
As my lord plans, I pray Heaven to temper.
So that the orphaned land and the prize
Of its name not be hateful—rendered
Empty through the sad, untimely demise
Of its children horribly dismembered.
Poor is the state, and sorrowful the crown,
Wherever a king tears his own kingdom down.

29   Quel che si vede è chiaramente aperto,
        Quel che si teme è dubbiamente oscuro.
        Or vorrai tu, già in tante prove esperto,
        Trar di danno presente util futuro,
        E per vano timor d'un rischio incerto,
        Procacciar, poco cauto, un mal sicuro?
        Un mal ch'apportator d'affanni estremi,
        Sarà forse maggior del mal che temi?

30   Temi la guerra insospettito, e vuoi,
        Che tanta gioventù sterpata mora?
        Chi sa se nato è già fra questi tuoi,
        Come il nemico, il difensore ancora?
        Dimmi, dimmi per Dio, chi fia, che poi
        S'armi in tua guardia e ti difenda allora,
        Se, germogliante a la stagione acerba,
        Un essercito intero or mieti in erba?

31   Che dirà poi la Fama? Ohimè la Fama,
        Che del falso e del ver divulga il grido?
        Dirà, che per sanguigna avida brama
        Ti fingesti rubello un popol fido.
        Popolo, che te solo onora ed ama,
        Ch'a te, lontano ancor dal patrio nido,
        Infra i tumulti de la regia sede
        Serbò mai sempre ubidienza e fede.

32   Né quel, come tu fai, creder fraterno
        Simulacro vogl'io, ch'aver ti parve
        Notturno innanzi: o fur, da gioco e scherno,
        Falsi sogni, ombre vane e finte larve,
        O, quant'io credo, il tentator d'Averno
        Con così fatta illusion t'apparve,
        Però che 'l Re del Ciel, sì come io lessi,
        Angeli e non fantasmi usa per messi.

29   "All that one can see is clear to the eye,
            But what brings menace is doubly obscure.
            Never, to you, has success been denied
            Yet what gain will your actions procure?
            If you pursue this course, which is ill advised,
            You trade possible risk for disaster that's sure.
            Is a woe that will bring you unheard-of evil
            Better than your mind's present upheaval?

30   "Suspicion makes you fear war, yet you would see
            Countless innocents stripped of their lives?
            Who knows, among them now there may be
            Your champion, who will not survive!
            Who, then, by God—tell me, tell me—
            Who in your guard will keep you alive?
            A whole army that has bloomed out of season,
            You would uproot and cut down without reason?

31   "Consider, also, your name for the ages:
            Reports spread abroad, whether wrong or right.
            Rumor will claim that lust for outrages
            Prompted you to concoct an outright lie:
            Of rebellious subjects, whose true wages
            Should be better, for they honored your might.
            In fact, they knew well they were not of your sort
            And respected orders that came from your court.

32   "Furthermore, I cannot rightly believe
            It true that your brother's likeness appeared.
            Perhaps—can it be—that you were deceived
            And mocked by a dream? Nighttime visions steer
            The senses in strange directions, indeed.
            Or else the Tempter it was you perceived;
            If what I read be fact, Heaven's commander
            Speaks through His angels, bright in their candor.

33   È poi, di questo re che temi tanto,
           Scritto, che 'l regno esser quaggiù terreno
           Non deve no, ma spiritale e santo,
           D'amor, di grazia e di dolcezza pieno.
           Re, che vestito di mendico manto
           Di tesori immortali ha pieno il seno.
           Temer dunque non dei che porti guerra,
           Se per dar pace al mondo è sceso in terra.

34   Mansueto, pacifico, innocente
           Verrà, deposti i fulmini celesti.
           S'armar volesse il suo braccio possente
           A' danni tuoi, deh qual difesa avresti?
           O come da l'essercito lucente
           De gli alati guerrier campar potresti?
           Chi può fuggir, come celarsi, o dove,
           Da lui, che tutto vede e tutto move?

35   O che falso è del tutto, o ch'è verace
           Quest' antico pronostico del regno:
           Se vano e' fia, perché turbar la pace,
           E de' tuoi suscitar l'odio e lo sdegno?
           Ben per me stimar vo' che sia fallace,
           Però ch' assai sovente astuto ingegno
           Sparge tai voci ad arte, invido e rio,
           Per irritar nel re gli uomini e Dio.

36   Se ne le stelle è poi scolpito e scritto,
           Se fermo è in Ciel, che 'l gran bambin sia nato,
           Studio umano che vale? a che l'afflitto
           Popolo affliggi? a che t'opponi al fato?
           Publichi indarno il dispietato editto,
           Premi, furia se sai, minaccia irato:
           Viverà, crescerà, sott'alcun velo
           Terrallo ascoso a tuo mal grado il Cielo.

33   "Of the one you so dread, it stands in Scripture:
His kingdom on Earth is not of the sword.
As it stands written, the picture is milder:
Grace, clemency, and still greater rewards.
This king, who is bound by poverty's strictures,
Holds, for us, undying treasures in store.
Do not fear, then, that he comes seeking a fight:
Peace—love for mankind—is his sole delight.

34   "Meek and innocent temper the Lord assumes.
Putting aside celestial thunder.
If He wished to brandish weapons of doom,
Then how could you fail to go under?
What means do you in your pride presume
Would prevail against heavenly wonders?
Does there live a man who could run and hide
From one who sees all the Earth and the Sky?

35   "If prophecy of the Kingdom be true
Or false—in the end, it does not matter.
If wrong, still how can it benefit you
To provoke subjects' resentful blather?
For my part, I think that it is untrue:
Spirits often our senses do flatter,
Spread whispers and lies by deceptive art
To drive kings from people—and God—apart.

36   "If it is declared by stars in the sky
That now shall be born such a child,
What then does it avail you to fight?
Why add further ills to your trials?
Do you believe you will see fate defied?
Your edict is in vain, wicked, and vile.
Still, he will grow and, in other guise,
Flourish elsewhere, concealed from your eyes.

37   Fuggi, Signor, di re crudele e folle
Titolo infame, e con real clemenza
Quel fervido valor ch'avampa e bolle,
Tempri maturo senno, alta prudenza.
Sospendi l'ire, e mansueto e molle
Usa giusto rigor, non violenza:
Cerchisi il reo più tosto, e di ciascuno
La pena universal porti quell'uno—.

38   Più oltre assai di sue ragioni il corso
Stendea forse in parlando il vecchio accorto,
Ma vide il re, del suo fedel discorso
Quasi sprezzante il dir facondo e scorto,
Crollare il capo, e più di tigre e d'orso
Volger lo sguardo dispettoso e torto;
E 'n fronte gli mirò scritto e nel ciglio:
Animo risoluto odia il consiglio—.

39   Burucco era un baron, d'astio e di sdegno
Roco mormorador, nodrito in corte,
Scaltro, doppio, fellon, che 'l rege e 'l regno
Per invidia e per altro odiava forte.
Precipitoso e fervido d'ingegno,
Vago di strage e cupido di morte,
Che pietà non conosce e che non cura
Tenerezza di sangue o di natura.

40   Questi, calvo la testa e raso il mento,
Era ancor di vigor fresco e vivace,
Ma 'l negro pel d'intempestivo argento
Seminato gli avea l'età mendace.
Poi che l'adulator gran pezza attento
Stette a quel ragionar saggio e verace,
Nel superbo tiranno i lumi affisse,
Sorse, inchinollo, indi s'assise e disse:

37   "Shun, my lord, title of king mad and cruel.
          Temper your spirit burning and ardent.
          Cease from your anger and remain cool
          In your rigor; do not be violent.
          Nothing is gained feeding the fire more fuel.
          Stay composed; you must exercise prudence.
          Seek the guilty party and punish him alone.
          Make him pay for his sins. Only he should atone."

38   Further reasons still the elder adduced,
          Unfolding his heart and mind as he spoke.
          And yet fierce Herod could not be induced
          To hear what he said. With disdain, he broke
          The man off and refused to make a truce.
          Like a tiger or bear when goaded or poked,
          The king's eyes shot hatred. It was clear from his face:
          He rejected the speaker as well as the case.

39   Baruch—a man harboring spite and scorn—
          Was a creature of the court to the bone.
          He was cunning and false, long had he borne
          Envy within and ill will to the throne.
          Of fervid mind, the counselor had sworn
          To see blood flow and ever had he shown
          Desire for death. Nature had so made him
          That appeals to mercy would never dissuade him.

40   His head was bare, and his face grew no beard.
          He was vigorous, though flecks of silver
          Here and there revealed the length of his years.
          Standing at attention the flatterer
          Listened a while but then sealed up his ears
          To avoid hearing words of discretion.
          Baruch bowed before his arrogant lord.
          His gaze narrowed; out his wickedness poured:

41   —Signor, sudasti e guerreggiasti, e quante
        La destra tua vittoriosa e forte
        Nel nemico feroce e ribellante
        Sanguinose stampò piaghe di morte,
        Tant'ella ha bocche lodatrici e tante
        S'aperse a gloria eterna eterne porte;
        Onde puoi dir, ch'hai con illustri affanni
        Vinti in un punto i tuoi nemici e gli anni.

42   Quinci, con pace altrui, creder mi giova,
        Che non senza ragion temi e paventi.
        L'invidia che 'n altrui spesso si cova,
        Esser può che gran cose ardisca e tenti,
        E che tratti congiure, e che sommova
        Ad armeggiar tumultuarie genti.
        Però che 'l Ciel ne la reale altezza
        Duo nemici congiuse, Odio e Grandezza.

43   Popolo rozzo, indomito e selvaggio,
        Gente vaga di risse e di rivolte,
        Vulgo incostante e presto ad ogni oltraggio
        Reggi Signor, che calcitrò più volte.
        Aviso fia di re discreto e saggio
        Frenar quest' ire impetuose e stolte,
        I rischi riparar de le sciagure,
        E i danni antiveder de le future.

44   Spegnesi di leggier breve favilla
        Pria che 'n fiamma maggior s'avanzi ed erga;
        Facil' è riversar picciola stilla
        Anzi che d'acque in legno empia e sommerga;
        Fresca piaga saldar, quand'altri aprilla,
        Vidi, e vidi piegar tenera verga,
        Ch'al fin, se l'una invecchia e l'altra indura,
        Vana la forza è poi, vana la cura.

41   "Great Sire, seasoned in battle and war,
      Your hand's mighty, conquering force
      Has left countless foes bloody and gored.
      And so your name, as a matter of course,
      Has grown famous for deeds of the sword.
      Fame eternal will adorn your court.
      Indeed, you can say your glorious endeavors
      Have beaten time and the enemy forever.

42   "Thus—I mean no disrespect to others—
      I believe that your cares are well founded.
      All too often, the envy discovered
      In mortal breasts has only compounded
      Scheming and intrigue. Given their druthers,
      People revolt with hopes that are groundless.
      Alas, it is but a too-certain thing
      That Hatred and Grandeur attend the King.

43   "Vulgar rabble—unruly and savage,
      A horde desiring riot and conflict,
      Fickle swarm, ever ready to ravage—
      Such people do you govern. They inflict,
      Perverse, stiff-necked, and stubborn, great damage.
      Thus, I conclude it is right to restrict
      The harm they can do. Take decisive actions.
      Thereby will you prevent future infractions.

44   "A small flame can be extinguished easily,
      Before the fire spills and spreads outside;
      One can stop water from filling a boat's keel—
      Unless, already, the leak has grown wide.
      And many times I have seen a wound heal
      When only a fresh compress was applied.
      But left untreated, it simply grows worse;
      Nothing can be done by doctor or nurse.

45   Opra fia di te degna e di quel senno
      Che sotto l'elmo incanutì pugnando
      E, fatto formidabile col cenno,
      Seppe trattar, pria che lo scettro, il brando,
      Far contrasto ai principii, i quai si denno
      Sempre curar, ma molto più regnando:
      Convien, ch'attento vegghi e che ben guardi
      A quel che poi vietar non potrai tardi.

46   Dice chi più non sa, che 'n petto regio
      Somma lode è pietà; ciò non negh'io.
      Al fido, al buon, l'usar pietate è fregio,
      Indegno è di pietà l'infido, il rio.
      Oltre che poscia onor non ha né pregio,
      Quando ancor non sia giusto, uom che sia pio.
      Son Giustizia e Pietà compagne e, quasi
      De la virtù real sostegno e basi.

47   Più ti dirò. Sai ben che in sua radice
      Ancor non fermo in tutto è questo impero.
      Tenero e fresco è il tuo dominio, e lice
      Sempre a signor novello esser severo.
      Anzi, a terrore altrui, non si disdice
      Farsi a torto talor crudele e fiero.
      La ragion del dever cede a lo sdegno,
      O cede almen a la ragion del regno.

48   Qualor di regno trattasi e d'onore
      Ragionevol partito è l'insolenza,
      E ne' casi importanti, assai migliore
      È la temerità che la prudenza.
      Ma prudenza par questa, ed è timore,
      Codardigia, che volto ha di demenza.
      Non, se non dopo 'l fatto, alcun pensiero
      Aver dee loco, ove ne va l'impero.

45   "It were an undertaking worthy of you—
       Whose hair has grown white on the field,
       Who have struck terror in more than a few,
       Who brandish the scepter, the sword, and shield—
       To offer resistance without further ado.
       Act to preserve the power you wield!
       See that, swiftly, you put a stop to events,
       Afterward, it will be too late to repent.

46   "Those who know no better say a pious heart
       Should beat in a king's breast. I do not deny
       It is true, yet it is true only in part.
       The disloyal deserve no indulgence—fie!
       Mercy's a disgrace if it does not start
       And end with a stern judge whom none dare defy.
       Clemency and punishment are allies; ever
       Have they held might and power together.

47   "Still more will I share. You know your position.
       It does not stand firm. Your rule must be sure.
       It is meet that one of your condition
       Be ruthless. Nor should a king ever spurn
       Ill repute, lest contempt and derision
       Attach to his name. That much is certain.
       Though it's true that duty has its own worth,
       Raison d'état should receive greater berth.

48   "When it's a matter of politics and power
       —To say nothing of honor—a strong nerve
       Is always required. Indeed, in the hour
       Of need, hesitation in no way will serve.
       Prudence is mere appearance: there cowers
       Behind it base fear, fatal lack of verve.
       Never give an impulse a second thought;
       By seizing the day, the future is bought.

49   Quand' altro ben da così fatto scempio
       Non segua ed altro effetto e' non sortisca,
       Per la memoria almen di quest' essempio
       Non fia più mai chi di tradirti ardisca,
       E se di tanti pur solo quell'empio
       Verrà che campi e che sue trami ordisca,
       Tutti, da strage tal già sbigottiti,
       Non avrà chi 'l secondi o chi l'aiti.

50   Ma poniam pur ch'alcun non fia giamai
       Ch'a la corona tua machini inganno:
       Da la fama a temer però non hai
       Titolo di protervo e di tiranno,
       Anzi di giusto e d'incorrotto avrai
       Loda immortal da gli uomini che sanno;
       Che se severo e formadibil sei
       Con gl' innocenti, or che farai co' rei?

51   Aggiungi poi, che 'l Re del Ciel custode
       Sempre è de' regi e protettor de' grandi.
       Son carissimi a Dio, però ch'ei gode
       In terra aver chi 'n vece sua comandi.
       Or se da lui favoreggiato Erode
       Con insoliti segni e memorandi
       Più d'un'aviso n'ebbe e più d'un messo,
       Questo mi tacerò, tel sai tu stesso.

52   La nova in Ciel misteriosa stella
       Stella non fu, che quivi a caso ardesse,
       Ma fu lingua di Dio, che 'n sua favella:
       —Guardati, o Re giudeo—parve dicesse.
       E gl'indovini eroi scorti da quella,
       Che con voci tra noi chiare ed espresse
       Cercando gian del re de' Palestini,
       Che altro fur che messaggier divini?

49   "If nothing else, action gives people a lesson;
As a result, no one in future days
Who minds the past will dare question
Your might and dominion in any way.
Should ever a traitor plan aggression,
Seek to bring others under his sway,
So deeply will they be marked by the slaughter,
Even the bravest will waver and falter.

50   "Let us suppose that there never appears
A man with designs on your throne.
Even so, there is no need to fear
The name of tyrant, for you'll have shown
That you are incorruptible. Men hold dear
Leaders to whom they know what they owe.
They always praise order, however stern:
Condemn the innocent, and the guilty will learn.

51   "Consider: the Lord in Heaven defends
Kings always, for He loves the good and the great.
They rule in His stead. He protects His friends.
You are marked to enjoy a lucky fate.
It can be seen by what the signs portend
Above. The sky augurs well for the state.
No need to count them or say what they tell—
Everyone sees them and knows them full well.

52   "The mysterious light newly shone
Was no star at all, but different in kind,
And its tongue speaks words to one of God's own.
Great Herod, King of the Jews, I remind
You of the three Sages wishing to know
Where to find the ruler of Palestine.
These pilgrims are in no way mortal;
They came here through a heavenly portal.

53 Ch'altri semplice plebe e sempre vaga
Di novità, volga a suo senno e giri,
Stranio non è; ma che sagace e maga
Gente e gente real dietro si tiri,
Sì ch'ella qual fatidica e presaga,
China l'adori e stupida l'ammiri,
Altrui lasciando i proprii regni in cura
Per via sì lunga e per stagion sì dura,

54 Questo è ben da temer. Punir l'aguato
Con supplicio commun, quand' altri il celi,
Gl'interessi affidar del regio stato,
Son giustissime leggi, e non crudeli.
Se certo è pur, che 'l traditor sia nato,
E non è chi l'accusi o chi 'l riveli,
Dunque tutti son rei, dunque dir puoi
Disleale e rubel ciascun de' tuoi.

55 Altri, cui molle il cor molce e lusinga
L'amor paterno e la pietà de' figli,
Ch' ama gli ozii domestici, depinga
Lievi l'ingiurie e facili i perigli;
Ciò che non è, pur come sia, s'infinga,
A suo senno e piacer parli e consigli:
O che molto timor de' danni sui,
O che poco pensiero ha de gli altrui.

56 Me, cui l'età non già, ma la fatica
Fatto anzitempo ha biancheggiar la chioma,
Che fra gente congiunta e fra nemica
Fui già teco in Arabia e teco in Roma,
Morso non riterrà sì ch'io non dica,
Ch'a gran re gran sospetto è grave soma.
Tanto mi detta il ver, non tesso inganno,
Né più miro al mio pro ch'a l'altrui danno.

53   "That the rabble, eager for anything new,
        Sees it in this way should be no surprise.
        But the wise men—and their followers, too,
        From over the sands—view with other eyes:
        Beholding the wonder, these sages do
        Obeisance to truth no one denies.
        They see fit to leave their kingdoms behind,
        And make this journey in season unkind.

54   "This great undertaking should give one pause;
        I think communal punishment is deserved.
        If the traitor hides, you have rightful cause:
        You should see to it the land is preserved.
        The matter now stands as firm as the law:
        They are guilty if they refuse to serve.
        No one will say where it is that he dwells,
        Justly you suppose that your subjects rebel.

55   "Others' hearts are softened by sentiment
        —Love for family, children, and the weak—
        Inhabiting some squalid tenement,
        They would ignore the ills of which I speak.
        That is to deny facts that now are patent.
        People murmur and low, stupid as sheep.
        It is only their concern for themselves;
        They do not care about anyone else.

56   "It is not age that has whitened my head,
        But too much labor in too little time.
        Among foe and friend abroad was I led
        In your service, while I was in my prime.
        I am not scared to speak, and I have said
        What I think: kings need an untroubled mind.
        Truth demands that I reveal myself straight,
        Disregarding my own—and others'—fate.

57   Io col mondo e col Ciel qui mi protesto,
Giudici e testimoni il rege e voi,
Ch'ai ripari del mal vuolsi esser presto:
Mozzar le lunghe e non dolersi poi.
Sire, star che ti val pensoso e mesto,
Se l'arbitrio hai del tutto? e che non puoi?
La cosa, a quel ch'espresso omai si vede,
Indugio non sostien, pietà non chiede.

58   Talor fisico esperto in braccio essangue
Fa volontaria e picciola ferita,
Né poche risparmiar stille di sangue
Suol, perché 'l corpo e 'l cor si serbi in vita.
Spesso accorto chirurgo, ad uom che langue,
Porge in atto crudel pietosa aita:
Incide, incende e ne l'infermo loco
Pon per maggior salute il ferro e 'l foco.

59   Sommergansi nel mar merci e tesori
Pur che campi la nave e giunga a riva;
Tronchinsi i membri ignobili e minori,
Sol che 'l capo real si salvi e viva;
Resti la pianta Ebrea di frondi e fiori
E d'inutili germi ignuda e priva,
Perché 'l ceppo maggior del regio stelo
Dritto s'inalzi e senza intoppi al Cielo.

60   Pera pur l'innocente, e pera il reo,
S'a l'innocenza in grembo il mal s'annida;
In sacrificio al regnator Ebreo
Tra mille giusti, un misfattor s'uccida;
Versi spada real sangue plebeo,
Caggian nemici e non nemici—ei grida—
Vita servil con gran ragion si spregia
Per sottrarre a gran rischio anima regia—.

57   "Before Heaven and Earth I must protest.
      May you, my Lord, witness. If you desire
      To see these ills repaired, do not dare rest:
      Respond quickly, before matters turn dire.
      What is there to gain from further distress?
      You can do as you please. Hear me, O Sire,
      The danger you face is as clear as the day:
      It forbids mercy and admits no delay.

58   "Studied physics make a cut on a limb—
      A small incision so the blood will flow.
      The wound releases the sickness that swims
      In the patient, so health again will grow.
      Often a skilled surgeon, when life's force dims,
      Seems cruel. Yet it is mercy he bestows:
      He cuts the flesh, burns the infirmity
      With steel and fire, and checks the malady.

59   "At sea, sailors cast off goods and effects
      So the struggling vessel will reach the shore.
      One also removes bodily defects,
      For the healthier parts to be restored.
      Strip needless growth from the people elect:
      Free it of the unwanted seeds and spores,
      So that the hearty plant straight up may rise
      And, without encumbrance, reach to the skies.

60   "Perish the blameless and the delinquent!
      Evil grows even in innocent womb.
      Let a sacrifice to the king be sent,
      With thousand others, the guilty be doomed!
      No matter if plebeian blood is spent:
      Kill foes present and future!" Baruch boomed.
      "No consequence holds the life of a slave,
      By his death alone can the realm be saved."

61   Così dic'egli, e con vie men turbato
      Ciglio a' suoi detti il re perverso applaude,
      Fermo in sua fera voglia e lusingato
      Da dolce suon d'adulatrice laude.
      Sorge e dà tosto a i principi commiato
      Machinator di scelerata fraude,
      E corre, in guisa pur di rigid' angue,
      Inferocito, inviperito al sangue.

62   Tace, e più ognor lo stimola e tormenta
      Mordace cura e fervido pensiero,
      E lo sferza la Furia, e lo spaventa
      Tema di morte e gelosia d'impero.
      Che non fa, che non osa, e che non tenta
      Un orgoglio tiranno, un cor severo?
      Presume sì, che temerario e stolto
      Vorria poter ciò che poter gli è tolto.

63   Già di Sion la notte empia sorgea
      Gravida d'armi e di mortali ecclissi;
      Né tanto orribil mai la terra Ebrea
      La vide uscir da' tenebrosi abissi.
      Quanto si stende il ciel de la Giudea
      Di tartarea caligine coprissi;
      Sì fosco il mondo appar, che par che debbia
      Disfarsi in ombra e convertirsi in nebbia.

64   Intanto il re, d'indugio impaziente,
      Da l'empia crudeltà spinto e commosso,
      Menade sembra, allor ch'orribilmente
      Rota se stessa al suon del cavo bosso.
      Da' timori solleciti si sente
      Tutto agitato il cor, tutto percosso.
      Ma in vista è tal, che da ciascun veduto
      Dee vie più che temere esser temuto.

61   Thus he spoke. The despot cruel and perverse
        Applauded, and calm returned to his gaze.
        The king's temper had gone to bad, from worse.
        Heartened by the flattery and the praise,
        He rose and bade the ministers disperse.
        Then the wicked fraudster, without delay,
        Darted—like a snake uncoiling and striking—
        Forth in a blaze of venomous lightning.

62   But soon Herod falls silent. Short of breath,
        Distressed, and now struck by apprehension,
        Lashed by the Fury, he fears his own death:
        Woes of the mighty fill him with tension.
        Thus, all will he dare to achieve success:
        Tyranny knows no bounds to invention.
        So vast and immense his foolish pride swells,
        What cannot be done, he yet would do well.

63   Over Zion loomed the unholy sky,
        Pregnant with imminent bloodshed and war;
        Never had the land seen such shadows fly
        Up from the banks of the Stygian shore.
        'Pon the vault of Judea blackness lies,
        Oozing night's pitch from Tartarean pores.
        The whole world appears, under the dark shroud,
        Ready to dissolve into fog and clouds.

64   Meanwhile the king, impatient of delay,
        Spurred by impious cruelty, shaking,
        Roves like a Maenad when the thyrsus waves:
        Convulsed, anguished, with all his limbs quaking.
        He feels, within, agitation and rage,
        His heart beats rapidly, sore and aching.
        Still, the way that he outwardly appears
        Shows he fears less, than he is to be feared.

65   Chiama i ministri, e del furor suo stolto
L'impeto è tal, che favellar mal pote;
E quasi fiume in se medesmo avolto
Ch'entro il rapido gorgo i sassi arrote,
Soffoga i detti, e 'l suon non ben disciolto
Rompe, e con quel fragor frange le note,
Con cui da l'ime viscere disserra
Prigioniero vapor concava terra.

66   Vuol che di quante madri il cerchio aduna
Di Betthelemme, entro la regia soglia,
Con qualunque bambin gli accenti in cuna
Oltra l'anno secondo ancor non scioglia,
L'altro mattin, senza restarne alcuna,
Tutto il numero sparso in un s'accoglia;
Così comanda, e 'l suo decreto esposto
La buccina real divulga tosto.

67   Tace il fellon l'ordita froda e vieta
Che 'l trattato crudel si scopra altrui,
E sotto altro color di cagion lieta
Vela l'insidie e i fieri inganni sui;
Nulla le donne san de la secreta
Machina, ch' apprestata è lor da lui.
L'editto altre conforta, altre sgomenta,
Parte pensa ubidir, parte paventa.

68   —Santa Pietà, s'estinta in Ciel non sei,
Poi che di terra in Ciel schiva fuggisti,
Mira i fasti quaggiù, mira i trofei
De la nemica tua flebili e tristi.
Perché non scendi omai? Gl'oltraggi Ebrei
Son da te non curati, o pur non visti?
Vedi che sermo o scampo, onde non pera
D'Israelle il buon seme, altro non spera—.

65   He calls his servants, but is so addled,
      He barely manages even to speak.
      Like a whirling river that does battle
      With itself, locked up between crags and peaks,
      The king's sputtering words, choked and babbled,
      Thunder—like the captive vapor that leaks
      From the Earth when, deep in its dark bowels,
      Underground caves emit grumbles and growls.

66   He decrees that Bethlehem's mothers should
      Appear on the next day in his presence.
      Furthermore, it is to be understood,
      That they bring along with them their infants.
      King Herod—who wishes the greater good—
      Desires to behold all in an instant.
      Thus does he command, and so straightaway
      The edict is published without delay.

67   The despot hides the fraud he has ordered,
      Forbids that one reveal his real demand,
      And so, he veils his insidious scheme
      Under colors of a happier plan.
      The poor women do not know the secret
      Design engineered by the wicked man:
      Some of them take comfort in the decree;
      Others grow worried and do not agree.

68   "Holy mercy, if you dwell in the skies,
      Having fled from the Earth's sorrowful lands,
      Witness the ceremony—the sad prize
      Held in the clutches of enemy hands.
      Why do you not rush down and alight?
      Why is it that your view does not expand
      To include the Jews? Verily, Israel's seed
      Has no other hope in its time of need."

69   Così, vicina a rimaner Rachele
Orba de' figli, in suon dolente e pio
Querelando sen giva, e le querele
Giunte lassù la dea benigna udio.
E vaga d'impedir l'opra crudele
Si stese a piè del tribunal di Dio,
Tolse il freno a la voce, e sciolse intanto
La vela al sospirar, la vena al pianto.

70.   —Occhi il tutto miranti, occhi divini,
Sete forse—dicea—rivolti altrove?
O de gl'innocentissimi bambini
V'è presente lo strazio, e non vi muove?
Vedete umani cori, anzi ferini,
A quali infamie inusitate e nove
Trae, mercè sol de l'empio infernal angue,
Nata di fame d'or, sete di sangue.

71   Padre già più non sei d'ira e vendetta,
Qual fosti un tempo, essecutor zelante,
Dunque perché vuoi pur la tua saetta
Scoccar severo e fulminar tonante?
Forse del puro Agnel l'ostia diletta
A la salute altrui non è bastante?
Non è di vivo umor stilla ch'ei versi
Largo prezzo a comprar mille universi?

72   Sovenir pur ti dee con quanto affetto
Già di Sion gli abitatori amasti:
Sacerdozio real, popolo eletto,
Città ch'appellar tua spesso degnasti.
Esser d'ogni sua porta e d'ogni tetto
Custode eterno e difensor giurasti:
Giuramenti d'amor, patti di zelo;
Or può le leggi sue rompere il Cielo?

69   Thus Rachel, fearing for her daughters' sons,
       Intoned pious and piteous lament.
       She mourned the approaching death of dear ones;
       To a kindly star her cries made ascent.
       There, the goddess—to halt ill to the young—
       Went before the tribunal of Heaven.
       Loosening the reins that held back her tongue,
       She now spoke to avert evils to come:

70   "Orbs that see all," she began, "Eyes divine,
       Does your gaze linger at some distant place?
       To the slaughter of babes can you be blind,
       Unmoved, untouched by the disgrace?
       Hard hearts that are unfamiliar in kind
       To savage beasts, even, quicken their pace:
       Spurred by the abyss and the serpent's wiles,
       They seek the gold innocent blood defiles.

71   "No more the father of vengeance and wrath,
       No longer are you a judge stern and dire.
       Why, then, is it that you open a path
       To grief instead of sending down your fire?
       Is the angelic host no longer enough
       To save mankind when the evil conspire?
       Is there not the living blood that, when spilt,
       Would redeem a thousand worlds of their guilt?

72   "Recall to your mind in what affection
       You hold the people of Zion, their high
       Priests, and the city of their election.
       Often have you called them your own. So why
       Would you, you who have sworn them protection,
       Forsake them now and withdraw to the sky?
       Why breach promises made without caution or clause?
       Can you, Empyrean, break your own laws?

73   Così tosto ti sdegni? È ver che sante
Sono e giuste quell'ire onde sfavilli.
Ma qual Angelo è puro a te davante?
O qual colonna in Ciel, che non vacilli?
Già non m'oppongo al tuo voler costante
Perché sì calde a te lacrime io stilli;
Sai, che tanto m'è bel quanto a te piace,
E che sol di tua voglia io fò mia pace.

74   Cheggioti sol, s'alcun giusto conforto
Fia dever ch'addolcisca i miei dolori,
Che la spada per me non vibri a torto
La libratrice de gli umani errori.
Qual dritto vuol che resti ucciso e morto
Il buon lignaggio Ebreo da' suoi furori?
E che, pur come reo, dannato vegna,
Chi non sa, che sia colpa a pena indegna?

75   Se piegar di costei non so pregando
L'implacabile sdegno e 'l fero orgoglio,
Pieghino te cui sol mercè dimando,
Queste supliche amare, ond'io mi doglio.
Vaglianmi questi gemiti ch'io spando,
Giovinmi queste lacrime ch'io scioglio.
Sovra l'incendio de' vicini mali
Piovano i fonti tuoi l'acque immortali.

76   Deh, se nulla in te può forza di prece,
Che 'l tutto vince e l'impossibil pote,
Che talor piover fiamme e talor fece
Fermar del Sol le fuggitive rote;
E se 'l preso flagel depor ti lece
Al tenor de l'altrui supplici note,
Volgiti a questi miei fervidi preghi,
Né voler ch'a Pietà pietà si neghi.

73   "Your brow darkens so quickly? It is true,
     Right, and good for your anger to be roused.
     Indeed, can even an angel stand pure
     Before you here in this heavenly house?
     Your authority inspires awe-filled view,
     See how, with hot tears, my eyes my breast douse.
     Humbly I come asking that rescue be sent
     I know nothing can be without your assent.

74   "I request only comfort and solace,
     Relief to lessen the grief and the pain.
     May your divine sword cut down the lawless,
     Strike with justice and now make your will plain.
     The Hebrew stock that is as yet flawless
     How is it that poor babes are to be slain?
     Luckless children requiring no absolution
     Are the very ones destined for execution!

75   "If words cannot soften your implacable rage,
     May you, whose mercy I hereby implore,
     Yield to my cries. May your wrath be assuaged
     By the laments that my tortured breast pours.
     Let the sobs I heave be compassion's gauge
     Let tears fling open a merciful door,
     Raining down on the fires of brutal force,
     Gentle streams that flow from an immortal source.

76   "If my supplications will not prevail
     On you, Majesty, who command all things,
     You who wield forces of fiery hail
     And can halt the Sun's circling rings,
     If ever 'gainst divine scourge did avail
     Sounds borne to the Heavens on prayer's wings,
     Please hear what I say now, and do not spurn
     Devotion that seeks devotion in turn.

77 Apri il grembo a le grazie, aprilo e movi
Quel braccio omai che l'universo folce;
Viva la Donna del Giordano e provi,
Fra tanti amari suoi, stilla di dolce;
Su l'incendio crudel diffondi e piovi,
Con la man, ch'ogni duol ristora e molce,
Da le non vote mai fonti superne
L'acque immortali, e le rugiade eterne—.

78 Pietà così dicea. Gli alati Orfei
Doppiaro il canto e su le lire aurate:
—Pietà, pietà de' pargoletti Ebrei
Pietà—sonaro, e risonar—pietate—.
Girò le luci il gran Motore in lei
Dal seggio ove, fra l'anime beate,
Siede Unità distinta e Triade unita,
Corda di tre cordon, man di tre dita.

79 Ne la sua fronte, a gli Angeli sì cara,
Vive la Vita e ne trae cibo eterno.
Questa sol è che 'ntorbida e rischiara
La tempesta e'l seren, la state e 'l verno:
Dal suo ciglio felice il Sole impara
De la face immortal l'alto governo:
Dal dolce de' sant'occhi ardente giro
Prendon le stelle e 'l Ciel l'oro e 'l zaffiro.

80 Le fila sue di non so che conteste
Ha quel ricco, che 'l copre abito santo;
Paion di Sol, se 'l Sol, che dal celeste
Sole ha sol lo splendor, splende cotanto.
Luminosa una nebbia egli ha per veste,
Nubilosa una luce egli ha per manto,
Riluce sì, che la sua luce il vela
E ne' suoi proprii rai se stesso cela.

77   "Open your bosom to blessèd acts of grace,
        Move your arm, the axis of the universe,
        Let My Lady of Jordan live and taste
        A little sweet in so much bitterness.
        With the great hand that all griefs can erase,
        Down upon fire and flames cruel and perverse,
        Rain, from supernal founts that never dry,
        Immortal waters, fresh dew from the sky."

78   Such discourse the voice of Piety made.
        The heavenly host redoubled its hymn:
        "Mercy! Mercy! For the poor Jewish babes,
        Mercy!" cried all the angels on the wing.
        Then the Mover of the Skies turned His gaze
        From upon high, from where all blessings spring—
        The tripartite Oneness, the Trinity single,
        As fingers and hand in a whole are commingled.

79   On His brow, to the angels dear, dwells Life,
        Who here draws her eternal provision.
        She sends forth storms, in anger and in strife,
        Or gentle calm, when free of division.
        The seasons come from her. She teaches the Sun
        With her radiance how light is given.
        From the sweetly burning orb of her eyes,
        Come the gold and sapphire of stars in the skies.

80   Her gown—what it is, is impossible to know—
        Gleams like the proud vestments of holy men,
        Shines like the Sun, with the majestic glow
        Of the One who confers sainthood upon them.
        A luminous cloud for a dress is thrown
        Over her frame supple and lithe. And when
        The goddess moves, she conceals her own light;
        Bright in her own rays, she escapes from sight.

81   Da sè solo compreso, in sè s'asconde,
       Tutto, e parte a sè stesso, e centro, e sfera,
       Immortal sì, ma non ha vita altronde,
       Non ha morte o natal, sempr' è qual era,
       E mentre si communica e diffonde,
       Tutto cria, tutto move, al tutto impera,
       Il tutto abbraccia, e pur sè sol contiene,
       Sommo bel, piacer sommo e sommo bene.

82   Nova pietà, ch'ogni rigor gli ha tolto,
       Par che nel cor del Creator si stampi.
       Par ch'i dolci occhi in lei fiso e rivolto
       Di doppio amor più vivamente avampi.
       Arse di zelo ed inondò dal volto
       Un abisso di fiamme, un mar di lampi.
       Onde tutto rigaro il sacro loco
       Torrenti di splendor, fiumi di foco.

83   Tremaro i poli a la sua voce, e l'asse,
       Che sostien la gran machina, si torse.
       De le sfere sovrane e de le basse
       Tacque il vario concento e 'l ciel non corse.
       Tigri con Gange in dietro il piè ritrasse,
       Curvossi Atlante e vacillaron l'Orse,
       E da l'alta immortal bocca di Dio
       Irrevocabilmente il fato uscio.

84   —O benedetta—ei disse—o sola avvezza
       Torcere il corso al mio divin furore,
       De l'eterne mie cure alta dolcezza,
       Sacro trastullo e mio celeste amore.
       Gloria mia, mio tesoro e tenerezza
       De le viscere mie, trafitto il core
       M'ha il tuo pregar; sono i tuoi preghi ardenti,
       Ferrati di pietà strali pungenti—.

81   By Himself alone comprehended, and hidden
      Within His own glory, both center and sphere,
      Immortal is He, without end or beginning,
      Beyond compass of birth, death, decade, or year.
      Unto Himself complete, yet imprinting
      His will—to make, to command, and to steer.
      All He embraces and offers: joy and beauty,
      The Highest Good that unites desire and duty.

82   New mercy, it seems, no hardness of heart
      In the Creator's great breast now is felt,
      His kindly orbs turn upon her and start
      To glow with twice as much love and to melt.
      He flashes in ardor, as the flames dart;
      A storm of fire pours forth as the light belts,
      Rushing to ignite and feed lucent pools
      Of the highest realm, both burning and cool.

83   The poles shudder, tremble as His voice sounds,
      And the center of the great wheel revolves.
      In the highest sphere and deep in the ground,
      Only calm: here it does not move at all.
      The waters of Tigris and Ganges turn 'round;
      Atlas bends low; the starry Bears nearly fall.
      God Himself now speaks in order to apportion
      What nothing can repeal, universal fortune.

84   "Blessèd one," He says, "You who endeavor
      To temper my fury and check my rage,
      Sweetly softening the woes that ever
      Beset me. Companion gentle and sage!
      Beloved glory, exquisite treasure,
      The worries of my heart you have allayed.
      With mild entreaties and burning prayers,
      Your tender darts have dispelled all my cares."

85   Ma come tanta gloria intende e spia,
Non che lingua l'esprima, oscuro ingegno?
Meglio quel ch'ei non è, che qual ei sia
Narrar può rozza penna e stile indegno.
—O—diss'egli e baciolla—o cara mia,
O caro, o dolce, o prezioso pegno,
Come rigido teco essere potrei,
Se tu mio parto, anzi me stesso sei?

86   Per te, figlia, dal nulla il tutto io tolsi,
L'aria distesi, il foco in alto affissi,
Nel gran vaso del mar l'acque raccolsi
Ed al suo corso il termine prescrissi;
I fonti e i laghi strinsi, i fiumi sciolsi,
L'ampia terra fondai sovra gli abissi,
E i fermissimi cardini del mondo
De la volta del Ciel supposi al pondo.

87   Per te la Luna e 'l Sole, e per te solo
Le stelle ornai di luce, ornai di moto;
Fei tra' giri del Ciel stabile il polo,
Criai, mobili e lievi, Africo e Noto;
Lo striscio a gli angui, a gli augelletti il volo
Diedi, a le fere il corso, a' pesci il nuoto,
Di fior, d'erbe e di piante il suol dipinsi,
E 'n quattro spazii il vago anno distinsi.

88   De le fatture mie fui poscia vago
Formar la somma, e sì fu l'uomo espresso,
Del teatro del mondo illustre imago;
Anzi del mondo è mio teatro ei stesso,
Ché 'n lui sol mi trastullo, in lui m'appago,
E la sembianza mia vagheggio in esso:
Nobil fabrica e bella in cui si scerne
La cima e 'l fior de le bellezze eterne.

85   Yet can intelligence less than divine
Ever compass or grasp such vast reason?
What it is not—and not what it is—define
Parties presumptuous and unseasoned.
"O," He says with a kiss, "Beloved Mine,
—You, who are my pledge precious and kind—
Could I ever refuse you, you who are part
Of Myself and therefore Thou Myself art?

86   "By you, daughter, I drew all from the void,
Spread the air, and lighted the fires on high.
Into the sea's vessels water I poured,
And I set, to make borders, shores nigh.
The springs, the lakes, and rivers I then scored
In land over the abyss by and by.
The poles I established to support Heaven's dome;
I anchored the globe, gave Creation a home.

87   "Through you are the Moon, Sun, and Stars given,
Through you alone exist light and motion;
The axis was fixed for the circles of Heaven,
And winds blew over the land and the ocean;
Serpents crawl, the birds fly, and fish swim,
—All lives and teems on the same condition.
Flowers and plants owe their colorful declension,
And the seasons their course, to your intervention.

88   "When all had been done, I then wished to shape
The loftiest being. And so Man was formed.
The glorious image of the world's stage,
He provides, for all, the measure and norm.
In his endeavors I Myself engage.
In him, I appear mirrored and transformed.
In this noble creature once did I see
The flower and crown of eternity.

89   Ma dapoi che 'l meschino a perder venne,
       Colpa sai ben di cui, grazia cotanta,
       Corsi tosto al riparo, onde convenne
       La tua mano allargar pietosa e santa.
       Chi morir non potea, mortal divenne
       E di spoglia terrestre ancor s'ammanta,
       Finch'ei venga a fornir laggiù quell'opra
       Che commessa da me gli fu qua sopra.

90   Fermo è quassù che, 'l sangue egli versando,
       Schiera ancor d'innocenti il sangue versi,
       Perché la Chiesa mia, ch'ei va fondando,
       Di fregi abondi e di tesor diversi,
       Né questa poi, ch'ha la bilancia e 'l brando,
       Meco mai d'alcun torto abbia a dolersi.
       Figlia, ciò non poss'io, né voler voglio,
       Ben sedar deggio in parte il tuo cordoglio:

91   Io vo' ch'a queste mie vittime prime,
       Ad onta altrui, l'oltraggio in gloria torni,
       Il duolo in gioia, e di splendor sublime
       Ogni lor piaga al par del Sol s'adorni.
       Vo' che se cruda man tronca ed opprime
       Lo stame in terra a i lor teneri giorni,
       In Ciel Parca immortale a la lor vita
       Torca di biondo fil linea infinita.

92   E farò sì che 'l re del mondo oscuro
       Resti, e seco il tiranno empio schernito,
       Tanto che sia quel tempo a pien maturo
       Ch' a lo scampo commun fu stabilito.
       Cercheran del gran parto; egli securo
       Fuggirà ben difeso e custodito;
       Fuga non di timor, ma ben di scherno,
       Per vincer Morte ed ingannar l'Inferno—.

89   "But alas, when the poor wretch came to lose
His grace (well do you know through whose bias),
Directly I sought to obtain from you
A fit remedy holy and pious.
The One who was—and is—to death refused
Turned mortal, went to lowest from highest,
So that he might do the work down on Earth
That My divine mind had conceived and birthed.

90   "On high stands written that his blood be spent,
And that the innocents', too, should be spilt.
For my Church must make its might evident.
Not just sword and scale, but riches that fill
Treasuries to honor the firmament.
May you never have doubt of my good will.
Daughter, I could not do else if I wanted to,
Yet I will lessen the pain that it causes you.

91   "The sacrifice of the babes without blame
Shall dishonor those who perform the deed.
Woe will yield joy, glory rise up from shame,
Just as, from night, the brilliant Sun proceeds.
When the hand that sunders, plunders, and maims
Uproots from the Earth the unblossom'd seed,
On high, immortal Fate will spin a thread
Of bright gold: eternal life for the dead.

92   "The cruel tyrant will remain in the dark
Pit with the king of the murk and the gloom,
Until such time as I will have marked
For all my children to rise from the tomb.
Let Herod try to hunt the one whose part
Is redemption; know, his efforts are doomed.
It is not fear that prompts him to take flight.
He'll beat Death and Hell. He wishes to fight."

93   Disse e fu fatto. Una pennuta luce
      De la beata angelica famiglia
      Vede il pensier di Dio che fuor traluce
      Dal cenno sol de le serene ciglia,
      E dal mondo, ch'eterno arde e riluce,
      Verso il fosco e caduco il camin piglia,
      E co' remi de l'ali in un momento
      Naviga l'aria e va solcando il vento.

94   Leggiadra spoglia in breve spazio ammassa
      D'aure leggiere e di color diversi.
      Poi dal colmo del Ciel volando, lassa
      Precipitosamente in giù cadersi:
      Pria de la sfera immobile trapassa
      I fuochi e i lampi fiammeggianti e tersi,
      Indi de' corpi lubrici e correnti
      Gli obliqui balli e i lievi giri e i lenti.

95   Viensene là dove 'l più basso Cielo
      Di bianca luce i suoi cristalli adorna,
      Né de l'umido cerchio il freddo gelo
      Sente, e sen va fra l'argentate corna.
      Giunge ove 'l foco il ruggiadoso velo
      Asciuga de la dea che l'ombre aggiorna;
      Né l'offendon però gli ardor vicini
      O le fulgide penne o gli aurei crini.

96   Porta gli omeri ignudi, abile vesta
      Gli scende in giù, sotto il sinistro fianco,
      D'un velo sottilissimo contesta
      D'azzurro e d'oro; e, fra purpureo e bianco,
      Fendesi in due la lieve falda; e questa,
      Succinta e breve in su 'l ginocchio manco,
      Mentre vola ondeggiando e si dilata,
      Morde con dente d'or fibbia gemmata.

93   The Deity spoke, and so it was done.
In the host of angels, a feathered light
Saw the divine thought shine bright like the Sun.
The messenger left behind the great heights,
And flew where the air became dark and dun,
Then onward to obscure realms of the night.
With a stroke of his wings, in the blink of an eye,
He sped through the air and parted the sky.

94   Weightless sum of incorporeal mass
—Light, floating air and colorful rainbows—
He took in the sights of the Heavens vast,
Then rushed on to the world lying below:
From the unmoving sphere quickly he passed,
Through the limpid fires that forever glow.
He descends to the perishable world,
Where baser matter dances, gyres, and whirls.

95   He comes to the place where the lowest skies
Array crystals that sparkle in splendor,
Not feeling the air's cold sting, he then flies
And alights on the horn of fine silver.
Here, the goddess hangs her veil out to dry,
Dispelling the shadows that offend her.
(She remains unperturbed, however—
The nearby flames do not disturb her.)

96   Her shoulders are bare; a delicate gown
Covers her form, suspended on the side,
Sliding its finely woven fabric down,
Ornamented in gold, purple, and white.
It descends in two gentle folds, and now
Is bunched where her slender leg makes its stride;
At her knee there shines a bejeweled clasp,
Biting the fabric with teeth like an asp.

97 Spunta dal vago tergo in su i confini
    Gemina piuma e colorata e grande.
    Sazio d'amomo il crespo oro de' crini
    Trecciatura leggiadra a l'aura spande;
    Di piropi immortali e di rubini
    Fascian l'eburnea fronte ampie ghirlande;
    Chiude il bel piè, che mena alte carole,
    Tra gemme che son stelle, oro ch'è Sole.

98 Già la notte sparia, benché sepolta
    Stesse sotterra ancor la maggior lampa;
    Ma la fiamma celeste a volo sciolta
    Fatta in ciel vicesole, arde ed avampa,
    E, ventilando i vanni, in sè raccolta,
    Lungo solco di luce in aria stampa.
    Ingannato il pastor lascia le piume
    Al tremolar del matutino lume.

99 Valle colà ne l'Ethiopia nera,
    Cui corona di rupi alte circonda,
    Ove per entro in su 'l merigge assera,
    Dilata i rami e 'ncontr' al Sol s'infronda.
    Qui con sua pigra e neghittosa schiera
    Il re de' sogni ha la maggion profonda,
    E qui fra cupe e solitarie grotte
    Suol ricovro tranquillo aver la Notte.

100 Stan su gli usci, un d'avorio ed un di corno,
    L'Oblio stordito e l'Ozio agiato e lento,
    Stavvi il Silenzio e fà l'ascolta intorno
    Cheto e col dito su fra 'l naso al mento,
    Quasi accenando al mutolo soggiorno,
    Che non scota le fronde o fera o vento.
    Vedi, non ch'altro, in que' riposti orrori
    Giacer languide l'erbe e chini i fiori.

97   From her ivory back, twinned wings extend,
Spreading radiant color as they ply.
Ringèd tresses of gold flow, curl, and wend,
And they diffuse sweet perfume as she flies.
On her alabaster brow garlands bend—
Eternal garnets and rubies that shine.
Assuring her foot's dainty step is a sandal
That flashes with light from heavenly candles.

98   The night was already fading away,
Though most of the light yet remained buried.
Now the starry fire of the angel blazed
Like another Sun up high. It carried
The day far and wide, into mortal gaze,
Shooting its flames brilliant and varied.
Deceived by the brightness that covers the skies,
The shepherds awaken and from their beds rise.

99   In Ethiopia, there lies hidden
A valley enclosed by great rings of peaks.
With thick brush the place is densely ridden:
Even at noontime, the Sun cannot peek
Where, with lazy, forgetful minions,
The King of Dreams has his castle and keep.
In the murky, isolated cavern,
Night herself finds a welcoming tavern.

100   At the gates—one of ivory, the second
Of horn—Idleness and Forgetting slump;
Silence stands guard and quietly forbids,
Finger at his lips, the slightest knock or bump:
No cracking twig, nor whispering wind,
Nor crashing beast is heard as it jumps.
A desolate land—here, there is nothing to see
Except wilted flowers and languishing weeds.

101   Taccion per entro il bosco ombroso e cieco
L'aure, né tuona ciel, né canta augello,
Né garrisce pastor, né rispond' eco,
Né can latra giamai, né bela agnello,
Se non ch'a piè del taciturno speco
Tra sasso e sasso mormora un ruscello,
Lo cui rauco sussurro, a chi là giace
Rende il sonno più dolce e più tenace.

102   Dentro l'opaco sen de l'antro erboso,
Romito abitator d'ombre secrete,
Steso in un letto d'ebeno frondoso,
Prende il placido dio posa e quiete.
Di papaveri molli ha il capo ombroso,
Ne la sinistra un ramo intinto in Lete,
Su l'altra apoggia la gravosa testa,
E di pelli di tasso è la sua vesta.

103   A pena il ciglio stupido e pesante
E la fronte sostien languida e lassa,
E traboccare accenna, e vacillante
Le tempie alternamente alza ed abbassa;
Vicina al pigro dio mensa fumante,
Che nappi e coppe in larga copia ammassa,
Gl'invia da cibi e vini eletti e rari,
Nube d'odori a lusingar le nari.

104   Là drizzò ratto da gli empirei scanni
L'Angelo il volo, e vide a schiere a schiere
Mille intorno vagar, con bruni vanni,
Simulacri fallaci, ombre leggiere.
Non è però ch'occhio celeste inganni
Illusion d'imagini non vere,
Anzi tosto a que' rai che gli feriro,
Morfeo, Ithatone, e Fantaso fuggiro.

101   In the dark grove, no breeze blows on the fronds,
Nor is movement of flying creatures heard.
No shepherd calls out, nor does echo respond.
No sound of hound or flock stirs.
Just one movement occurs: into a pond,
There, where one hears not a single word,
Between rocks and stones, a brook flows;
In its meandering course, a soft murmur grows.

102   Deep in the heart of the overgrown cave
Lies the dweller lonesome among shadows.
Sprawled on a leafy bed of ebony,
The god takes wonted rest in the hollow.
A wreath made out of poppies crowns his head.
He holds a branch dipped in dark Lethe's flow,
And upon his heavy brow, the other arm rests.
Only a badger's pelt covers his nakedness.

103   His cloudy eyelids he scarcely can lift,
And his weary head droops sluggish and dumb,
Nodding up and down, he listlessly drifts
In and then out of sleep, torpid and numb.
Next to the god, a regal banquet sits
Overflowing with delectable crumbs:
From the rich plates, heady scents waft and blow,
Perfumes of fine wines that tickle his nose.

104   Thither, from Heaven, the angel made way.
When he came, there scattered throng upon throng
Of deceptive likenesses—fleeting shades—
Which flapped, flew, fluttered, and scampered along.
His heavenly eyes were not led astray
By the illusions misleading and wrong.
As soon as the messenger's beams struck the host,
The brood of Morpheus fled, vanished like ghosts.

105   Tra 'l negro stuol di quelle larve alate
Vola bianca e lucente una donzella,
Che di spoglia diafana velate
Porta le membra, a meraviglia bella.
Ali ha d'argento e, qual pavon, fregiate
D'occhi diversi, e Vision s'appella:
Scorta del vero e de' profeti amica,
Del Re celeste ambasciadrice antica.

106   Di cristallo la fronte ha tersa e pura,
Dove scritte son tutte e lineate
Quante produce o può produr Natura
Forme giamai creabili o create.
Dio di sua man le scrisse, e la scrittura
È d'inchiostro di luce a lettre aurate.
Quì spesso ai cari suoi ciò ch'altrui cela,
Quasi in candido foglio, apre e rivela.

107   Qui 'l peregrin Ebreo l'alto mistero
De la scala del Ciel vide e comprese;
Qui de l'Egitto il santo prigioniero
De le spiche adorate il senso intese;
Qui del popol diletto il gran guerriero
Mirò le fiamme in verde spina accese;
E quì lesser del Ciel mille secreti
I veraci di Dio sacri poeti.

108   Qui l'amato discepolo, ripieno
Di quel che 'n carte espresse alto furore
Essule in Pathmo, e prima a Cristo in seno,
Gli occhi chiudendo, aprì l'ingegno e 'l core.
Qui rapito dal carcere terreno
Il dottor de le genti al Ciel, d'amore
Vide, ai sensi mortali in tutto ascose,
Non mai vedute e non sentite cose.

105   In the midst of the swarm of wingèd things,
There floats a maiden glowing bright and fair.
A transparent veil adorns the limbs
Of the beauteous girl in the air.
Her name is Vision; from her silver wings
—Like a peacock's tail—colorful eyes stare.
Friend of the prophets, escort to the Truth,
God's ancient herald, though still in her youth.

106   On her crystalline brow, clear and pure,
All has been written and all defined
That Nature has made or will yet mature
—All that can be conceived in form and kind.
God Himself put it all there, written sure
For the ages, in bright ink and gold lines.
What to profane eyes is ever concealed,
Here to His chosen He often reveals.

107   Here, Jacob beheld the great mystery
Of the ladder and understood its sense;
The riddling harvest, Egypt's history,
Joseph gathered from a dream dark and dense;
Moses viewed his people's delivery
From bondage—the means to lead them thence.
All that thousandfold secrets have said,
Poets belovèd to God here have read.

108   In this place, the disciple of Christ filled
Himself with what holy fury expressed;
On Patmos, yet here, John grasped divine will:
He opened his mind and was blessed.
And the evangelist who sought to build
God's Church for all the nations found rest.
What mortal sense fails to grasp, Paul discerned:
Things no one had seen, truths as yet unlearned.

109 Con questa il divin nunzio in aria ascende,
   Indi sovra la terra e sovra il mare
   Dritto ver Betthelem l'ali distende,
   Ed a Giuseppe addormentato appare.
   L'alba, che sfavillante in ciel risplende,
   Quell'auree impression mostra più chiare,
   Con tutto quel, che nel mirabil viso
   Scarpel celeste ha nuovamente inciso.

110 Ama l'alba costei, brama l'aurora,
   E, più ch'altra stagion, la mattutina,
   Perché meno aggravata, e più in quell'ora
   L'anima da la carne è peregrina.
   Ella volgendo al santo vecchio allora
   La traslucida faccia e cristallina,
   D'ogni specie segnato, il bel diamante
   Del libro spirital gli offerse avante.

111 Fermò Giuseppe entro le note impresse
   Che l'Angel gli additò, l'interno sguardo,
   E distinto di Dio l'ordin vi lesse,
   Zelante ch'al suo scampo ei sia sì tardo.
   Ah fuggi, fuggi—era scolpito in esse—
   Già non è sogno il tuo, sogno bugiardo;
   Oracolo è di Dio vero e fedele,
   Fuggi la terra avara e 'l re crudele.

112 Troppo pur tu fra tante insidie e tante
   Giaci lento e securo; or sorgi, e pria
   Che del gran pegno le vestigia sante
   Rintracci Erode o chi per lui ne spia,
   Tronca gl'indugi, e col celeste infante
   Dritto verso Canopo or or t'invia.
   Là, fin ch'abbi del Ciel novo messaggio,
   Porrai termine e meta al tuo viaggio.

109 With her at his side, the herald takes flight,
  Soars toward Bethlehem over land and sea,
  To where Joseph lies resting, then alights
  And appears before him in a dream.
  Dawn, who sparkles and shimmers in the sky
  Makes the bright forms even clearer to see:
  Her luminescence now intensifies
  The sights and sounds that materialize.

110 Vision loves daybreak more than other hours:
  At this time, less burden weighs down the soul,
  Which soars up at the height of its powers
  And escapes the lowly body's control.
  When she arrived, the sleeper encountered
  Prophecy as if set down in a scroll.
  The characters glistened like bright diamonds,
  Spoke eloquent words long held in silence.

111 Joseph's inner eye turned on the writing
  That was contained in the angelic shapes.
  There he beheld the will of God shining:
  He should not delay to make his escape.
  "Flee, flee!" the sacred letters incite him,
  "The dream you witness is real and not fake.
  Trust an oracle of God, it is true:
  Flee the land whose king is hostile to you.

112 "With treachery near, too long do you rest,
  And lie about idle. Quick, awaken!
  Before one acting at Herod's behest
  Finds you out and hunts down your sweet burden.
  Do not delay, rather bring the child west.
  Straight to Canopus should he be taken.
  When a sign in the skies has made it plain,
  You'll know that the journey's end is attained.

113   Ben del tuo grande allievo il gran cugino
Nato d'Elisabetta, anco in secura
Parte condur lontano e dal vicino
Esterminio campar, del Ciel fia cura;
Ei, chiuso in selva, il precursor divino,
Benché in tenera etate e non matura,
Guarderà da l'insidie; ivi coverto
Gli fia l'antro città, casa il deserto.

114   Va pur, né d'aversari empi e felloni
Timor t'affreni o di tiranno rio.
Tra le fere, tra l'armi e tra' ladroni
Salvo n'andrai per tutto; è teco Dio—.
Qui 'l Sonno e 'l Sogno a l'atre lor magioni
Ratto volar, qui Vision svanio,
E qui l'Angiol lasciollo e sparve e sparse
Luce che l'abbagliò, fiamma che l'arse.

115   Destasi, e sbigottito e stupefatto
Parla a la Vergin, sua sposa e compagna,
Che informata dal Ciel di tutto il fatto,
Non si turba, non teme e non si lagna:
Corre il vecchio a la culla, e quindi tratto
Lo Dio bambin, per tenerezza il bagna
Tutto di pianto, e con paterno affetto
Sel reca in braccio e se lo stringe al petto.

116   E 'l bacia e dice:—E dove andrenne, o figlio,
O, di padre in pietà, figlio in amore?
Fuggir n'è forza il già vicin periglio,
O di quest'alma afflitta anima e core.
Deh, come intempestivo è quest'essiglio,
O del tronco di Iesse unico fiore.
Co' piedi in fasce e con non salde piante
Gir ti convien peregrinando errante.

113   "Your holy charge's cousin, who was born
        To Elizabeth, will see he stays safe and sound—
        He will save him from slaughter and perform
        The celestial duty to which he is bound.
        Though tender of years and as yet unformed,
        The babe knows of the perils all around.
        Let the kinsman guard him from hurt and the grave—
        His mansion the desert, his quarters a cave.

114   "Go forth! And do not be deterred by fear
        Of the merciless foe or wicked king.
        Through beasts, battles, and bandits will you steer
        A sure course, secure under divine wing."
        Then, Sleep and Dream hurried back to their sphere,
        And Vision joined them in vanishing.
        The angel, too, disappeared from sight,
        Flew off in a flash of blinding light.

115   Joseph rose up stupefied and amazed,
        With worry he addressed his maiden bride.
        But Heaven instructed her in its ways,
        And so she neither lamented nor cried.
        With tears of paternal affection he bathed
        The child he held in his arms. From his eyes
        The waters poured down and over his chest;
        He cradled the babe, hugged it to his breast.

116   With a kiss, he asks: "To where are we bound?
        Love makes you my son, but a higher law
        Makes you my father. The danger all 'round
        We must flee; nearer and nearer it draws.
        O, my troubled mind and worried brow,
        How untimely this exile does fall!
        Branch from Jesse's trunk, your feet are unsteady,
        You must wander, though not at all ready.

117   Fuggiam pur; verrò teco, al corpo infermo
       Darà spirto e vigor celeste aita;
       Promette il Ciel per calle alpestre ed ermo
       Al nostro tapinar la via spedita.
       Padre e Signor, tu gli sia guida e schermo,
       Guarda tu mille vite in una vita.
       Fa tu, ch'a buon cammin drizzino il passo,
       Fra 'l bambin, debil donna e vecchio lasso—.

118   Così mentre parlava il balio santo,
       Già tutto accinto a maturar la fuga,
       Giù gli scorrea senza ritegno il pianto,
       Per la guancia senil, di ruga in ruga.
       Il pietoso fanciul l'abbraccia in tanto
       E di sua man le lacrime gli asciuga,
       E compiangendo a le miserie umane
       Lava del vecchiarel le bianche lane.

119   Egli, che l'aria ancor tra chiara e bruna
       Vede, e che tutti ingombra oblio profondo,
       De gli arnesi megliori un fascio aduna
       E ne commette ad umil bestia il pondo,
       Dove in un cesto a guisa pur di cuna,
       Pon la salute universal del mondo.
       —Deh perdona—dicea—se d'ostro o d'oro
       Non t'accoglie, Signor, nobil lavoro.

120   Prema pur re superbo empio tiranno
       Le ricche moli e gli ornamenti illustri.
       Te difenda dal gel povero panno,
       Opera vil di rozze mani industri.
       Se malagiata qui sede ti fanno
       Aride paglie e calami palustri,
       So, che lassù trionfi, e che ti sono
       Reggia il Ciel, manto il Sole e i Troni trono.

117   "Let us hurry and go; may Heaven's hand
Lend us vigor and force to speed our way
As we cross mountains and the desert sand,
Until at last we arrive where we may.
O Father, be our guide through the land,
Shield one life that is pawned for thousands—Yea,
A frail woman and old man pass through the wild;
Smooth the path for us, as we escort the child."

118   As the holy steward utters his prayer
And readies his family to flee,
Tears flow down his cheek, and there
They fill up the wrinkles and seams.
In his arms, the pious child is aware
And dries them off with his hand instantly.
Pitying the misery of the old man,
The babe wipes his beard clean, the best that he can.

119   Hanging between dark and light, the air is all gray.
Nothing moves. Mortals are dead asleep
As Joseph collects the humble array
Of his effects and loads them on a beast.
Carefully, the world's salvation he lays
In a basket—a cradle made of reeds.
He speaks: "Pardon, my Lord, the humble bed;
Better were work of silk and gold instead.

120   "The arrogant, impious tyrant lies
Down on embroidered pillows soft and full.
Against the cold, alas, you must rely
On tough rags that are worked of shaggy wool.
Swampland grasses and hay brittle and dry
Can scarcely provide much comfort to you.
Yet while down here, you exult there above:
Your heavenly kingdom warms you with love.

121 So che sprezzi ogni fasto, e che non hai
   Più pregiato tesor ch'un puro affetto,
   E t'è sovr'ogni pompa in grado assai
   L'amor d'un core e l'umiltà d'un petto—.
   Così ragiona, e ben acconcio omai
   Tra le ruvide piume il pargoletto,
   La soma annoda, e con la Diva, a piedi
   Segue pian piano i poverelli arredi.

122 Struggi la terra tua dolce natia,
   Tiranno io non dirò, mostro d'Averno;
   Pasci pur la tua rabbia iniqua e ria
   Di civil sangue e di dolor materno.
   Ecco in tanto da te per destra via
   Sen va sicuro il Redentor eterno,
   E giunge là dov'egli mira e sente
   Da l'alte cataratte il Nil cadente.

123 Il Nilo, assordator de' suoi vicini,
   Inondator de le feraci arene,
   Che porta, quasi un mar che 'n mar ruini,
   D'orgoglio e di furor sett' urne piene;
   Ch'a partir d'Asia e d'Africa i confini
   Di sconosciuta origine sen viene,
   E, mentre al mondo i termini prescrive,
   Pon due nomi diversi a le sue rive.

124 Vede l'alte piramidi famose,
   Quasi monti de l'Arte e quasi altere,
   Per le stelle assalir, scale sassose,
   Farsi colonne al Ciel, basi a le sfere,
   E ricoprir sotto le spalle ombrose
   Le piagge tutte e le colline intere,
   Vietando ognor, con la lor vasta mole,
   A le selve la luce e 'l passo al Sole.

121   "You disdain pomp and finery. For you,
       No wealth is dearer than gifts of the heart:
       Kindness and modesty alone will do."
       Speaking these words, Joseph sets down his ward
       On the makeshift cushions rough, coarse, and crude.
       All is ready for the team to depart.
       Joseph ties the bundle. His holy bride
       And he walk along at the donkey's side.

122   Ruin your beloved land and birthplace
       (A worse word than "tyrant" I must employ),
       O beast of Avernus—engorge your rage
       On the countless lives and loves you destroy!
       Know that while you do so, he makes his way:
       The Savior gains safety, and he enjoys
       Refuge now where the rushing waters fall,
       Spilling from cataracts mighty and tall.

123   Here, the Nile enriches the fertile fields,
       Inundating the hot sands that burn;
       It seems a sea that another sea yields,
       Gushing torrents forth from its seven urns.
       Between Africa and Asia it keels
       From an unknown source. The great river turns
       And twists, drawing the borders with its flanks:
       There are different names for the facing banks.

124   Behold the great pyramids that tower
       Like artful mountains built up to the skies,
       Stairs of stone that confer strength and power
       To the lofty summits to which they rise.
       They give shade, with their vast shoulders,
       To the slopes and the hills at their sides.
       Even at high noon the immense masses block
       The Sun from reaching the trees and the rocks.

125   E vede il Faro per gran tratto intorno
L'acque segnar di luminosa face;
E de la Sfinge il simulacro adorno,
De lo scarpel miracolo verace;
E 'l laberinto illustre, ampio soggiorno,
Ch' ha di ben sette regie il sen capace;
E 'l gran muro fabril, che sì da lunge
Pelusio ed Eliopoli congiunge.

126   E quasi parto del superbo fiume,
Meride, il lago immenso indi discerne,
E le scole e i musei, del chiaro lume
Che la Grecia illustrò, memorie eterne;
E di cedro e di pece e di bitume
E d'umani cadaveri caverne,
Preziose conserve, onde vien poi
De la mummia salubre il dono a noi.

127   De l'eterna progenie il lume e 'l caldo,
Ch' ovunque va, soavemente irraggia,
Quasi del vero Sol verace araldo
Vide e sentì la Paretonia piaggia.
Nacque zaffir, topazio, ostro e smeraldo
Per la contrada inospita e selvaggia;
L'orso, il tigre, il leon conobber Dio
Ed a lambirlo il cocodrillo uscìo.

128   Con stupor di Natura, il manto vile
Spogliossi il verno e la canicie antica.
Sue pompe in lui la cortesia d'Aprile
Tutte versò con larga mano amica,
Et arricchì d'un abito gentile
La terra ignuda, e la stagion mendica.
Le spine ornò d'impestivi onori
E maritò con le provini i fiori.

125   See Pharus reflect on the gleaming face
Of clear waters that shine bright through the waves,
See the Sphinx and how the chisel has traced
Its wondrous features so noble and grave;
See the great sprawling Labyrinth, the space
So vast, seven cities fit in its maze;
And the high wall that extends far and wide
And connects capitals to either side.

126   Behold the immense lake, how it fuses
Its blue waters with the mighty river.
See academies and shrines to the Muses
Built by the Greeks, memorials forever
To the light that learning diffuses.
See the deep tombs where lie cadavers
Preserved by cedar, bitumen, and pitch:
The art of embalming is Egypt's gift.

127   Light and loving warmth the eternal child
Radiates everywhere that he goes.
Into cold winter the Sun now smiles,
And so Pharaoh's land blossoms and grows:
Sapphire and emerald fill the wild,
Inhospitable lands down below.
Bear, tiger, and lion recognize God;
Even the crocodile voices its awe.

128   Nature marvels, winter casts off its shroud,
This gray garment which is ancient and bare.
April pours forth, with a generous hand,
Her splendors to brighten the air.
The beggarly season and the bleak land
Put on rich garments, elegant and fair.
Among the thorns, blossoms lie embedded:
To frost and ice, now flowers are wedded.

129   Anime lieve di vezzose aurette
E con musici fiati allettatrici,
Tra laureti e palmeti amorosette
Sussurrando scotean l'ali felici.
Con molli seggi d'odorate erbette
Lusingaro il Fattor valli e pendici,
Piegaro il crin per riverenza i monti
E mormorando il salutaro i fonti.

130   Fuor del chiuso la testa il Nilo trasse
Per baciar l'orme virginali e sante;
S'inchinar l'onde, ed a le membra lasse
Alimento, e ristoro offrir le piante;
Ogni erba e fiore, ovunque il piè posasse,
Con gli odori adorava il suo Levante;
Belle gare movean da gli arboscelli,
Per benedirlo e gli Angeli e gli augelli.

131   Mille e di mille fiamme intanto accesi,
Sparse con varie danze in varie torme,
Amoretti canori in aria stesi
De' santi peregrin secondan l'orme.
Quai son del volto ad asciugar intesi
L'umor notturno al fanciullin che dorme,
Quai dal rigor de le gelate brume
A schermirlo con manti e con le piume.

132   Spirto guerrier, fra l'altre eteree scorte,
Cura ha dal Ciel d'assicurar la strada,
E, di lucido scudo il petto forte
Ed armato la man d'ardente spada,
Quasi forier, per le vie dubbie e torte,
L'umil coppia precorre ovunque vada,
Simile a quello, al volto ed alla vesta,
Che l'un vide sognando e l'altra desta.

129   Cheerful spirits sing on the charm-filled breeze
      With a sweet musical breath in their throats,
      Darting adorably between the trees,
      Gentle birds flutter their wings as they float.
      Praise resounds on high cliffs, in deep valleys
      As fragrant herbs whisper their perfumed notes.
      The mountains now bow in adoration,
      Gaily, fountains babble adulation.

130   The Nile lifts up its swelling head to kiss
      The delicate step of the untouched bride,
      The waves bend down low as the soft grass slips
      Smoothly underneath to relieve her stride.
      The herbs and flowers upon which she trips
      Exhale sighs wherever the virgin glides.
      Sweet chattering sounds from the trees and the scrub
      —Angels and birds' benediction and love.

131   Colored flames flash and sparkle in the air,
      As they dance in rich and colorful throngs.
      Hear the delightful melodies they share,
      Assembling to speed the pilgrims along.
      They wipe, from the face of the baby fair,
      The chilly dew of night with their gay song.
      Others extend their wings and give cover
      From frost that makes him shiver and shudder.

132   At the fore of the ethereal host parades
      A spirit who assures their safe passing.
      His armored chest makes a dazzling display;
      In his firm hand, a bright sword is flashing.
      The footman, over unsure, twisting ways,
      Offers Heaven's guidance and compassion.
      His face and dress shine, so that they do seem
      What *she* saw waking, and *he* in a dream.

133   Qual di se stesso e genitore e figlio,
Move l'augel, ch'al par del Sole è solo,
Di foco il capo e di piropo il ciglio,
Con l'ali d'ostro e di zaffiro, a volo.
Ammirando il diadema aureo e vermiglio,
Del pomposo suo re, l'alato stuolo
Lieto il corteggia, e con canora laude
Al miracol d'Arabia intorno applaude.

134   Cotal sen va fra cori eterni e santi
Il campione immortal. Tutto confuso,
Mira Giuseppe i lumi, ascolta i canti,
Stringe le ciglia, aguzza il guardo in suso.
Ma vinto al folgorar di raggi tanti
E tali accenti a sostener non uso,
Chiude, cadendo attonito e smarrito,
De la vista i meati e de l'udito.

135   Ma divina virtù l'egra pupilla
Rinforza e 'l debil senso al santo vecchio,
Ed a l'occhio che manca e che vacilla,
L'oggetto affrena, e a l'infermo orecchio.
Sorge, e 'ncontro al balen ch'arde e sfavilla
Con la tremula man si fa solecchio,
E del corpo senil l'antico incarco
Sul nodoso baston incurva in arco.

136   Poiché 'l vigore ha racquistato, in guisa
Che 'n su le piante i gravi membri appoggia,
Gli occhi leva pian piano, indi gli affisa
Verso il balcon de la stellata loggia,
E, da festive lacrime recisa,
Apre il varco a la voce, in questa foggia:
—O del celeste essercito pennuto
Fulgentissime squadre, io vi saluto.

133   As the bird that is its own child and sire—
The phoenix, which matches the Sun's bold light—
Has eyes of gemstones and a head of fire,
And flashes purple and sapphire in flight—
Which is by the wingèd host so admired
That they will follow it to any height
In a cheerful train that flocks all around
The wonder that in Araby is found—

134   Thus does the immortal champion walk,
To song of eternal and holy choirs.
Joseph looks, he listens, and then he gawks;
He furrows his brow and squints at the fires.
The sights and the sounds deliver a shock
To his poor senses, which promptly expire.
Overwhelmed, he falls as if struck by thunder:
His vision and his hearing rent asunder.

135   With divine aid, sight returns to his eyes.
The saintly old man's senses are restored.
His wavering vision and ears had tried
And failed. Now, his efforts have their reward.
He faces again what made the sparks fly.
With shaking hand—yet firmer than before—
He shields his dim view from the burning Sun
And clutches his staff with the other one.

136   Then he regains a semblance of vigor
To support his stiff gait and heavy limbs,
Slowly, he lifts his eyes to consider
The sight that hangs suspended above him.
Choking down tears of joy, he delivers
An address to the angels he hears sing:
"Celestial army marching on high,
Accept my salute, you who dwell in the sky.

137   Vi saluto e v'inchino, e se le luci
Stupide alzar presumo a sì gran raggi,
Tutto è sol mercè vostra, empirei duci,
Del gran Re de le stelle alti messaggi.
Tu, possente drappel, reggi e conduci
Lo stanco piè per boschi ermi e selvaggi;
Tu per rigide vie d'aspre montagne
Ne guida e guarda—. E così parla, e piagne.

138   Allor per quanto stende infra duo mari
L'ampio confin, dal manco braccio al dritto,
Le statue eccelse, i celebrati e chiari
Idoli suoi precipitò l'Egitto.
Cadder di Tebe e Menfi i sozzi altari
Di Faria, e d'Asna, e quei del greco invitto;
Giacquero Osiri ed Isi, e tacque Anubi,
Fiaccati in pezzi e dileguati in nubi.

139   Qual suol, ne la stagion tacita e nera,
Vigilante a l'insidie ed a le prede,
Di ladroni fuggir turba leggera
S'improviso splendor gli occhi le fiede;
O qual d'augei notturni infame schiera,
Se rosseggiar ne l'Oriente vede
I principii del dì che fa ritorno,
Teme il Sole e la luce, e cede al giorno:

140   Tal d'ogni nume perfido e profano
L'ombre, di forza e di baldanza vote,
Sparver dinanzi al vero, ond'altri in vano
N'attese il suon de le bugiarde note.
Pien di spavento e di stupor, dal piano
Le reliquie raccolse il sacerdote,
E de' suoi dei, ch'altro tremoto infranse,
Le ruine e i silenzii indarno pianse.

137   "I salute you, and I kneel before you.
       Great host, if I make bold to lift my gaze,
       Please accept the gratitude that is due,
       You, who execute all that the Lord says.
       Bear the banner; lead us across and through
       The wilderness, for we are tired and dazed.
       Over the steep, rocky, and mountainous steps,
       Guide and preserve us." Thus he spoke as he wept.

138   At the same moment, throughout Egypt's whole,
       From East to West, by act of Providence,
       The land's idols—statues famous and tall—
       Topple from the weight of their senselessness.
       In Memphis and Thebes, the foul altars fall,
       As do Greek temples, for their offenses.
       Osiris, Isis, and Anubis lie in dirt—
       Silent, broken in pieces, forever inert.

139   As deep in the quiet darkness of night,
       Prowling and on guard against ambushes,
       Fleet-footed companies of thieves take flight
       If suddenly a light flashes
       —Or as the ill-rumored band, at the sight
       Of the dawn, of nocturnal beasts dashes
       Away, seeing that now the Sun has returned,
       And fearing the day like a fire that burns—

140   Thus did the shadows of idols profane,
       Which drew from obscurity their substance,
       Vanish before the Truth. Bootless and vain
       Was it to seek their power and presence.
       Full of dumbstruck terror, from where they lay,
       The priests gathered up the broken remnants.
       They bewailed the silent gods without worth,
       Dashed down by Heaven when it shook the Earth.

141 Quindi de' riti antichi a mancar venne
   La superstizion vana e fallace,
   E ne' petti credenti il seggio tenne
   Di ferma e stabil fè culto verace.
   Dietro al fulgor de le celesti penne
   Sen gìa la cara al Ciel coppia seguace,
   E, già da l'altrui froda empia e villana
   Libera in tutto, in tutto era lontana.

142 Non è però, per sì solinghe strade,
   Che 'l cor pur non le scota alta paura.
   Non Tebe la magnifica cittade,
   Ricca di cento porte e d'alte mura,
   Non Ermopoli ancor, da l'altrui spade
   Stima ai sospetti suoi patria secura;
   Quindi Siene aprica adietro lassa,
   E, nel centro d'Egitto, a Menfi passa.

143 Qui fin che 'l Ciel, ch'al patrio nido il tolse,
   Altro volgesse, il vecchiarel mendico
   Trasse il figlio e la sposa; e qui l'accolse
   Povero tetto di cortese amico.
   Qui poi, sagace artefice, rivolse
   La man rugosa a l'essercizio antico,
   E qui lasciò del suo scarpello industre,
   Dotto scultor, più d'un intaglio illustre.

144 Fabro era esperto, e nel lavor fabrile
   Possedea nobil arte, alto disegno;
   O prendesse a trattar con pronto stile
   L'argento e l'oro, o pur l'avorio e 'l legno.
   Oltre che poi, de l'animo senile
   La miseria sferzava il pigro ingegno;
   Però ch' assai sovente altrui consiglia
   Necessità, di cui l'Industria è figlia.

141   The old rites and ancient superstitions
Without a foundation weaken and fail;
In faithful hearts, still-older traditions
Now renew worship vigorous and hale.
Light of guides on a heavenly mission
Leads the voyagers along on the trail.
The threats of the tyrant lie far away;
Freed from his clutches, they escape the fray.

142   But though taking lonesome roads, not at all
Are they free from apprehension and fear.
Neither Thebes, which stands a hundred gates tall,
Nor does the city of Hermes appear
To guarantee safety within in its walls.
No place seems to provide a safe repair.
Therefore, they pass through all habitations,
'Til they reach Memphis, their destination.

143   Far from his native soil, the poor old man
Left—until Heaven saw fit—wife and child.
The humble, thatched-roof hovel of a friend
Offered a haven that was warm and mild.
The skilled artisan applied his rough hand
To venerable crafts. The sculptor styled
Handsome figures, and he could rightly claim
To have made, with his art, a respectable name.

144   He was truly a master of his trade
And in art pursued the highest designs.
Not just to wood did he apply his blade:
He worked silver, gold, and ivory fine.
Poverty had spurred him on, and it made
Him sharpen his wits and refine his mind.
It is often so, that necessity
Begets both diligence and industry.

145   D'ebeno e cedro e d'altri legni egregi
Ampie tavole scelse, e varie in esse
Formando e vaghe imaginette e fregi,
De' Tolomei la lunga serie espresse;
La lampa de' nocchier, l'urne de' regi,
E del gran Nilo la feconda messe;
E per mercar con la fatica il vitto,
Tutti gli onor v'effigiò d'Egitto.

146   Da quest'opre, talor famose e conte,
D'una in altra città vulgate e sparte,
Mercenario sudor de la sue fronte,
Solea d'oro ritrar non poca parte.
Di fortuna a schernir gli scherni e l'onte
Questo studio gli valse, usò quest'arte,
Procacciando a se stesso alcun sostegno,
A la dolce consorte, al caro pegno.

145   Of ebony, cedar, and noble woods
He wrought broad tables. A variety
Of images he carved; among them stood
The long line of the royal Ptolemies,
Sea-faring vessels and all of their goods,
The kings' tombs, and harvest festivities.
All that Egypt can boast—the glorious array
Of treasures—he sculpted to keep hunger at bay.

146   Over the land, one city to the next,
The reports grew and spread of his great skill.
The money he earned by toil held in check
Greater hardship and more serious ill.
To mock fortune's mockery and to vex
Vexation, he applied his art and will.
By this means he supported those in the house,
His belovèd burden of children and spouse.

LIBRO TERZO

Da sublime palagio Erode mira
De la strage crudel l'orrida scena;
Lo stuol, ch'infellonito il ferro gira,
Altri sbrana, altri pesta ed altri svena.
Trafitta nel figliuol piange e sospira
E dimostra ogni madre amara pena;
Lasciata il re crudel l'eccelsa reggia
Su gl'innocenti uccisi empio passeggia.

BOOK THREE

Herod, from his palace's sublime heights,
Beholds the horrible scene of carnage.
The gang of murderers, whom blood excites,
Stampedes, tramples, and treads like savages;
The mournful mothers all wail at the sight,
Choked by tears at witnessing such ravages.
The king descends from his lofty eminence,
And makes his way to the slaughtered innocents.

1   Deh perché la mia lingua e lo mio stile
       Non punge al par de le crudeli spade,
       Perché potesse in ogni cor gentile
       Mille piaghe stampar d'alta pietade?
       O perché la mia penna oscura e vile,
       Ch'a ritrar tanti orror vien meno e cade,
       Del gran martirio Ebreo l'istoria amara,
       Arpin, dal tuo penello or non impara?

2   Quella tua nobil man, che senso e vita
       Dar seppe a l'ombre ed animar le tele,
       Onde la schiera lacera e ferita
       Ancor sente dolor, sparge querele
       E, quasi a nuova strage, ancora irrita
       L'empio tiranno e 'l feritor crudele,
       Or ai miei 'nchiostri i suoi color comparta,
       Sì ch'emula al tuo lin fia la mia carta.

3   Sorse l'Aurora e d'Israelle i figli
       Volse onorar di lacrime pietose;
       Insanguinò le violette e i gigli,
       Impallidì le porpore e le rose.
       Cinto di lampi torbidi e vermigli,
       Sotto il vel de la notte il dì s'ascose;
       Pareva il Sol, con volto afflitto e smorto,
       Giunto a l'occaso, e pur sorgea da l'orto.

4   Fuggite o madri, e i dolci pegni amati
       Portate in braccio a più sicuri nidi;
       Ecco a lor danno e vostro, ecco ch'armati
       Mille ne vengon già fieri omicidi.
       Ecco i lor ferri in alto, ecco vibrati
       Fendon l'aure, odo i pianti, odo gli stridi,
       Veggio i vostri sembianti almi e leggiadri,
       Volti in pianto, in orror: fuggite o madri.

1 Alas! That neither my tongue nor my quill
 Cuts as deep as a crueler implement
 To mark readers' hearts with wounds that are filled
 Full of pious and righteous sentiment!
 Why is it that my unworthy pen still
 Should prove but a useless instrument?
 To paint the grim martyrdom of the Jews—
 What, Arpino, can it not learn from you?

2 With what bold strokes has the brush in your hand lent
 Quick life to shadows and vigor to blows
 —Blows striking at victims' breasts, blows that rent
 Tender flesh and laid the innocent low—
 Seeing which, the tyrant on evil bent,
 Then felt his ungodly appetite grow!
 May ink and page take a colorful sample
 From your painted hues, follow your example.

3 When Dawn rose, to honor the nation
 Of Israel, she shed pious tears.
 Lilies turned a brownish carnation;
 Purple and rose blanched as she came near.
 A hazy and bloody coloration
 Shrouded the day as soon as it appeared.
 The Sun showed a face woeful and deadened,
 Drew back its rays as soon as it spread them.

4 Flee, o mothers! Carry, to safer roost,
 The gentle burdens that lie in your arms!
 Behold, now are a thousand butchers loosed
 To bring the children—and you—grievous harm!
 Behold the sword raised high and how its tooth
 Cuts the air! Hear cries and sounds of alarm!
 Now, your kindly semblance chokes and smothers
 In horror and sorrow. Flee, o mothers!

5   Fabrica in Betthelem, ch'alta s'appoggia
      Sovra cento colonne, in mezzo siede,
      Spaziosa e capace, e quasi a foggia
      Fatta di tempio sferico si vede.
      Che sala fosse anticamente, o loggia
      Del re de' Cananei certo si crede;
      Di quel gran re che la città reina
      Primiero edificò di Palestina.

6   Non volse il fier tiranno a cielo aperto
      La tragedia mirar crudele e mesta,
      Ma quel portico scelse, al Sol coverto,
      Opportuno teatro a l'empia festa.
      Quivi su d'un balcon sublime ed erto
      A riguardar l'uccision funesta
      E de le morti altrui le varie guise,
      Giudice e spettator, lieto s'assise.

7   Pensò fors'egli in cotal modo ascose
      Tener sue frodi a la pietà celeste;
      Ma non l'ascose a voi schiere pietose,
      Angeli, che 'l miraste, e ne piangeste;
      E le piaghe stillanti e sanguinose
      Di propria mano ad asciugar correste,
      Intenti ad arrichir di sì begli ostri
      Il lucido candor de' manti vostri.

8   Qui, come prima il novo dì s'aperse,
      Venner citate, e, quasi in chiuso agone,
      Caterve innumerabili, diverse
      Si raccolser di madri e di matrone.
      Tosto ch'entraro e 'n vista lor s'offerse
      Strano apparecchio d'armi e di persone,
      Tra pensiero e stupor dubbie e sospese,
      Repentino terror tutte sorprese.

5   In Bethlehem rises a high fortress
     Held aloft by a hundred columns.
     There, at the center, a round temple sits,
     A structure vast, capacious, and solemn.
     The reports of the popular chorus
     Hold that long ago the king of Canaan
     Laid the foundation, so that for all time
     She might rule here, the Queen of Palestine.

6   The haughty tyrant did not wish to behold
     The cruel tragedy under an open sky;
     Instead, he chose a shady portico
     From which to view the play he had contrived.
     Up on the balcony, he saw unfold
     The festive event that he so desired:
     Judge and audience, he enjoyed the show
     Of manifold deaths occurring below.

7   Perhaps he thought thereby that he would hide
     All the fraud that he had perpetrated—
     Away from what Heaven's eyes could espy.
     But you, angelic host, contemplated
     The impious sight he made, and you cried.
     You held forth undefiled, consecrated
     Hands in order to bathe your white raiment
     In red jewels tendered as unowed payment.

8   Thus, when the first rays of the new day shone,
     Countless mothers summoned there by the king,
     As if all into the arena thrown,
     Huddled in a fearful, trembling ring.
     As they entered the palace, a strange show
     Awaited them: soldiers bearing weapons.
     They stopped in their tracks, and dread filled their hearts.
     Then, an unforeseen terror made a start.

9   Aveano, al bando ubidienti, in schiera
Tratto di figli un numero infinito,
De' quai ben atto ancora alcun non era
A scior lingua perfetta o piè spedito.
Forma quei, non intesa e non intera,
La parola tra voce e tra vagito.
Questi con passo dubbio e vacillante
Accennando cader, move le piante.

10   Or come tra carnefici rinchiuse
Le sventurate donne si trovaro,
Tutte ammutiro, e 'n lor pensier deluse
Quasi calcati fior si scoloraro.
I fanciulli, che timidi e confuse
Le videro languir, le stride alzaro:
Qual fuggia tra le mamme e qual nel grembo,
Chi col vel si copriva e chi col lembo.

11   Stavasi in alto soglio Erode intanto
Coronato di gemme, e 'l petto e 'l tergo
Sotto il fin'ostro del reale ammanto
Guernito avea di luminoso usbergo:
Ma, vago pur del fanciullesco pianto,
Più si compiacque, in quel funesto albergo,
Ferro e sangue, il crudele, aver d'intorno,
Che di porpora e d'or vedersi adorno.

12   Come predace augel, che d'alto mira
Stuol d'incaute colombe, i foschi cigli
Là drizza, arrota l'armi, aguzza l'ira
Del curvo rostro e de' pungenti artigli,
Così, torvo e traverso il guardo gira
A le pallide madri, ai mesti figli;
Indi a suo banditor cenna dal palco,
Che dia la voce al concavo oricalco.

9   Tiny sons they had brought in vast number:
        Not one of the babes who had come along
        Could even speak or walk unencumbered.
        The confused sounds from their mouths and their tongues
        Were half-cries, barely a murmur or mutter.
        The children could barely crawl, much less run,
        And so the poor souls wavered and tottered,
        Trying to escape the nearing slaughter.

10   Soon, the unfortunate women perceived
        Executioners storm into the place.
        They all fell silent, dismayed and deceived.
        As from cut flowers, life drained from each face.
        The cry of the babes, seeing them bereaved,
        Rose into the air and filled the great space.
        Some hid at the bosom, others below.
        Their mothers shielded them with veils and clothes.

11   The while, Herod stood near, wearing a crown
        Of jewels, resplendent in garb finely worked.
        Beneath the crimson of his royal gown
        Glistened and sparkled a wrought chainmail shirt.
        To feast his eyes on such carnage all 'round
        Counted, for him, as the richest dessert:
        The despot preferred the cruel steel and gore
        To all the wealth that his treasury stored.

12   When a quick falcon, in the lofty haze,
        Sees a flock of mild, unsuspecting birds,
        At first, the quick hunter sharpens his gaze,
        And then his beak and his fierce talons' spurs—
        Thus, with a grim stare, Herod's eyes appraised
        The pale mothers and sorrowful children.
        He gave the herald a wave of the hand,
        A sign to perform the awful command.

13   Quei, dal tergo onde pende, in mano il toglie;
      Pon su gli orli le labra, e, mentre il tocca,
      Nel petto pria quant'ha di spirto accoglie;
      Quinci il manda a le fauci, indi a la bocca,
      Gonfia e sgonfia le gote, aduna e scioglie
      L'aure del fiato, e 'l suono ne scoppia e scocca;
      Squarcia l'aria il gran bombo e 'l ciel percote,
      E risponde tonando eco a le note.

14   Udito il segno de la regia tromba,
      Ecco alzar mille man, mill'armi orrende,
      Già sopra mille capi il ferro piomba,
      Già fuor di mille piaghe il sangue scende.
      Del pianto feminil l'atrio rimbomba,
      Al grido pueril l'aria si fende.
      Là tinti d'ira e qui di morte i visi,
      Fremono gli uccisor, gemon gli uccisi.

15   Quanti l'ultimo spirito spiraro
      Ch'a i primi sospiretti aprien l'uscita?
      Quanti morte acerbissima provaro
      Che conosciuta a pena avean la vita?
      Quanti del Limbo pria l'ombre miraro
      Che del mondo la luce alma e gradita?
      A quanti fu con disusato modo
      Tronco il filo vital sul far del nodo?

16   O qual era, a veder fuggir tremanti
      Per la reggia crudel, fanciulli e donne;
      Tali furo i lamenti e i gridi tanti
      Che non pur l'ampia cupola tremonne,
      Ma, molli al sangue, intenerite ai pianti,
      Contan che statue intorno anco e colonne
      Pianger fur viste, e da pietà commosse,
      Al suon de le durissime percosse.

13   The man draws the bugle from where it rests
      And places his lips to the instrument.
      As much as he can, he gathers his breath,
      Then releases a sound most dissonant.
      Forth from lungs, which have expanded his chest,
      Out through his cheeks, as if fleeing a cage,
      The blast roars and hammers at Heaven's gate.
      There follows an echo, almost as great.

14   Just as soon as the royal signal sounds,
      Behold a rush: myriad arms of war.
      Blows of iron rain down upon thousands,
      And from as many fresh wounds the blood pours.
      The desperate women shriek all around;
      The piercing screams cleave the air as they soar.
      The killers grow fierce, gaze burning with fury.
      The victims lie still, dead eyes glazed and blurry.

15   How many were there who then breathed their last,
      Children who scarcely had drawn a first breath!
      How many little ones who had just passed
      Into life, just as soon entered death!
      How many beheld the next world—alas—
      Before this one even welcomed their step!
      In what cruel manner hitherto untried
      Was life's thread cut short before it was tied!

16   What horror: women and children took flight,
      Running in terror throughout the great hall.
      How awful the sobs, how awful the cries,
      The mournful clamor shook even the walls.
      They say statues, as if softened by sighs
      And warmed by flowing blood, also did fall
      And lie weeping, moved by mercy to tears
      By the wails of victims dying so near.

17   Miracoli dirò: fama è che molti
Già di senso e di vita e d'alma privi,
Dal ferro micidial torsero i volti,
Forse dal gran timor tornati vivi.
Con le materne lacrime disciolti
Correan de' figli i sanguinosi rivi,
Onde parea che pallido ed essangue,
Fuggisse anch'egli impaurito il sangue.

18   Trema il gran tetto al suon di tante spade.
Ahi tetto infame, ahi scelerata mole,
Come il copre e 'l sostien? Forse non cade,
Per non tinger di sangue i raggi al Sole.
Tu Sol, perché non torci or per pietade
L'usata via, se ciò veder ti dole?
Perché non celi almeno i chiari rai,
Se sospirar, se lacrimar non sai?

19   Le spade che pur or terse e lucenti
Con lunghe bisce balenar fur viste,
Or, con orribil tratto il ciel fendenti,
Veggionsi rosseggiar, di sangue miste.
Ascolta Erode i queruli lamenti,
Vede le morti spaventose e triste,
E, quasi assiso a dilettosa scena,
Si fa gioco e piacer de l'altrui pena.

20   Non così suole a lo splendor de l'oro
Talor rinconfortarsi animo avaro,
Come de' ferri, onde perian coloro,
L'infausto lampo a la sua vista è caro.
Né men gli apporta a l'anima ristoro,
Il ramarico acerbo e 'l pianto amaro,
Che soglia altrui tra' fiori e gli arboscelli,
Canto di ninfe o melodia d'augelli.

17   Hear now wonders. The dead, so goes the report,
Who had been robbed of sweet breath by the knife,
Averted their gaze from the king's cruel sport,
Felt such fear, they almost came back to life!
With their mothers' tears, the children's blood poured
In wild rivers running rampant and rife.
Blood gushed away, as if it were sickened
By its own sight, the horrors it quickened.

18   The roof trembled at the clash of the swords.
Wicked structure, abominable mass,
How could it bear what occurred on the floor?
Could it be that it refused to collapse
So the Sun wouldn't be splashed by the gore?
And why did the Sun still follow its path?
It should have halted its course in the sky,
If it did not hide behind clouds to cry.

19   The glistening gleam of the polished blades,
Flashing sharp teeth like serpents that dart,
Wove in the choked air a ruby brocade
With the crimson gushing from bleeding hearts.
Herod heard gladly the shouts of dismay,
Saw limbs lying severed and torn apart;
Seated before a magnificent stage,
He found pleasure in the torments displayed.

20   To no hard-hearted skinflint is so dear
The vision of golden riches that gleam
As to Herod the cold steel shining here,
When hot blood tempers it and it steams.
Like the wanderer whose fortunate ear
Catches nymphs singing their song by a stream,
Or the birds' sweet melody in the wood,
The tyrant hearkened; he saw it was good.

21   Giovinetta gentile, prodigo in cui
      Pose ogni grazia Amor, s'ode in disparte
      Patteggiar con ministro, e pregar lui
      Con le man giunte e con le treccie sparte:
      —Me, me ferisci, e campami costui,
      Ch'è de l'anima mia la miglior parte—.
      Promette il disleal, promette e ride,
      Poi rompe il patto, e 'n vista sua l'uccide.

22   Trionfa il feritor sopra il ferito,
      E poi che l'ha ferito anco il minaccia;
      Geme e vagisce l'un, l'altro il vagito
      Col ferro in bocca e 'l gemito gli caccia;
      Quei, svelto a forza e con furor rapito
      Da le braccia materne, apre le braccia,
      E la semplice bocca a chi l'impiaga
      Sporge, e rende al crudel bacio per piaga.

23   Qual giovenca talor, se da pesante
      Maglio o mazza percossa, avien che caggia,
      Il torel non spoppato a lei davante,
      D'angosciosi muggiti empie la piaggia;
      O come rossignuol tra verdi piante,
      Cui de l'amata sua stirpe selvaggia
      Abbia avaro villan votato il nido,
      Ferisce il ciel di doloroso strido:

24   Tal divenne colei, così la punse
      Punta d'acuto duolo, e venne meno,
      Sul caduto figliuol cadde e congiunse
      Mano a man, volto a volto e seno a seno;
      Stillò dal cor licor pietoso ed unse
      Le piaghe acerbe, ond'era sparso e pieno;
      Sciolse ella gli occhi, egli le vene; e quanto
      Egli di sangue, ella versò di pianto.

21   A graceful young girl—a wonder in whom
        Love placed all the graceful charms known to man—
        Begged a soldier spare the fruit of her womb,
        Undoing long tresses, she clasped her hands:
        "Strike me instead! This boy is my life's bloom,
        My own soul! Heed not the dreadful command!"
        The faithless rogue agreed—agreed and smiled,
        Then he broke the pact and impaled the child.

22   The triumphant dealer of death exults
        As he towers over the hapless babe,
        Whose wailing protests against the insults
        The butcher deals with the offending blade.
        Choking on the cries pushed back down his throat
        And torn from his mother's tender embrace,
        The poor boy opens and extends his arms;
        He offers love yet receives only harm.

23   As a heifer, when her calf is struck down
        Before her eyes by the blow of a club,
        Fills, with her bellows, the land all around;
        Or when a nightingale, in the green scrub,
        Sees a poacher sneaking toward her dear young
        In the nest, intent on snatching them up,
        Shrieks loudly to sound alarm far and wide,
        So that her plaintive cry pierces the sky—

24   So is it for the mother. Benighted
        By anguish too awful for her to stand,
        She falls on her fallen son, uniting
        Face and face, breast and breast, hand and hand.
        Her torn heart's merciful balm she applies
        To the wounds made by the murderous brand.
        All that flows from his veins, streams from her eyes:
        As much as he bleeds, so much does she cry.

25   In altro lato (ahi ferità!) si mira
Pugnar la madre e 'l manigoldo insieme;
L'una tiene il fanciullo e l'altro il tira,
L'una nel piè, l'altro nel braccio il preme;
Di pietà ferve quella e questi d'ira,
Quei rugge e latra, e questa langue e geme;
Ed è la spoglia al fin di quel contrasto
La spoglia di un bambin lacero e guasto.

26   —Perché, perché—dicea colei nel pianto—
Quel che nacque di me, da me dividi?
Io l'ho con tanta cura e studio tanto
Allevato e nudrito, e tu l'uccidi?
Parte de la mia carne è questo manto
Da natura contesto, e tu ne ridi?
Ch'io ami quel che del mio ventre è nato,
Lassa, è forse tua ingiuria, o mio peccato?

27   Uccidi almen col caro suo germoglio,
Sola non la lasciar, la genetrice;
Sfoga pur nel mio sangue il fero orgoglio,
Ch'assai n'ha più di lui questa infelice;
Due morti almeno accoppia, altro non voglio;
Conceder tanto a crudo cor ben lice;
S'egli ha colpa, è mia colpa; egli errò meco,
Or mi vaglia a mercè ch'io mora seco.

28   Crudel, che cerchi? E perché pur cercando
Nemico o reo, chi non t'offese, offendi?
Ma tu perché più indugi? E 'n fino a quando?
Come il folgor temuto in man non prendi?
Vienne, ma vien, Signor, l'asta vibrando,
Redentor già promesso, omai deh scendi.
Veggiati e tema il dispietato mostro,
L'avido spargitor del sangue nostro—.

25   Elsewhere (such horror it is to behold!),
A woman grapples with an assassin.
She clutches the child, the wicked man pulls,
The grip of both on legs and arms fastened.
She acts from pity; anger fires his soul.
He howls and barks; she sobs, pale and ashen.
See now the spoils of the terrible wrangle:
A baby maimed, mutilated, and mangled.

26   "Why, oh why," the mother cries out, half-crazed,
"Do you take the child born of my loins?
So carefully has he been nursed and raised—
And yet now you would murder my boy?
He is flesh of my flesh! You act amazed
And laugh that I defend my only joy—
Are you surprised to find love in my heart?
Does it offend you? Is it sin on my part?

27   "If we must, let us go at the same time,
Don't leave me alone and miserable!
My blood will satisfy your fearsome pride—
My very life stands at your disposal.
Mother and son: together may we die,
At least that much should be admissible.
Has he done any wrong, I too have erred—
We are one and the same; our destiny is shared.

28   "Wicked man, what is it you seek to do?
And why, in your search for an enemy,
Would you wrong one who has never wronged you?
Lord, how much longer will this torment be?
If only—at long last—your lightning flew!
Descend, Lord, brandish the spear against villainy!
Your coming, Savior, has long been foretold
Strike down this fierce fiend without any soul!"

29   Così languia la sconsolata, e 'n questa
    Il mal difeso corpo, onde languia,
    Cade sbranato, e parte in man le resta,
    Sì fu troppo crudel, per esser pia.
    Sul cadavere danza e fa gran festa
    Colui ch'ha in forma umana alma d'Arpia;
    Né sente altro dolor, se non, ch'egli abbia
    Troppo picciole membra a tanta rabbia.

30   Al repentino inaspetatto insulto
    Stupide l'altre e sbigottite stanno;
    Già d'or in or, del tradimento occulto
    Miran gli effetti e la cagion non sanno;
    Né meno a sè ch'ai figli, in quel tumulto,
    Temon la morte; anzi timor non hanno,
    Perché ciascuna, per minor martire,
    Con la sua vita in braccio ama morire.

31   Tanto in una di lor l'affanno acerbo
    Pose d'ira e d'ardir, che tra' crudeli
    Ferri si spinse e disse: —O re superbo,
    E perché questo ai servi tuoi fedeli?
    Ma vendetta a vederne ancor mi serbo,
    Se gli altrui giusti pianti odono i Cieli,
    Se 'l gran Rettor de' fulmini sovrani
    Mira con occhio dritto i torti humani—.

32   Giovane donna onestamente bella
    Pargoletto tremante in piè reggea
    Quasi guida e maestra; ed egli ed ella
    Somigliavano Amore e Citerea.
    Ma né questi da poi parve, né quella,
    Né 'l più bel dio, né la più bella dea,
    Ché non avria di Marte empio sergente
    Lasciato ucciso l'un, l'altra dolente.

29   In this way the unhappy woman spoke
As she held to the dear body. Alas,
The worn limbs of the boy finally broke,
And fell; just a piece remained in her grasp.
The beast in the form of a man was soaked
In gore and danced on the disfigured mass.
He felt neither remorse nor regret—except
When nothing remained to crush under his step.

30   Other witnesses of the gruesome scene
Gasp stupefied; they are dumbstruck and mute.
Worse and worse are the effects they have seen
Of the treachery contrived by the brute.
The frail women do not know what it means,
Yet they all stand fearless and resolute.
The light of sacrifice shines in their eyes,
They hold in their arms their very own lives.

31   In the breast of one flames such choler,
She thrusts her slight body between the blades.
"Arrogant king, why do you dishonor
Your own faithful subjects in such a way?
Heaven's vengeance you, my king, will yet learn,
For the Lord knows how you've gone astray.
The great Redeemer sees all that men do.
He will send down His thunder to destroy you!"

32   A virginal beauty, as escort and teacher,
Led a child who stumbled unsteadily.
The young pair seemed like Venus and Amor,
But the bright sight vanished too readily.
Soon, outrage had defiled both their features,
They ceased to resemble divinities:
The impious sergeant of the god of war
Left the girl mourning the child on the floor.

33   Vestia quel masnadier giuppa contesta
Di sottil maglia, a guisa di corazza;
L'avanzo ignudo avea, di ferro in testa
Rugginoso cappello, in mano un'azza;
Fra quelle miserabili con questa
Larga s'apriva e spaziosa piazza,
Quasi cinghial, le sete aspre, pungenti,
Sporgea dal grugno, e fuor del grugno i denti.

34   Pianse la sventurata, ei non udilla,
E di man le rapì l'amato amore,
Orfanetto pupillo, anzi pupilla
De gli occhi, occhio de l'alma, alma del core.
Mentre con piè non fermo egli vacilla,
L'orme segnando con incerto errore,
E' preciso al meschino in un istante
Il camin de la vita e de le piante.

35   L'impiaga e svena e fa che d'ogni vena,
Non ancor ben formata, il sangue piova;
Snida dal dolce albergo, anzi scatena
Da l'amara prigion l'anima nova;
Ma ne' membri minuti ancora, a pena
Loco a la piaga il piagator ritrova,
Ché maggiore il pugnal del picciol busto
E minore è del colpo il corpo angusto.

36   La madre il prende e se l'accoglie al petto,
Peso che già le piacque ed or l'aggrava,
E i freddi spirti e 'l volto pallidetto
Con lacrime di cor riscalda e lava.
Ella sì nel sembiante e ne l'aspetto
A l'estinto fanciullo egual sembrava,
Che distinguer da lui mal si potea,
Se non forse però ch'ella piangea.

33   The garb the murderer wore had been worked
        In heavy ironclad armor of mail;
        On the man's head, a rusty helmet jerked
        As he marched forth wielding a massive flail.
        When he drew near, the frightened crowd dispersed
        And fled. Alas, it was to no avail.
        A boar's bristles sprang from his mouth, prickly and rough.
        Great tusks protruded between them, beastly and tough.

34   The sad woman wailed, but he did not hark.
        He grabbed her dear child—the light of her eyes,
        The eyes of her soul, the soul of her heart.
        Struggling on his feet, the sweet cherub tried
        To steer his small steps, but he missed the mark
        And stumbled forward to his own demise.
        In a single movement, the giant blocked
        The course of his life and the course he walked.

35.   Promptly, the killer dealt a mortal blow.
        From every vein of the boy's tiny frame
        The tender sap erupted, gushed, and flowed.
        The soul of the child, no longer in chains,
        Flew free, released from its earthly prison.
        The executioner was only pained
        That the slight body had not still more room
        For his hand to inflict another wound.

36   The mother seized her son and clutched him near.
        Her joyful burden now bringing her woe.
        She bathed his cold body in the hot tears
        That she had warmed in her heart's kindly glow.
        So much like the child's did her face appear,
        —For the girl's traits in his features did show—
        One could hardly tell one from the other,
        But for the sobs that came from the mother.

37   Una ve n'ha, che del bel fianco ignudo,
Misera! e del bel petto e del bel volto,
Come può meglio, al caro suo fa scudo,
Né soffrir sa, che le sia morto o tolto.
Ma le sta sovra uom minaccioso e crudo,
Che l'aureo crin s'ha intorno al braccio avolto,
E del crespo e fin or le bionde pompe
A scossa a scossa le divelle e rompe.

38   Ella, sì come tronco edera cinge,
Al dolce pegno abbarbicata stassi,
Ma lui nel piè, lei ne la chioma stringe
Sì forte il fier, ch'alfin convien che lassi;
Poi con robusta man lo scaglia e spinge
Contro il muro vicin fra duri sassi;
Pria però che l'aventi e che 'l percota,
Tre volte e quattro intorno intorno il rota.

39   A quell'orrenda e dispietata scossa
Nel fanciullo tremante e sbigottito
Precorsa dal timore è la percossa,
Onde morto riman pria che ferito.
Al fin, rotto le membra, infranto l'ossa,
Steso al suol tutto pesto e tutto trito,
Per le labra e le nari in copia grande
Con la bianca midolla il sangue spande.

40   Né, di ciò pago ancor, l'uom crudo e rio,
Con le piante calcandolo lo spezza.
Ella, ch'altro non sa, rivolta a Dio
E scoppiandole il cor di tenerezza,
Gridò: —Meravigliar non mi degg'io
Ch'alberghi in petto uman tanta fierezza,
Né men d'ingiurie tante e tanti morti,
Ma di te, Re del Ciel, che lo sopporti—.

37   See a poor soul of fair figure and face,
      Trying to shield, just the best that she can,
      Her exposed son with her naked embrace.
      But looming above her, a butcher stands,
      Rough, crude, depraved, menacing, cruel, and base.
      He holds her hair coiled up in his hand
      And twists and turns the beautiful locks
      'Til the gold comes out in bloody shocks.

38   Like the green ivy that grows on high trees,
      To her beloved charge the mother clings,
      But the monster pulls so vigorously
      At him and at her, that at last she gives in.
      Then, the brute seizes the child with a heave,
      And against the rocky wall he flings him.
      Three or four times, before letting him go,
      He whirls the boy 'round to speed up the throw.

39   The poor babe is so scared that he expires
      Even before he has reached the brick wall.
      He slumps on the ground in a fearful pile
      Of bones and limbs lying broken, dashed, sprawled,
      And trampled to mash—in a sticky mire
      Of head, arms, legs, and guts, all gored and mauled.
      Blood pours from nostrils and lips as from a sluice.
      Gray bits of brain bob in the ooze and the juice.

40   By this the ogre is not satisfied,
      And with his boot he squashes the remains.
      The mother can but appeal to the skies.
      As her heart breaks in pieces, she exclaims
      "Lord, I should not marvel or be surprised
      That such wantonness and savagery reign
      Among men, and that so many perish—
      Yet it astounds me that you should bear it!"

41   Non lunge era un villan di fier visaggio,
Rozzo a gli arnesi e spaventoso a gli atti.
Non credo, che sì rigido e selvaggio
Là ne' monti lucani orso s'appiatti.
Porta l'ira ne gli occhi, in man l'oltraggio,
Fiero ne le fattezze, e più ne' fatti;
E grave tratta e boschereccia ronca,
Ch'usa a podar già tralci, or membri tronca.

42   Questi contr'un de' miserelli Ebrei,
Che dei labri materni i vivi spirti
Suggea, si volse e disse:—Or a costei,
Che t'ha sì caro, io vo di sen rapirti.
Vo sviscerarti, e così poi di lei
Sviscerato figliol potrai ben dirti—.
Così dice, e l'assal. La donna ardita
S'oppon a lui, ma più quell'ire irrita.

43   Lassa, e che val contro furore armato
Feminil debolezza a far contesa?
Timor scudo le fa del proprio nato,
Amor poscia l'arretra e tien sospesa;
Mentr'ella è in forse e stassi in tale stato
Fra la sua propria e fra l'altrui difesa,
Ecco l'irreparabile ferita,
Che lei toglie di dubbio e lui di vita.

44   Impiaga, ahi crudo, il figlio e non ben anco
Sazio sol d'una morte, allora allora
Trapassato a la madre insieme il fianco,
Fa che colà di nova morte ei mora:
Passa ove dentro il cor nel lato manco
L'amor materno il mantien vivo ancora,
E due volte gli uccide il suo diletto,
La prima in braccio e la seconda in petto.

41   Nearby stood a rogue of grimacing mien,
With filthy garments and horrible ways.
Not even in the highlands, I believe,
Does beast more savage roam and prey.
His eyes flame in rage, his hand bears cruelty.
Fierce in seeming, but fiercer still in deeds,
He carries a great woodsman's tool. Instead
Of branches and logs, it splits limbs and heads.

42   Onto one of the wretched Jewish babes,
Drawing sweet life from his young mother's breath,
The wicked forester turned the sharp blade:
"Now are you torn from the maternal breast,
Felled and chopped up. She speaks true when she says
That she is holding her own blood and flesh!"
Then he makes a start and attacks the child.
The more the mother fights back, the more he grows wild.

43   Poor thing, how can a small woman compete,
Meek and frail, with a giant man's rage?
Fearfully, she holds her son as a shield,
Before love checks her. The mother is caged
By conflicting emotions, and she reels:
Is it herself or her own she should save?
Then, behold, comes the irreparable blow:
The case is closed when the child is struck low.

44   The soldier stabs the boy, but just one death
Does not yet satisfy his burning thirst.
In the same motion, he swings at her chest,
Kills him a second time after the first.
On her other side, the blade strikes a cleft
Where her son is cowering and once nursed.
Twice is destroyed what the woman loves best:
Once he dies in her arms, then at her breast.

45   Contr'una, che chiedea piangendo aita,
Soldato empio qual aspe, aspro qual orso,
Per privar lei di figlio e lui di vita
Già levato avea 'l braccio e steso il corso;
Quando colei, fatta dal duolo ardita,
L'unghia adoprando infuriata e 'l morso,
Il brando allor, che 'n lui torcere il volse
Con intrepida man di man gli tolse,

46   Fra se stessa dicendo:—Ah non fia vero,
Figlio, di questo core unica doglia,
Non fia che man sì sozza e cor sì fero
Trionfi mai di sì leggiadra spoglia.
Pria vo, con atto rigido e severo,
Che chi latte ti dà, sangue ti toglia:
Vedranno or or queste malvagie squadre,
S'io so meglio omicida esser, che madre—.

47   Ciò detto, di sua man, nova Medea,
Il trafigge, l'uccide e 'n due lo spara,
E 'n faccia al malandrin, che ne ridea,
Gitta in pezzi la carne amata, e cara:
—Saziati—disse—e da la madre Ebrea
Incrudelir ne' propri figli impara;
Impara di ferir più fere guise
Da questa destra—. E qui se stessa uccise.

48   Eran qui due, l'una d'un parto solo,
L'altra ricca di due germane belle;
Premean queste in silenzio il grave duolo,
Torcendo al Ciel le lacrimose stelle.
Verso colei, che l'unico figliuolo
Timida si stringea fra le mammelle,
Mosse il passo veloce e 'l braccio crudo,
Un giudeo tutto scalzo e mezzo ignudo.

45   Another soldier, as fierce as a bear,
      Wicked as a serpent, raises his knife
      To rob a mother of her sweetest care
      By taking her child and from him his life—
      But she, emboldened by her grief, tears
      At him with her nails. She scratches and bites.
      She leaps suddenly, makes a daring start,
      And seizes the blade aimed for the boy's heart.

46   She speaks in her soul: "Oh, let it not be,
      Dearest son, you, the sole care of my days!
      Neither hand so defiled, nor heart so fierce
      Will triumph; nothing will take you away.
      Before that occurs, I intend to see
      One final, decisive action essayed:
      I, who nursed you with milk, your blood will spill.
      Let them see: a gentle mother can kill!"

47   So the new Medea, with her own hand,
      Transfixed her child, and she split him in two.
      Into the face of the villainous man,
      Who stood there laughing, she gathered and threw
      The slaughtered remains that came from her son.
      "Monster, glut yourself," she cried, "And may you
      Do to your brood what you have learned from me!"
      Then, she struck her breast and died instantly.

48   Two women were there—the one with one child;
      The other mother had been blessed with twins.
      Mute, they stood and stared through tears at the sky,
      Silenced by their bitter grief and chagrin.
      Toward the first of the pair—the one shyly
      Clasping her son—drew a man tall and grim.
      The barefoot and half-naked ogre ploughed,
      Frothing and seething, his way through the crowd.

49   Lacero avea, quasi farsetto, indosso,
         Ch'a pena il ricopria fin sui ginocchi,
         Purpureo cencio; e, di pel crespo e rosso,
         Dal mento gli pendean duo lunghi fiocchi;
         Sgangherato la bocca e i labri grosso,
         Rabbuffato le ciglia e bieco gl'occhi,
         Di sozzo ceffo e di sparuta cera:
         In somma, tal ch'era uomo e parea fera.

50   Tacque la bella donna e non disciolse
         Voce, pianto o sospir: tacque e sofferse,
         Ma sì pietosa in atto il figlio tolse
         E volontaria al mascalzon l'offerse,
         Che, se non ch'egli altrove i lumi volse,
         Se non ch'ella d'un velo i suoi coverse,
         Vincealo il dolce sguardo, e 'l ferro acuto
         Fora di mano al feritor caduto.

51   Ma che, contro furor, che val bellezza?
         Strins'egli il ferro e nel fanciul l'affisse.
         Quei come suole ad uom che l'accarezza,
         Ridendo a l'assassin, babbo gli disse;
         E spinto pur da pueril vaghezza,
         La man stese al coltel che lo trafisse,
         Credendo dono, imaginando argento
         L'acciar, che era di morte empio stromento.

52   Ei non mirollo o non curollo, e dritto
         Là, donde il riso usciva, il ferro mise;
         Ma come vide il poverel trafitto
         Languir morendo in sì dolenti guise,
         Fatto quasi pietoso angue d'Egitto,
         Si dolse e lacrimone, ei che l'uccise;
         Ma sedate le lagrime e 'l cordoglio
         Tosto poi la pietà cesse a l'orgoglio.

49   As a doublet, the brute wore a torn rag,
Tattered and red; it hardly reached his knees;
From his chin hung braids of ruddy, coarse shag.
In his great mouth gaped a graveyard of teeth.
With pallor of death, his filthy face sagged,
His livid skin was dirty and sickly.
From his wild eyes, he cast sinister beams—
He was less a man than a beast, it seems.

50   In silence, the fair woman made no noise—
Neither lament, nor a sigh, nor a wail.
Dutifully, she raised and offered the boy
To the foul fiend who had scented his trail.
Had his gaze not been otherwise employed,
Had the mother not been wearing a veil,
The sight would surely have bested the man:
The blade would have fallen out of his hand.

51   How can rage by beauty be defeated?
He clutched the steel, and he stabbed the laddie.
Whene'er a man approached, the boy greeted
Him by smiling and calling out "Daddy!"
And so, to the knife the butcher wielded,
The child extended his hand playfully.
The babe thought it a present of silver—
Iron held in the grip of a killer.

52   The man didn't see or else didn't care.
He planted the blade where the smile appeared.
Yet when he saw the poor thing writhing there
In the throes of death, the brute shed a tear.
As the kindly crocodile weeps, he stared
At the hapless child whose body he had speared.
But his heartache relented and eyes dried—
Mercy gave way to his natural pride.

53   Volgesi a l'altra e fra suo cor discorre
      Qual de' due figli, e di quel colpo ei fieda.
      Che dee far, lassa lei? Chi la soccorre?
      Dove sarà ch'aita invan non chieda?
      Fuggesi intorno, e quei la segue, e corre
      Quasi ingordo mastin dietro a la preda;
      Ella, vagante in questa parte e 'n quella,
      Sembra da lupo insidiata agnella.

54   Con quell'affetto che, dal patrio regno
      L'alte fiamme fuggendo, il buon Troiano
      Il vecchio genitore e 'l picciol pegno
      Reggea col tergo a un punto e con la mano,
      Fatta de' cari suoi schermo e sostegno,
      Per involargli al predator villano
      Quinci e quindi traea, pietoso impaccio,
      Suavissima soma, i figli in braccio.

55   Misera, ma che pro? Fugge il periglio,
      Non scampa già, ché 'n novo mal trabocca;
      Tal augel del falcon sente l'artiglio
      Mentre sottrarsi al can tenta di bocca.
      Ecco un altro crudel, ch'al primo figlio,
      Che il sen le sugge, un dardo aventa e scocca,
      E passa oltre le labra, onde la poppa
      Già di latte, or di sangue è fatta coppa.

56   Giunge in tanto più presso e la minaccia
      Con più forti armi il barbaro omicida.
      Vede l'altro bambin, che tra le braccia
      Stretto le giace, e la motteggia e grida:
      —Poiché cotanto amor teco s'allaccia,
      Ragion non è ch'io te da lui divida,
      Ma perché non si scioglia il caro nodo,
      Fia gran pietà s'io nel tuo sen l'inchiodo—.

53   Seeing the mother of twins, he wondered,
      Which one of them would he kill first, and how?
      What could the woman do? Who will help her?
      What can the poor soul even ask for, now?
      And so she flees—behind, his step thunders—
      She runs as if chased by ravening hound.
      She darts here and there; he follows her way.
      He seems a wolf in pursuit of his prey.

54   As the noble Trojan, fleeing the fires
      That burned to the ground his native land,
      Took upon his shoulders his agèd sire,
      And led his son, his sole hope, by the hand
      —In like fashion does the woman desire
      To shield and to protect those of her clan.
      Seeking to deliver her boys from harm,
      She pulls them this way and that by the arm.

55   It is no use. She escapes danger's claws
      Only to find a new menace draw near—
      As when a swift bird eludes a dog's jaws,
      Then, all of a sudden, a hawk appears.
      Behold: a second villain pins one son
      To the soft white teat where he has been reared.
      The spear pierces her breast and strikes his lips:
      No longer milk, it is blood he now sips.

56   The barbarous killer makes his approach;
      More—and more terrible—weapons he bears.
      Seeing how she holds the other child close,
      He shouts out in mockery, and he swears:
      "Such loving embraces! It would be gross
      Wrong for me to separate such a pair!
      Never should a couple be divided,
      So I'll make sure you're forever united."

57   Quel meschinel, qual timidetta damma
       La qual ricovri a le sue siepi ombrose,
       Dentro il solco di neve, in cui di fiamma
       Vivaccissimi semi Amor ripose,
       Smarrito, allor fra l'una e l'altra mamma
       Da la faccia del ferro il volto ascose;
       E tanto ebbe di senno acerbo ingegno,
       Che temer seppe morte e sfuggir sdegno,

58   Quantunque invan: che 'n lui la punta orrenda
       Drizza il fellon, ma falle il colpo ed erra;
       Crudel l'error, ma più crudel l'emenda
       Che lui trafigge e lei trafitta atterra.
       Egli le braccia aperte avien che stenda,
       Ella in giù cade e nel cader l'afferra,
       Onde, immobile tronco e senza voce,
       Al figliuol crocifisso è fatta croce.

59   Arpin, chi vide mai con dotto stile
       Da la tua man la Carità dipinta,
       Che di vaghi bambin schiera gentile
       Abbia nel seno e ne le braccia avinta?
       Cotal parea leggiadra donna umile,
       Scompigliata il bel crin, scalza e discinta;
       E 'ntorno le fiorian, teneri e molli,
       De la progenie sua cinque rampolli.

60   Benché del regio editto il fier tenore,
       Fuor che 'nfanti da latte, altri non cheggia,
       N'avea costei, di età poco maggiore
       Parte condotti a la spietata reggia,
       Sì perché, stretti di fraterno amore,
       L'un con l'altro trattiensi e pargoleggia,
       Sì perché ella, ove mova o fermi il piede,
       Disgiunti ancor mal volontier gli vede.

57   As a timid fawn repairs to the wild
And in the woods seeks forested cover,
The child crawls deep into the snowy hills
That are warmed by the love of his mother.
He cowers, hiding himself from the steel,
Now lost between one breast and the other.
Though yet so young, the boy has enough sense
To fear grim death and to flee in defense.

58   The first swing misses and the heave goes wide—
A mistake, but what follows is far worse,
For the next blow pierces both through the side;
As the pair goes down, the poor lad falls first,
Then the mother lands on top of her child
In an arrangement that is most perverse.
Under her dead weight, the boy now lies pinned:
The corpse of his mother crucifies him.

59   Who, Arpino, has not seen your painting?
Sweet charity as portrayed by your hand,
Gathering to herself and embracing
All her dear children in a gentle band—
Her beautiful tresses flow, cascading
From her ivory brow, modest yet grand;
All around her there blossom tenderly
The flowers of her lovely progeny . . .

60   Herod's royal edict had only called
For the slightest infants to be brought here;
Nevertheless, there appeared in the hall
Children who were slightly older in years.
For their brotherly love held them in thrall,
And so they clung to each other dearly;
All their steps followed those of their mother,
Who would not take one boy from the other.

61   Stavasi il primo in picciola tabella
Le note ad imparar de la prima arte
Discepol novo, e de l'Ebrea favella
Leggea le righe in lei vergate e sparte,
Quando la testa ecco gli è tronca, e quella
Gli cade in sen su l'innocenti carte,
E l'estremo suo fatto a lettre vive
Con vermigli caratteri vi scrive.

62   Move colui ver l'altro il passo orrendo,
Poi ch'l capo ha de l'un sciolto dal busto.
Vedelo là ch'un pomo ei sta rodendo,
Pomo mortale, ahi troppo amaro al gusto.
Drizza a le fauci, ond'inghiottia ridendo
L'esca dolce e matura, il ferro ingiusto,
E gli fa con un colpo acerbo e forte
Trangugiando il pugnal, morder la morte.

63   Iva il terzo trescando a salto a salto
Sovra un finto destrier di fragil canna.
Miser, né sa qual repentino assalto
A morte crudelissima il condanna.
Ecco quel cor d'adamantino smalto,
Pria con man lo schermisce, e poi lo scanna,
Ne lo spazzo l'abbatte, e quivi il lassa
A giostrar con la Morte, e ride, e passa.

64   Del bel drappel reliquie assai leggiadre
Avanzavano ancora il quinto e 'l quarto,
Coppia che fu de la dolente madre,
Madre più non dirò, gemino parto.
L'un rotando sen gìa fra quelle squadre
Mobil paleo per entro il sangue sparto,
E, tutto intento al fanciullesco gioco,
Al periglio vicin pensava poco.

61   The eldest sits at a little tablet,
Studying the elements of grammar.
He knows the letters of the alphabet,
Yet he still reads in a halting manner.
In an instant, the boy's head is severed,
Falls to the earth as the pupil stammers.
Thus, the last lesson of the budding scholar
Has been written in words crimson in color.

62   Having chopped off the boy's head, the great brute
Lumbers and steers his way to his brother,
This child sits and is nibbling a red fruit
—The apple proves sourer than all others!
The juice dribbles down from his smiling lips,
But soon, in his throat, he chokes and sputters.
A massive blow falls, and the child ingests
An iron mouthful, the bitterest of deaths.

63   The third of brothers was hopping about,
Pretending to be a knight on a horse.
The guileless boy playing did not suspect
The cruelest of fates that waited in store.
Behold: the giant with a granite heart
Grabs him as he pursues innocent sport.
He laughs and strikes him before proceeding.
The boy jousts with Death, battered and bleeding.

64   Now hear: the last two of the five brothers
In the lonesome company that remained
Were born together, twins to their mother
(Alas, she no longer merits the name!).
The one ran around between the others
Throughout the hall, which seemed a bloody plain.
His gay diversion filled him with such cheer,
He failed to notice the danger so near.

65   Contro costui la destra e l'armi stese
Rapidamente il feritor villano,
Ma la piaga mortal colà non scese
Dov'ei mirò, se ben non scese in vano,
Ché, frapostosi a caso, in sè la prese,
Non aspettata, il suo vicin germano.
Diss'egli allor:—La tua follìa s'incolpi,
Non la mia man, se vai furando i colpi—.

66   Sotto la gonna allor colei si cela
L'ultimo, che di cinque ancor le resta.
Ma che? Del proprio scampo ei si querela
E col proprio vagir si manifesta,
E la froda pietosa altrui rivela,
Ch'ascoso il tien, de la materna vesta,
Semplicetto ch'egli è, né sa tacere,
Perché non ha imparato anco a temere.

67   La malaventurosa e malaccorta,
Cui dà senso l'amor, vita il dolore,
Altro non sa che, sbigottita e smorta,
Piover per gli occhi amaramente il core;
Ma l'avanza il vagito e si fa scorta
Del cieco ferro, de l'ostil furore;
Segue la voce e là, donde deriva,
Per la traccia del suon la spada arriva.

68   Non così contro 'l nibbio empio e maligno,
La domestica augella i polli cova,
Come colei dal barbaro sanguigno
Il malcauto schermisce e non le giova;
Però che 'l fier, che petto ha di macigno,
Brandisce il brando e ne la strozza il prova.
Giac'ei nel sangue orribilmente involto,
Tra i fraterni cadaveri sepolto.

65   The villain raised up his right fist,
       Meaning to leave the poor boy slain.
       And even though the cruel blow missed,
       It was not delivered in vain:
       It hit his twin as he ran past
       In the course of their childish game.
       Mockingly, the rogue snorts: "Why so stunned?
       Don't you think playing soldier is fun?"

66   The last of the five sons now hides
       Crouching under his mother's skirts.
       What good does it do him? His cries
       Consign him to lie in the dirt.
       The scoundrel hears him as he tries
       To stay unnoticed and unhurt.
       Simple thing—it will cost him dear
       Not to know the true value of fear!

67   The mother unfortunate and ill starred—
       She lives to love, yet is living in pain—
       Stands powerless, can do nothing at all,
       Except shed tears abundant as rain.
       The frightened wail of the child carries far,
       Leading the cruel enemy back again.
       The brute hears and sets himself on the trail,
       Then he hammers the source dead as a nail.

68   Against the fierce hawk, malign and depraved,
       The motherly hen does not guard her young
       With more resolve than the woman displayed,
       As she endeavored to shield her dear son.
       However, the bloodthirsty fiend, whose ways
       Were hard as stone, grasped the sword fast and swung:
       The blade cut his throat and down the boy went
       To join his brothers; his life was now spent.

69 Qual fu Niobe a veder, quando dal Cielo
  Vide scoccar le rapide saette,
  Onde in un giorno i due Signor di Delo,
  Orba la fer di sette vite e sette,
  Che, visto al fin cader l'ultimo telo,
  Al dolente spettacolo ristette,
  E 'l corpo per dolor stupido e lasso,
  Venne gelida selce, immobil sasso;

70 Tal fra la stirpe sua, mentre moriva,
  Restò la tapinella instupidita,
  Di color, di calor, di senso priva,
  Senza moto, senz'alma e senza vita;
  Parea morta non già, ma men che viva,
  Di bianco marmo imagine scolpita;
  Di bianco marmo, se non quanto i figli
  Fatto i candidi membri avean vermigli.

71 Pur, tanto di vigor le dà pietate,
  La mistura crudel volge sossopra
  E va cercando le reliquie amate,
  Ove la varia uccision le copra;
  E le lacere membra insanguinate,
  Reggendo amor la mano a sì fier' opra,
  Per onorarle de l'essequie estreme,
  Sparse, raguna e le commette insieme.

72 E col pianto le lava, e dice:—Ahi lassa,
  Lassa, chi fia che i miei soavi pegni,
  La cui vista infelice il cor mi passa,
  Di riunir, di risarcir m'insegni?
  Altro non veggio ch'una orribil massa
  Di frammenti avanzati a gli altrui sdegni,
  Altro ch'un mucchio di sanguini e monchi
  Squarciati brani e dissipati tronchi.

69   As Niobe looked when the sky rained arrows
       Sent down in one day by the Delian pair,
       Bolts that left her alone and in sorrow,
       Of two-times-seven lives stripped bare;
       When the last of her brood was laid low,
       She just froze on the spot and stared:
       Overcome by sore grief, worn out, and shocked,
       She turned to cold stone, to immobile rock.

70   And so, the poor mother, among her sons,
       Remains stupefied and without defense;
       They lie about her colorless and dumb,
       Mute and motionless, and robbed of all sense.
       She is not dead, yet death surely will come.
       It seems like a scene a sculptor has dreamt
       In marble, except that the once-white limbs
       Are covered now in vermillion skin.

71   Convulsed—moved by the pity in her heart—
       She fishes about in the red puddle
       Seeking in the mess the beloved parts
       That lie scattered in a gory muddle;
       Mutilated limbs, in fits and in starts,
       She brings together again and cuddles.
       Filled with motherly love, she holds them tight,
       Praying to give her poor children last rites.

72   She asks, washing the bodies with her tears:
       "Woe, wretched me, where and how might I learn
       To piece back together my vanished cheer?
       The sad looks on their faces pierce and burn
       My heart. I see just the horrible smear
       Of bodies others ripped apart in scorn.
       Everywhere now lie the chunks torn and threshed,
       Strewn about in a mass of ravaged flesh.

73   Già solev'io, non è gran tempo avanti,
Trattando di mia man serici stami,
Nel lin, che vi copria, poveri infanti,
Con sottil ago ordir fregi e ricami;
Or da ferro crudel ne' vostri manti
Quali, ahi quali vegg'io lavori infami?
Fiera man vi trapunse, ed ecco in vui
Ricucir mi convien gli squarci altrui.

74   Son queste, ohimè, le forme altere e vaghe,
Che da la genitrice in prima aveste?
O stelle, del mio mal sempre presaghe,
Le mie misere carni, ohimè, son queste?
Queste son pur, tra 'l sangue e tra le piaghe;
Riconosco pur io l'amate teste.
Dunque così mi ritornate innanzi,
De le viscere mie miseri avanzi?

75   O specchi del mio cor, volti amorosi,
Ov'io me stessa vagheggiar solea;
O soli di quest'occhi, occhi pietosi,
In ch'io mille dolcezze ognor avea,
O labra, onde pur or baci vezzosi,
Misti fra dolci risi, amor traea;
Ahi qual selvaggio, ahi qual tartareo mostro,
Ha sparso il sangue mio nel sangue vostro?

76   Dato mi fusse almen toccar distinti
Que' membri, ohimè, che più, toccando, infrango;
Lassa, ch'io pur miseramente estinti
Piango i miei figli, e non so quale io piango,
Perché d'atro pallor siete sì tinti
Che dubbiosa e confusa io ne rimango,
E l'effigie gentil del volto mio,
Cancellata dal sangue in voi vegg'io.

73   "Not long ago, my hand would have, instead,
        Worked fabric of delicate silken sheets.
        To make blankets for my poor children's beds,
        I used to weave patterns pretty and sweet.
        But now the cruel steel traces strands of red
        Between them as they lie dead at my feet.
        Whatever seams the killers have unsewn,
        I'll stitch together and make whole on my own.

74   "Are these, woe is me, the charming features
        That you, my child, from your mother received?
        O stars in the sky, whose bright orbs teach us
        Misfortune, is this my own flesh I see?
        I recognize well the luckless creatures,
        The dear heads lying in bloody debris.
        Is it thus that we are to be rejoined,
        My beloved children, fruit of my loins?

75   "O you, my heart's mirror, my soul's dear lights,
        In whom I saw my own self in a glass!
        O eyes like the Sun, shining clear and bright
        Where once a thousand charms did flash!
        O lips, whence Love himself took flight
        With kisses and smiles in his sash!
        What savage fiend has flown out from Hell's doors,
        To spill your blood in mine, my blood in yours?

76   "Were only it granted me, at least,
        To know which of the limbs belong to whom!
        Poor wretch that I am, I wail and I weep,
        Yet am standing before an unmarked tomb.
        In the black pallor of death, all have ceased
        To display to my eyes their wonted bloom.
        And so I remain baffled and confused:
        I do not know them, so battered and bruised.

77   Se' tu colui, ch'io generai primiero?
Già non è questo il capo tuo reciso.
Chi fu, che nel tuo busto, ahi scambio fiero,
Trasportato e commesso ha l'altrui viso?
Figli, miseri figli, or che più spero?
Sepolto è ne' vostr'occhi ogni mio riso—.
Qui le cresce la doglia e manca il pianto,
Secca han gli occhi la vena al pianger tanto.

78   E sviene, e 'l volto oscura, e la favella
Perde, e fiato non spira, occhio non move.
Sanguigna in tanto e torbida procella
Da mille spade in altra parte piove.
Ben fu sotto re tale e 'n tale stella
Felice chi non nacque o nacque altrove;
Felice chi non nacque o, nato, poi
Diè fine il primo giorno ai giorni suoi.

79   Di che ti lagni poi, di che ti sdegni,
Mondo vil, secol rozzo, oscura etate,
Che 'n te viva l'inganno il vizio regni,
Che sien lungi da te fede e bontate,
Che virtù pianga e seco i chiari ingegni
Languiscan tutti e l'anime ben nate,
Se la bella Innocenza in cotal guisa
Quaggiù fin da quel dì rimase uccisa?

80   Già scorre in fiumi il sangue, altro non s'ode
Che voci di dolor, strepiti d'ira;
Tutt' orror, tutt' è morte, e solo Erode
Lieti al tragico oggetto i lumi gira.
La fiera strage, ond'ei festeggia e gode,
Tra se lodando i colpi, intento mira,
E vedesi con voglie ingorde e vaghe
Contar le morti ed additar le piaghe.

77   "Are you the first one to have seen the day?
This severed head does not belong to you.
Who is it that made this awful trade
And put the wrong one where yours grew?
Children, all my hope is gone away;
It is now buried, my joy is through."
The pain grows until her weeping subsides:
So many tears flow, it dries out her eyes.

78   She falls to the ground. As her face grows pale,
She loses voice, breath, and sight. And then,
At that instant, erupts a stormy gale:
Swords rain down over and over again!
Happy he who enters this tear-filled vale
Without such an unlucky star or king.
Happy the one not born in the first place,
Or else dies at birth and is spared such disgrace.

79   Why do you grow so angry? Why complain,
You vile world—dark age and corrupted times?
World where treachery and vice reign,
And faith and charity are crimes,
Where virtue languishes in chains,
And the righteous lament and pine.
Does it at all bother you that innocence
Has perished and will be dead from this day hence?

80   The blood flows everywhere, red and turbid.
Nothing is heard but voices of anguish.
All is bathed in horror. Only Herod
Takes pleasure in the murder and carnage.
He savors tragedy rich and florid.
The scene appears impressively savage.
Lust for gore—to see more blood being shed—
Makes him crane his neck to count all the dead.

81 Mentre la plebe addolorata e trista,
  Con pietosi ramarichi languisce,
  Terror de la memoria e de la vista,
  Ostinato in sua voglia il re gioisce.
  Qual serpe, che dal Sol veneno acquista,
  Più la stessa pietà l'infellonisce;
  Ha spumante la bocca e gli occhi ardenti,
  E si morde le labra e batte i denti.

82 Sorto Erode dal loco, onde pur dianzi
  Fu spettator de' suoi furor perversi,
  Più da presso si fece, e volse innanzi
  Il macello tirannico vedersi.
  Parean gli sparsi corpi orridi avanzi
  Di naufragio mortal, legni sommersi,
  Il sangue pueril flutto crudele,
  E le membra e le fasce arbori e vele.

83 Su per gl'immondi e sanguinosi monti,
  Spaventoso a pensar, spazia e passeggia;
  Da i fianchi aperti e da le rotte fronti
  Vede che sangue in gran diluvio ondeggia;
  Pur come in chiari fiumi o in vivi fonti
  Là per entro si specchia e si vagheggia,
  E vuol de' miserabili infelici
  Misurar di sua man le cicatrici.

84 Sembra a punto, di tana uscito, drago
  Con ale verdi e con sanguigne creste,
  Ch'al novo Sol, presso il natio suo lago,
  Le fauci aprendo orribili e funeste,
  Terga le scaglie, in un feroce e vago,
  Di squalid'auro e rigido conteste,
  Et al dolce del Ciel lume sereno
  Saetti da tre lingue ira e veneno.

81 While the people of the land, afflicted,
  Exhale piteous wails and aching groans,
  Terrorized by all that they have witnessed,
  The king struts around with pride overblown.
  As sun gives serpents venomous substance,
  The righteous tears make his wickedness grow.
  Fire burns in his eyes, in his mouth foaming froth seethes;
  Herod bloodies his lips as he gnashes his teeth.

82 The great tyrant descends from where, before,
  He beheld the fruits of his perverse rage.
  He draws nearer and nearer on the floor,
  To the slaughter he has put on the stage.
  Bodies lie everywhere, scattered and gored,
  Like victims washed up by the ocean's waves.
  It seems a shipwreck is brought in by the tide
  On great swells of blood, the severed limbs ride.

83 As if over bloodied alpine passes
  (Horror to see!), it seems he makes his way:
  From skulls split open and mangled gashes
  Geysers and fountains of welling blood spray.
  As if at a limpid pool, he pauses,
  And he admires the delights on display;
  He stands before the dead piled in a mass,
  And inspects ev'ry wound, down to the last.

84 He looks like a dragon quitting its lair
  Fanning green wings, with sanguineous crests,
  A serpent opening its jaws to bare
  Its horrid fangs as it rises from rest
  And uncoils its length in the Sun's bright glare,
  Flashing a golden back and scaly breast:
  Into the serene eye of the Heavens
  Three tongues project its bile and its venom.

85 Vede di brutte macchie altri coverti,
Languidi, moribondi e palpitanti,
Tra' confin de la morte ancora incerti,
Stringer le madri ed anelar spiranti.
Altri già senza vita, i cori aperti
Mostrano ancora, e mostrano i sembianti
Effiggiati di pietà, d'amore,
Atteggiati di pianto e di dolore.

86 Altri il vital umor, che largo abonda,
E dal cor, non stagnato, ancor deriva,
Vomita per la bocca in su la sponda,
Quasi nave sdruscita e giunta a riva.
Vorrebbe a nuoto alcun su per quell'onda
Morte fuggir, che 'l segue e che l'arriva,
Ma debile, mal vivo e semimorto
Cade nel sen materno e more in porto.

87 De le donne meschine, altra le gote,
Altra le man si batte e 'l crin si frange.
Questa, mentre che 'l sen squarcia e percote,
Ulula, non sospira, urla, non piange;
Quell'altra fa con dolorose note
Del petto un Mongibel, de gli occhi un Gange;
Chi del re, chi del Ciel si lagna e stride,
Chi si duol del suo duol che non l'uccide.

88 Altra ve n'ha, che taciturna e sola,
A l'estinto figliuol prostesa avanti,
Stupida in atto e senza far parola
Si distempra in sospir, si strugge in pianti.
Altra al pianto pon freno e si consola
In tor da terra i figli ancor tremanti,
E le fredde cogliendo aure fugaci
Stampa ne' labri lor gli ultimi baci.

85   Some Herod sees wounded, bruised and livid,
Who twitch in agony at death's door.
Too tired to go in—and still too timid—
They cling to their mothers all the more.
Others lie dead, their bodies are rigid.
They seem, although they are steeped in gore,
Statues of compassion and affection
To which pain and grief have lent perfection.

86   Elsewhere a child spits out the vital stuff
Pumped by a heart that still beats and yet pounds.
The red vomit spills out from the boy's mouth
As from a ship that has run aground;
Another little sailor tries, on rough
Seas, to swim to where safety may be found.
Death pursues him and snuffs out his ardor:
He reaches his mother, then dies in the harbor.

87   Of the poor women, one claws at her face,
A second rips her hair, and a third beats
Her breast, for no child is left to embrace;
Neither sighs nor sobs are heard—only shrieks.
Chests heave in earthquakes, rivers of tears race
Down as they lie on the ground, pale and weak.
Wailing to the skies, the mothers regret
The horrible pain has not killed them yet.

88   Another lies still before her dead son.
A blank and empty stare sits in her eyes;
At first she is stupefied and struck dumb,
Then she dissolves into weeping and sighs.
Yet another one stops the tears that run
By gathering the remains of her child:
She holds him and then sucks up in a kiss
His departing soul with quivering lips.

89   Altra, del corpicel pallido e brutto,
Le squallidette e lacerate spoglie
Dentro alcun vel, che sia di sangue asciutto,
Pietosissimamente in braccio accoglie.
E mentre in acque il cor distilla tutto,
Mentre tutta in vapor l'anima scioglie,
Gli fa del petto suo, stringendol forte,
Già cuna in vita, or sepoltura in morte.

90   Stanchi già di mirar, ma non satolli,
Volgea cupido gli occhi Erode il magno,
E 'n quei torrenti sanguignosi e molli,
Dolce al cor si facea tepido bagno.
Già de' vermigli e torbidi rampolli
Omai tutto tranquillo era lo stagno,
Se non quanto il crespava in lievi giri
Auretta di mortiferi sospiri.

89   A woman collects the parts pale and soiled
Of her poor son's body wounded and maimed.
With her veil she dries off the bloody spoils,
And hugs close at his piteous remains.
In her eyes, the liquors of her heart boil,
As her soul ignites in a grief-filled flame.
Her arms are clutching the corpse without breath—
A cradle in life, now a grave in death.

90   Tired by what he has seen, but not sated,
Herod happily takes in the slaughter,
The torrents of blood he has created;
The king bathes himself in the warm waters
Of the Dead Sea. Motion all but abates:
The spiraling whirls become fewer.
Softer and softer grow the murmurs there,
Muffled sobs gasping in the quiet air.

LIBRO QUARTO

Spinto da Erode, il fier Malecche toglie
A viè più d'un bambin l'alma e la vita.
Quegli intanto su'l figlio e su la moglie
Piange e sente nel cor l'alma smarrita.
Il gran Poeta Ebreo la lingua scioglie,
E i vecchi Padri a rallegrarsi invita,
Mentre lo stuol de gl' Innocenti ei mira
Ch'unito verso il Limbo il volo gira.

BOOK FOUR

At Herod's command, fierce Malachi takes
More than one poor child's breath and life.
But soon, the king's own heart must break:
He loses his son and his wife.
The great Hebrew Poet awakes
And bids the Patriarchs revive.
Bear witness: the host of the Innocents
Finally ascends in deliverance.

1   Carca di nembi e fuora l'uso intanto
Mesta la notte al mesto dì successe,
Onde de' pargoletti il bruno manto
Parve l'essequie accompagnar volesse.
Pioggia versando gìa, quasi di pianto
Da l'ombre sue caliginose e spesse,
E de' confusi suoi muti lamenti
Eran gemiti i tuon, sospiri i venti.

2   Contento sì, ma non a pien contento,
In palagio a ritrarsi il re ne viene,
E qual fucina che del dianzi spento
Foco il calore ancor vivo ritiene,
Contro i miseri pur l'empio talento
Fresco nel cor nodrisce e ne le vene,
Temendo non ne sien per l'altrui case
Non piccole reliquie ancor rimase.

3   Malecche a sè chiamò. Tra' più felloni
Uom più fellone il mondo unqua non ebbe,
Né, se gli Antropofagi e i Lestrigoni
Risorgessero ancor, forse l'avrebbe.
Malecche, il Gebuseo, che tra' ladroni
Nacque e tra fere visse e fero crebbe.
Difforme sì che le sembianze istesse
Avria, credo, il Terror, se corpo avesse.

4   Oltre il mento pelato e 'l capo raso,
Oltre le tempie anguste e 'l ciglio irsuto,
Tre denti ha meno ed ha schiacciato il naso
E ne gli occhi ineguali il guardo acuto;
Benché 'l miglior de' duo, rigato a caso
D'un gran fregio a traverso, abbia perduto.
Ne la fronte e nel volto ha per trofeo
Il carettere greco e 'l conio ebreo.

1   Laden full with unseasonable clouds,
The sad night follows the sorrowful day,
As if it were veiled in a shroud,
It sends down thick, mournful rains.
Wrapped in dense and dark shadows
The groaning hour voices its pain.
Cries and whispers of the wind
Express woe that chokes it within.

2   Herod, though he is pleased, is not content,
And so into the palace he retreats.
Like a smith, even when his forge is spent,
He still feels, in his breast, burning heat.
Fresh rage and hate for the innocent,
In royal heart still have a seat.
Herod worries that a house may yet shield
Another child hiding somewhere concealed.

3   He summons Malachi, a wicked man:
So wicked, never would one find his sort
Where anthropophages dwell in the land
Or where Lestrygonians hold their court.
A Jebusite born to a thieving band,
Malachi grew wild as the beasts' consort,
So ugly that Terror, had it a face,
Would appear to have sprung from the same race.

4   From his great jaw jut bristles, coarse and rough;
Likewise, his temples and brow are hirsute.
Three teeth he lacks, and his nose has been crushed.
From mutilated eyes, cruelty shoots:
It is horrible to see: a scar cuts
Over the whole countenance of the brute.
His mangled features, which are scarred and ripped,
Seem to have been branded by foreign script.

5   —Va, spia—dice—per tutto, e teco mena
       Squadron d'armati, e se nascosto o chiuso
       Trovi alcun vivo infante, uccidi e svena,
       Segui in ciò del tuo stile il solit'uso—.
       —Farò—risponde—ho ben dispetto e pena
       D'esser steril di figli, e 'l Ciel n'accuso,
       Per altro no, se non perch'io vorrei
       Sol per piacerti, incominciar da' miei—.

6   Mentre de' suoi furori infra se stesso
       Lasciar dispone Erode eterno essempio,
       Malecche, a cui dal perfido commesso
       L'ordine fu de lo spietato scempio,
       I satelliti guida al fiero eccesso,
       Non di re crudo essecutor men empio:
       Ma di signor sì rigido e protervo
       Non devea più pietoso esser il servo.

7   Sì come allor, che dopo i tempi adusti
       A librar l'anno, o bell'Astrea, ritorni,
       E 'l Sol con raggi temperati e giusti
       Matura i pomi e 'ntepidisce i giorni,
       Vanno schierati a depredar gli arbusti
       A fila a fila turbidi di storni,
       Onde, mentre calar lunge gli mira,
       L'uve sperate il villanel sospira:

8   Tal dopo sè lasciando, ovunque avisa
       Esser riposto alcun germoglio Ebreo,
       Traccia crudel di quella turba uccisa,
       Lo stuol si sparge insidioso e reo.
       I palagi e le rocche, in quella guisa
       Che suol da gli Austri il combattuto Egeo,
       S'odon sonar di fanciulleschi accenti,
       Di donneschi ululati e di lamenti.

5   "Go forth," the king orders, "and take along
    Soldiers in arms. If a child is revealed,
    You should do unto him your wonted wrong:
    Kill him and bleed him; his fate has been sealed."
    "As you command," the good sergeant responds,
    "Curse God for denying a son to me:
    Would only I did—may Heaven be damned—
    For you I would kill him with my own hand!"

6   Setting an example for the ages,
    Of infamy, Great Herod sends him out.
    At court, the tyrant paces and rages,
    While Malachi gathers soldiers and scouts.
    Then he sets off to earn gruesome wages.
    Such a henchman suits his master, no doubt:
    A king thoroughly fearsome and depraved
    Deserves discipline from servants and slaves.

7   As when Astraea, after summer heat,
    Returns in the fall to balance the year,
    And the fruit that hangs on the boughs of the trees
    Is growing rich and ripe in wholesome cheer,
    And a dappled host of birds comes to eat
    The bounteous crop just as it appears
    (The farmer, all the while, looks on and sighs
    That his labors vanish before his eyes)—

8   Thus the treacherous horde fanned out and looked
    For the smallest shoot of the Hebrew stock,
    To uproot what might yet grow in a nook
    Undetected, whether seed or stalk.
    All houses, small and great, high and low, shook
    With cries at the approach of the flock;
    Throughout all the land they flew and they swarmed,
    As when battling winds bellow and storm.

9   Non altrimenti che, se prese ed arse
        L'alte mura vedesse e l'alte porte
        E le schiere nemiche intorno sparse
        Scalare i tetti e gridar sangue e morte,
        Parea l'afflitta Betthelem lagnarse,
        E percotersi il petto e pianger forte;
        E sì alte mandò le voce a Dio
        Che da' colli di Ramma il suon s'udio.

10   Sotto la falce le tremanti biade,
        Sotto l'aratro i tenerelli gigli
        Cader soglion talor, sì come cade
        Presso le madri il numero dei figli.
        Spandendo van l'ingiuriose spade
        Di sangue cittadin fiumi vermigli,
        E la misera plebe a mal sì grave
        Altro, salvo il morir, scampo non have.

11   Fra gli altri alberghi, in picciola casetta
        L'oltraggioso Malecche a forza entrando,
        Vede due figli, a vaga giovinetta
        L'uno a' piè l'altro in sen starsi posando;
        A l'un con liete nenie il sonno alletta
        E col piè leggermente il va cullando;
        L'altro da' fonti candidi e vivaci
        Le sugge il latte e più che 'l latte i baci.

12   In cambio di saluto, ecco, veloce
        A quel che dorme il traditor s'aventa,
        Alza la fiera e formadibil voce
        E lo sveglia dal sonno e lo spaventa.
        Cala la spada orribile e feroce
        E 'n perpetuo letargo l'addormenta,
        E gl'insegna a saper come vicini
        Hanno il sonno e la morte i lor confini.

9   Bethlehem—as if the city were breached
By a horde that penetrated its walls
And now set fire to all standing in reach
Among shouts, commands, and furious calls—
Seems to tear its breast, to wail and screech
In horror and grief as, broken, it falls.
The cries ascend so far and reach so wide,
One can hear them even on Ramah's side.

10   As trembling wheat is cut under the scythe,
Or tender lilies fall beneath the plough,
Thus, lying lifeless at their mother's side
Number innumerable children now.
The swords of killers, mercilessly plied,
Leave behind rivers of blood as they mow.
The wretched people, gasping and gaping,
Have, except death, no way of escaping.

11   Malachi thrusts his way into a shack
That lies tucked away on a humble street.
He sees a girl with her sons in the back.
The one, in a cradle, lies at her feet;
Gently, the mother rocks him back and forth,
Sings a lullaby so that he will sleep;
The other she nurses and caresses,
Giving him milk and stroking his tresses.

12   The false-hearted ogre, to say hello,
Rushes first to the one who lies dreaming.
There, at the crib, he emits a bellow,
Wakes the terrified boy with his screaming.
Then, from his horrid and fierce sword, a blow
Returns him to the state of nonbeing:
Now the tiny lad will rest forever,
So close do sleep and death lie together.

13   Poi che ne l'un le prime prove ha fatte
Nel poppator fanciullo il brando rota,
E da la nuca, ov'egli il fiede e batte,
Gliel fa per bocca uscir, tra gota e gota.
Quei sputa il cibo, e dentro il sangue e 'l latte
L'anima pargoletta ondeggia e nuota;
Scorre la punta ingiuriosa e fella,
E conficca la lingua a la mammella.

14   Misera avea colei di non perfetto
Altro parte immaturo il ventre pieno.
Passa il già nato, e giunge ove al concetto
Era vital sepolcro il cavo seno:
L'un chiuso in grembo e l'altro in braccio stretto
More, ed ella in un punto anco vien meno.
Chi mai caso sì strano intese o vide?
Un colpo, un colpo sol tre vite uccide.

15   Quindi in altra magion s'apre l'entrata
E 'ncontro a nobil giovane si spinge,
Che la fresca ferita e non saldata
D'un circonciso suo ristagna e stringe.
Ed ecco alzando allor la mano armata,
Nel sangue, ch'ella asciuga, il ferro tinge,
Ed a piaga di legge il braccio forte
Accoppia a quel meschin piaga di morte.

16   Allor colei per ravivarlo alquanto,
Porge la poppa al miserel che langue;
Versa in grembo a la madre il figlio intanto,
De la madre medesma il latte in sangue;
Versa del figlio stesso il sangue in pianto
Su 'l sanguigno figliuol la madre essangue;
Lava il candido umor, mentre il vermiglio
Macchia il seno a la madre, il volto al figlio.

13   Having dealt in this fashion with the first,
He now turns the blade on the other boy,
He hacks at his neck as he stills his thirst.
Under the cruel blow, his mouth is destroyed.
Blood and milk flow from his mother, his nurse.
On the billows, the child floats like a toy
Until the fiend's second swing does him in
And to her breast the poor child's tongue is pinned.

14   The mother of the pair has in her womb
A third babe still not entirely formed.
Piercing his brother, the sword makes a tomb
For the one her body and heart yet warm.
The unborn child dies before it can bloom,
And the mother dies before she can mourn.
Is there a case so strange otherwise known—
Three birds that are killed by a single stone?

15   Another doorway the butcher tears wide;
There, he sees a noblewoman attend
To her son but recently circumcised.
His wound is unhealed, and it must yet mend.
Even so, where the blood has not yet dried
His steel opens it more when it descends.
Unlike the first cut, which the Law fulfills,
The next incision is sinful and kills.

16   The woman tries to stem and stanch the flood,
Give him her breast to ward off death so near.
The boy sheds her milk as though his own blood;
As if pouring his blood, she sheds her tears.
Alas, her efforts do her son no good,
Nor do they benefit her, it appears.
Whenever white washes away the red,
The red returns, only now it has spread.

17 L'abbandona ciò fatto, e passa audace
    Di stanza in stanza a più secreti ostelli.
    Cerca gli accessi, e con lo stuol seguace
    Lini e lane rivolge e coltri e pelli.
    In cavo letticiuol trova che giace
    Coppia di similissimi gemelli;
    E l'un a l'altro in guisa era congiunto
    Che i Gemelli del Ciel pareano a punto.

18 La forma è pari e differente il sesso
    De la mal nata e mal guardata coppia;
    Vive in due corpi vari un spirto stesso,
    Una vita in due cor gemina e doppia.
    Natura ha in loro ugual sembiante espresso,
    E pueril simplicità gli accoppia;
    E qual Giano novello in duo diviso
    Hanno il letto commun com' hanno il viso.

19 Quella cara union ruppe e distinse
    Malecche, e disse:—O fortunata sorte,
    Ecco pur quell'amor, ch'ambo vi strinse
    Sì dolce in vita, ancor v'unisce in morte.
    Se somiglianti il Ciel sì vi dipinse,
    Non vo' che l'un a l'altro invidia porte,
    Ma questo e quel, come di par v'entraro,
    Vo' che del mondo ancora escan di paro—.

20 Ciò dice e nel primier prima si cala,
    E con la forte incontrastabil destra
    L'arrandella colà, d'onde a la sala
    L'aria e 'l lume introduce alta finestra.
    Precipita col piè giù per la scala
    L'altro, e la scala è d' una selce alpestra,
    Sì ch'ei viene a pagar, rotto e battuto,
    Di sangue a ciascun grado ampio tributo.

17   The task done, onward Malachi proceeds
      From room to room, and then from hall to hall,
      He rifles through carpets, linen, and sheets
      Lest anything remain hidden at all.
      Finally, he discovers what he seeks:
      Tucked into their bed, a pair like two dolls.
      Brother and sister, together they lie,
      Angelic twins like those up in the sky.

18   They are of different sex, but look the same—
      The unfortunate children, babes ill starred.
      In their two bodies a sole spirit flames,
      There is but one life that beats in two hearts.
      A single likeness their faces contain
      Nor are they old enough to grow apart.
      Like the god Janus divided in two
      They lie side by side, separate yet fused.

19   Malachi tears the union asunder:
      "Blessed fortune, by celestial light,
      Such a love you share! Greater wonder
      Still were it if the dark, eternal night
      Surrounded you and heightened your splendor.
      Both of you have been made equally bright,
      So the one should not envy the other:
      Die, then, together—sister and brother!"

20   He barks out these words, and he grabs the male.
      Cast with the killer's incomparable might,
      Off into the air the hapless boy sails,
      Through the same window through which enters light.
      Malachi kicks his sister down the stairs,
      Down onto the hard rock, polished and white.
      Bruised, broken, battered, and gored through and through,
      To each of the steps she pays bloody due.

21   Parea ciascun con gli ultimi tributi
      Gemendo accompagnar l'essequie altrui.
      Quasi innesto reciso in duo virgulti,
      Egli per lei languia, ella per lui.
      Così, non rei, sentiro, e non adulti,
      La pena de gli adulteri ambidui;
      Ebber ne le prime ore e ne l'estreme
      Un ventre, un letto ed un sepolcro insieme.

22   Viensi dove modesta umil fanciulla
      Custode a duo bambin siede e compagna.
      L'una in conca dimora e l'altro in culla:
      L'uno in lavacro tepido si bagna,
      L'altro fra bianchi lini si trastulla;
      Ride per vezzo l'un, l'altro si lagna.
      Nati già di due ventri e d'un sol padre,
      Ond'a l'uno è madrigna, a l'altro è madre.

23   Quando la miserella entrato scorge
      L'assalitor, che d'improvviso arriva,
      Lascia figliastro entro la cuna e porge
      Soccorso al figlio, onde si salvi e viva.
      Prendelo in braccio incontanente e scorge
      Stupefatta, smarrita e fuggitiva;
      Pur ver l'altro fanciul ritienla a freno
      Pietà se non materna, umana almeno.

24   Corre con quel che partorì da l'alvo
      Verso colui che di campar desia,
      Ahì folle, e le convien che quel che salvo
      Tolse pur dianzi a l'acque, al ferro dia.
      Malecche il fier con Barabasso il calvo
      Punì la pietosissima follia,
      E fece ad ambo, avante al suo cospetto,
      Sepolcro il vaso e cataletto il letto.

21   It seems that both, in the final drama,
Performed the one for the other last rites.
The sounds they made—in inverted commas—
Meant words that only they could hear: "Sleep tight."
Though not adults, they suffered the trauma
That is reserved for adulterous plight:
Never was there sinful thought in their head,
Yet in birth and death they shared the same bed.

22   The monster next finds a maid who attends
To the charge of watching over two cubs.
Nestled in a cradle, the first extends
Tiny limbs; the other sits in a tub.
Each one, in turn, of the two little friends
Brings forth laughter and cries as the girl scrubs.
In fact, only the first boy is her son,
Another woman had the second one.

23   But now, suddenly, when she sees the brute
Bursting in, arriving unexpected,
She leaves her stepson where he is and scoots
Off in mad haste that is unreflected.
Her child in her hand—her fear is acute—
She wants for her own to be protected.
The mother leaves the other boy behind:
Alas, such is the nature of humankind.

24   She runs with the child to whom she gave birth
Back to the other one—to save him, too.
But in so doing, she hands over the first
The very boy that she has just rescued!
Malachi and Barabbas, full of mirth,
Applaud the fatal compassion they view.
The poor woman beholds the children's doom:
The bath is a grave, the cradle a tomb.

25 Vinta colei da la soverchia ambascia
   Gela, e trema nel cor, nel volto imbianca,
   Piombar nel suol si lascia, e già la lascia
   A vista sì crudel l'anima stanca.
   Quei, strangolato da la propria fascia,
   Si contorce e dibatte e more e manca;
   Questi, tra 'l latte e 'l pianto e 'l sangue e l'onda
   Svenato cade e soffocato affonda.

26 Giunse, ove poi di cittadine inermi
   Povera famigliuola era raccolta:
   Una fra lor ne gli anni suoi men fermi
   Imeneo, stretta a pena, avea disciolta;
   Ma di ben quattro assai leggiadri germi
   Fecondata la prima in una volta,
   Or in un anno sol fatta si vede
   Sposa, vedova, madre e senza erede.

27 Duo di lor per lo collo ha tosto preso
   Malecche, un per le gambe, un per le braccia.
   Un ne lancia col calcio al fuoco acceso,
   Un battuto nel suol co' piè ne schiaccia,
   Un ne tracolla ad una trave appeso,
   Un nel pozzo domestico ne caccia:
   Così con vario universal tormento
   Ebbe ciascuna morte un elemento.

28 Chi contar potria mai le varie spoglie,
   Onde Morte sen gìa superba e ricca?
   Qual dal tenero busto il capo scioglie,
   Qual da l'omero molle il braccio spicca,
   Quei del fiato a la gola il varco toglie,
   Quei nel fianco tremante il ferro ficca.
   E fra rabbia e terror, fra doglia e lutto,
   Il Furor con le Furie erra per tutto.

25   Struck by overpowering grief
She freezes and shudders and pales;
Finally, she falls down like a leaf,
Struck dumb by the horror, wan and frail.
Strangled within the winding sheets,
One of the children twists and wails;
The other splashes in red-white water:
Drowning, he sinks and drinks in the slaughter.

26   The killer then arrives at a place where
More fearful women cower unarmed.
There, he beholds a girl barely married,
So young, yet denied all of her groom's charms.
Still, she has had time enough to carry
The fourfold fruit of brief union to term.
And so, in just a year, she has become
Wife, orphaned mother, and widow in one.

27   Soon, Malachi has seized two by the scruff,
One by the arm, the other by the feet.
In the burning flames the first child is snuffed,
And the second trampled into the street.
The third hangs from a beam. Still not enough:
The fourth goes down a well; work is complete.
He has used a full array of torments,
They die by all four of the elements.

28   Who could recount the terrors that adorn
Grim Death as it struts among the flames?
From tender busts heads have been torn,
Arms have been ripped from tiny frames.
The pathway of breath is cut short,
Trembling flanks are mangled and maimed.
Through the scene of rage, terror, and pain,
Stalks Fury, with the Furies in train.

29   Braccia, da' busti lor tronche e recise,
      Seminate hanno il suol, gole strozzate,
      Teste, quai da secura aspro divise,
      Quai con man rotte e quai con piè calcate.
      Trescar Morte veggendo in tante guise,
      Se medesma abhorrì la Crudeltate,
      Né lasciava però d'esser crudele,
      Ma 'l dispetto al suo tosco accrescea fele.

30   Et ecco già, ch'omai si leva ed esce
      L'alba da l'Indo e 'l Sol non molto è lunge,
      E 'l ciel l'ombre co' rai confonde e mesce,
      E marito a la notte il dì congiunge.
      Si rode Erode e l'aspettar gl'increscе,
      Tale stimolo ardente il cor gli punge.
      Sorge e riveste i regi arnesi e toglie
      L'aurata verga e le purpuree spoglie.

31   Intanto il gran palagio ode repente
      D'alti strepiti e fiochi ulular tutto,
      E di servi e di ancelle intorno sente
      Suoni di palme e gemiti di lutto;
      Ed ecco arriva un messagier dolente
      Pallido in vista e d'atro sangue brutto,
      Ch'anelando e sudando in apparire
      Al re s'inchina, e poi comincia:—O Sire,

32   Un son io di color ministro indegno,
      Cui de la fiera uccision commesso
      Fu iersera l'incarco; ed or ne vegno
      Poco a te lieto e fortunato messo;
      Lungo a narrar del tuo sublime sdegno
      Fora distintamente ogni successo;
      Istoria memorabile di cui,
      Vagliami teco il ver, gran parte io fui.

29   Scattered limbs lie over the ground
      Among shredded throats in the soot;
      Severed heads lie in piles all around,
      Crushed either by hand or by foot.
      Indeed, Cruelty itself has found
      Such horror that it cannot stay put.
      Running wild, it grows more and more savage,
      Seeks everywhere fresh victims to ravage.

30   Behold, the pink Dawn rose and gleamed,
      And the bright Sun ascended, too.
      Mixing in one shadows and beams,
      Day and night together she drew.
      Herod roved and he raved; it seemed
      That his rage would never be through.
      At court, he again donned royal attire:
      Took up the scepter, burning like fire.

31   And all the while, the great palace's walls
      Filled more and more with high-pitched sounds of woe.
      The servants and the maids are held in thrall,
      Wringing their hands fretfully as terror grows.
      Lo, a messenger arrives in the hall:
      His face is pallid, no blood seems to flow.
      He is white as a sheet, though caked in gore.
      Panting, he kneels down and begins: "O Lord,

32   "I am a vassal unworthy and base,
      Ordered to fulfill your ev'ry command.
      I fear I must bring bad news of the chase
      And report that not all has gone as planned.
      It is not fitting for me to narrate
      Every deed performed by my hand—
      But for all that, I should not leave aside
      That I have discharged my duty with pride.

33   Sotto il vessillo tuo, sì come imposto
Da te stesso ne fu, partimmo noi,
Duce e capo Malecche, e gimmo tosto
Veloci ad esseguir gli ordini tuoi.
V'era tal, ch'era padre, e pur disposto
Ne venia per gradirti a i danni suoi.
Piani dunque n'andammo e taciturni,
Chiusi da l'ombre e da gli orror notturni;

34   Presa fu la gran piazza e tutti i lati;
Quinci e quindi, sbarrando ambe le porte,
Chiusi fur d'ogni intorno e circondati
Da custodi fedeli e guardie accorte,
Acciò che altrui fra vigilanti armati,
Non potesse la fuga aprir la sorte.
Fece per tutto il capitano allora
Squillar la tromba garrula e canora.

35   E 'n virtù commandò del regio editto,
A ciascun, che per uso armi vestisse,
Che de l'albergo e del confin prescritto
In guardia fuor de la cittade uscisse.
Né, mentre un reo di capital delitto
Cercando ei giva, altro impedirlo ardisse:
Un reo che quivi occulto in grande impresa,
Avea del re la maestate offesa.

36   Alcun non fu de' cittadin né lento
Ad esseguir, né ad ubidir ritroso.
Quindi di borgo in borgo in un momento
Si spiò de' bambin per l'aere ombroso.
E sappi, che del numero già spento
Trovammo assai maggior l'avanzo ascoso;
Onde fu con diverse aspre ferite
Rotto il tenero stame a mille vite.

33   "Under your standard (as you instructed)
      We proceeded, Malachi at the fore.
      We followed his lead, as he conducted
      The team, and we readied ourselves for war.
      Fathers among us were uncorrupted
      By whatever paternal love they bore.
      In the darkness our band slinked down the street,
      And no sound came from our voices or feet.

34   "The great city square on all sides we barred.
      All the gates in front and back were secured.
      At every point, the soldiers stood guard
      —The men were trained to be watchful, alert—
      To stop anyone from making a start
      And trying to scamper off in a spurt.
      When it was time, our captain gave the sign
      That the trumpets sound and blast their shrill whine.

35   "As per royal edict he commanded
      Those parties who bore any arms at all
      To leave their houses and be remanded
      To custody outside the city walls.
      But one guilty person he demanded:
      None should seek to halt the criminal's fall.
      This party, to be denied all defense,
      Had given His Majesty grave offense.

36   "The citizens all responded quickly.
      They wasted no time, so great was their fright.
      Soon we found more babes, over the city,
      Than already had fallen to the knife.
      Know, Sire, that we denied them all pity
      And dispatched ev'ry one of them on sight.
      Myriad tender lives did we cut low
      Dealing as many bitter and fierce blows.

37   Fuor che strida e sospir, pianti e singhiozzi,
       Altro non si sentia per ogni parte.
       Vedeansi entro gli alberghi immondi e sozzi
       Trionfar Morte orribilmente e Marte.
       Colà fascie squarciate e membri mozzi,
       Qui nel sangue nuotar viscere sparte;
       Se ciò ch'allor fec'io silenzio or copre,
       Bello è il tacer là dove parlan l'opre.

38   Stamane poscia in su 'l ritorno, quando
       Già l'eccidio notturno era fornito,
       Impensato accidente e miserando
       Ne si fè incontro, e caso empio, inudito.
       Deh stato fosse il tuo real commando
       Da' tuoi servi, Signor, meno ubidito!
       Ma che sapea simplice turba, e quale
       Colpa aver può d'involontario male?

39   Troppo la nostra man fu presta e pronta,
       Troppo la voglia a sodisfarti intensa.
       Ebri di sangue i cori e d'ira e d'onte,
       Ciechi eran gli occhi e cieca l'aria e densa.
       Fu scusabile error—. Così racconta,
       E qui lega la lingua, e tace e pensa.
       Ma lo stimola Erode e quei, risciolta
       La voce, il parlar segue, e 'l re l'ascolta.

40   —Mentre, esseguito a pien l'alto statuto,
       Sì come io dissi, il nostro stuol venia,
       Ne venne ad incontrar scudiero astuto,
       Secreta di Malecche e fida spia;
       E ne scorse colà, dove veduto,
       Disse, furtivamente aver tra via,
       Con duo bambini avvolti entro la gonna,
       Fuggirsi in chiusa parte ignota donna.

37   "Nothing except for dull sobs and sharp screams
      Was to be heard in the city at all.
      Black Death and red War in glory were seen
      Parading before and throughout its walls.
      Bedding and limbs torn at the seam,
      Raw viscera that snaked and sprawled . . .
      I now fall silent, for there is no need
      To speak in words what has been done in deeds.

38   "Then, in the morning we made our way back
      —The night's battle had already been won—
      When suddenly we were stopped in our tracks
      By an ill that was foreseen by no one.
      Would only we, your servants, had lacked
      Such savage desire to see your will done!
      Are simple men not to be acquitted,
      When unawares a wrong is committed?

39   "Our hands were overly quick to engage,
      The wish to do your bidding too intense.
      Our hearts had been made drunk with blood and rage,
      Our eyes were blind in the night dark and dense.
      Forgive an error . . ." the messenger said,
      Hesitating to reveal the words' sense.
      Herod, of course, felt his interest piqued.
      He urged the man to continue to speak.

40   "As our squad was carrying out
      Your Highness's royal command,
      We were joined by Malachi's scout,
      His keen and trusty right-hand man.
      He led us where, he had no doubt,
      A woman with two children ran.
      The fugitive, our comrade suspected,
      Sought out a place to hide undetected.

41 Non lunge dunque da quest'alta reggia
    Verso quel lato, onde 'l real giardino
    Di sovra 'l fiume il Libano vagheggia
    Presso un uscio ne trasse empio destino;
    Vago pur di saper ciò ch'esser deggia,
    Il nostro condottier si fe' vicino
    Là 've tra legni perforati e scissi,
    Luce per noi si vide e voce udissi.

42 Femina v'era dentro, e parve in vista
    Lo spavento portar dipinto e 'l duolo;
    E di due fanciullin, timida e trista,
    L'un si tenea nel sen, l'altro nel suolo;
    Voce tremante e di sospir commista
    Dal cor traendo, a l'un dicea:—Figliuolo,
    Figliuol, come ti scampo? Ove t'ascondo?
    E chi m'apre l'abisso o 'l mar profondo?

43 Donne un tempo Samaria ebbe sì felle,
    Fama è tra noi, che da la fame astrette
    Risepelir ne le materne celle
    Carni, ch'eran di lor nate e concette.
    Lassa, e perché ciò che per rabbia a quelle,
    Ora me per pietà non si permette,
    E celar voi da queste ingorde Arpie
    Ne le viscere mie, viscere mie?

44 Ma con l'essempio già di tanti eccessi,
    Figlio, ben mi vedresti il seno aprire,
    Quando in tal guisa poi speranza avessi
    La tua vita campar col mio morire.
    Così l'anima aprirmi anco potessi,
    E 'l corpo tuo con l'anima coprire,
    Ch'io non sarei di ricettarti avara
    Dentro l'anima stessa, anima cara—.

41   "Not far away from the great palace here,
       Where the royal gardens look down upon
       The flowing river that appears
       Beneath the hills of Lebanon
       —At this site, a fatal moment drew near.
       Our leader told us all to come along:
       We heard voices and saw light through the cracks
       Of a small hovel, a broken-down shack.

42   "There we found a woman trembling inside,
       Terror and pain were painted on her face.
       She was clutching two babes to her side;
       When she spoke, her voice quivered and quaked.
       She heaved a great sigh and said to one child:
       'Alas, my son, there is no hiding place.
       Why won't the gaping abyss down below
       Or the deep sea's waters swallow me whole?

43   "'Samaria was once home, it is told,
       To a race of women fearsome and tough;
       Driven by hunger, they even made bold
       To bury their own children in their guts.
       Why can I not do the same out of love,
       If, for them, bitter want was enough?
       And hide you away deep beneath my heart,
       Again flesh of my flesh, never to part?

44   "'When I now contemplate such infamy
       As rages, my son, I'd pierce my own breast,
       If only I might hope in this way
       To preserve your life through my death.
       I would tear open my soul instantly
       So that there your body might at least rest.
       Then would I welcome and warmly enfold
       Your dear spirit from my own spirit's mold.'

45 E, così ragionando, il pargoletto
Ch'ha in braccio entr'una veggia ampia e capace,
Che del licor di Bacco era ricetto,
Non di tutto ancor vota asconde e tace;
Poi sospira e soggiunge:—A te commetto,
Vaso fedele, ogni mia gioia e pace;
Tu 'l mio tesor fra tanti fieri orgogli,
Cortese almen depositario accogli—.

46 Oltre seguir volea, ma si rivolse
Del nostro duca a l'impeto, a la voce,
Ch'urtò la porta e, poi che ruppe e sciolse
I ferrami e le sbarre, entrò feroce.
L'un ne l'urna appiattò, l'altro s'accolse
Colei nel grembo, indi fuggì veloce,
Ove di quell'albergo era nascosta
La camera più interna e più riposta.

47 Quivi l'ascose. E ben sottrarlo allora
Potea volendo al sovrastante male,
S'aperto avesse altrui senza dimora,
Di cui si fosse il fanciullino e quale.
Ma sperò forse il suo più caro ancora
Prima salvar dal rischio aspro e mortale,
O, con inganno almen spietato e scaltro,
Far l'uno al fin vendicator de l'altro.

48 Meraviglia fu ben ch'a noi non fosse
Nota costei; ma tra per l'aer bruno
E per l'alto terror che la percosse,
Non valse allora a ravisarla alcuno;
Oltre che dal furor che ne commosse,
Fatto cieco e baccante era ciascuno;
E 'l vederla poi fuor del regio tetto
Ne tolse del gran caso ogni sospetto.

45   "She picked up the babe, all her hope was spent,
        And off into a cask—one still half filled
        With the sweet nectar of Bacchus—he went.
        She put him in the barrel, and she fell
        Quiet for a while, then ended her silence:
        'Receive now, most faithful receptacle,
        My sole delight, my great treasure, my joy
        Be gracious, vessel, and please keep my boy.'

46   "More prayers still would she have said but she stopped
        When she heard the voice boom of our captain.
        He broke down the door and shattered the lock—
        She left one son behind as he barged in.
        Towering Malachi lumbered and stalked;
        At her soft breast, the poor babe was flattened.
        One room to the next, she fled left and right,
        Looking where they might hide, out of his sight.

47   "She would have saved the boy from all danger,
        If only she had revealed in time
        That the child was a native, no stranger
        —Indeed, he belonged to the royal line.
        Perhaps in her fright the woman wagered
        She might avert disaster by lying.
        Or perhaps she had thought she could thwart
        Our chase by playing a trick of some sort.

48   "It is strange that she was not recognized.
        However, in the dark gloom of the night,
        With grim fear twisting her features and eyes,
        It was impossible that we see right;
        Worse still, the hunt had made all the men wild,
        Blinded by rage, they were deprived of sight.
        When we found her outside the royal walls,
        There could be no doubt in our minds at all.

49   Malecche dunque, ancor che espresso intanto
Sapesse il loco ov'era il furto ascoso,
Per riportar d'ogni fierezza il vanto,
Sì come aspro che egli era e dispettoso,
Volse, gioco di lei prendendo alquanto,
Spaventevole in atto e minaccioso,
Schernir, pria ch' uccidesse i cari pegni,
Con astuzia crudele i suoi disegni.

50   Ed ecco il braccio e 'l piè contro lei move,
E le straccia le vesti e streccia i crini.
—Dimmi—dice—malvagia, or dimmi, dove,
Dove dianzi celasti i duo bambini?
—E tu, da la cui destra il sangue piove,
Di'—dic'ella—ove son tanti meschini?
Tanti di tante madri occhi e pupille?
Tu cerchi di duo soli ed io di mille.

51   Fusse in grado a le stelle, o cari figli,
Ch'a mio talento in mia balia v'avessi;
O qual nido vi accoglie e quali artigli
Dal mio sen vi rapiro, almen sapessi:
Ché, fra ceppi e catene, armi e perigli,
Se flagellata in vive fiamme ardessi,
Mai questo cor, che luce altra non vede,
Non spoglierei de la materna fede.

52   Figli, deh qual fortuna o pur qual loco
Vi possede infelici e vi nasconde?
V'ha forse, lassa, inceneriti il foco?
O sepolcro vi dier l'acque profonde?
Cibo ai cani, a gli augelli? o fatti gioco
Siete de' venti instabili e de l' onde?
O col sangue innocente estinta avete
De le spade barbariche la sete?

49   "Malachi, of course, who knew that the boy
Had been artfully concealed from our view,
Immediately saw through the mother's ploy,
And he countered with his own wicked ruse;
He wanted to drink a full cup of joy
By seeing how her vain hopes were abused.
And so, before killing her progeny,
He concealed his plan diabolically.

50   "The ogre advanced and he grabbed her fast,
Tearing her clothes and ripping her hair.
'Tell me,' he shouts, 'tell me at last
How you hid the two boys, and where!'
'Why don't you tell me,' in turn she asks,
'Where are all the children—where?
The sole delight of so many mothers—
Two you seek; what became of the others?

51   "'Would that the stars saw fit, beloved sons,
To let me hold you in my warm embrace;
If I but knew where it is you have gone,
Or who has taken you, or to what place!
Were you put in irons and chains, or drawn
On the rack, or tortured by whips and flames?
Never will my motherly heart be stripped
Of the devotion that dwells within it.

52   "'My poor children, alas, where are you held?
What is your fortune, where is it you lie?
Did the flaming pyres consume you, as well?
Or did the deep waters silence your cries?
Do the bellies of wild dogs or birds swell
With your flesh? In what manner have you died?
Were winds or the waves your fatal curse?
Has your blood slaked a sword's scorching thirst?

53   Estinta? Ahi no, del barbaro inumano
      Son l'ire ancor, per quel ch'io veggio, ardenti—.
      Qui l'incalza Malecche e dice:—In vano
      Ciò che negar non puoi, negar mi tenti.
      Stolta fè, pietà folle, amore insano
      Occultar quel che palesar convienti.
      Violenza di ferro, a viva forza,
      Pietoso affetto in cor materno ammorza.

54   Tu, qual madre magnanima ed ardita,
      Quel ch'è pur noto, appalesar non vuoi,
      E sprezzar morte e non curar la vita
      Ti fa forse l'amor de' figli tuoi;
      Ma questo stesso amor muove ed invita
      Erode ancora a provedere ai suoi—.
      Così le dice, la minaccia ed ella
      Con audacia viril freme e favella:

55   —Ponmi tra 'l foco e 'l ferro; ardi, se sai,
      Uccidi pur, morir mi fia gran sorte.
      Se spaventarmi vuoi più che non fai,
      Minacciami la vita e non la morte—.
      Mentre parla così, vie più che mai
      Ostinata in suo cor, la donna forte,
      Ecco il primo fanciul, da l'urna chiusa,
      Con voce pueril se stesso accusa.

56   Rise Malecche e, preso il doglio, il trasse
      Per lo palco rotando e ne fe' gioco;
      Ma però che di ferro ha i cerchi e l'asse,
      Danneggiar non si può molto né poco.
      Vuol egli al fin provar, s'almen bastasse
      Ciò che 'l braccio non valse, a fare il foco.
      Nel foco il caccia, e fa che versi e stilli
      Misto il sangue col vin per cento spilli.

53   "'Is it over? Alas, no. Fire still burns,
     I see too well, in the cruel monster's breast ...'
     Then Malachi addresses her in turn:
     'In vain do you deny the truth. Confess,
     —Such stupid faith you show, pity unearned!—
     You harbored criminals under arrest.
     Now my steel's force will offer correction
     To your wayward maternal affection.

54   "'O mother so kind in both heart and soul,
     You won't reveal what is already known?
     Does your love for your brood make you so bold,
     That you scorn death—be it even your own?
     The same feeling inspires Herod. Behold,
     See how he provides for seed he has sown!'
     Thus the sergeant spoke darkly—fearsome and grim.
     But she shook with manly rage and answered him:

55   "'Bring hot fire and cold iron, go ahead.
     If you wish to kill me, gladly I die.
     For if you really want to inspire dread,
     Then you should threaten to leave me alive!'
     Holding firm to all the words she has said,
     The proud woman all but spits in his eye.
     Alas, just then the boy she has concealed
     Is betrayed by his own voice and revealed.

56   "Malachi laughs and takes the wooden drum,
     He kicks it this way and that on the ground;
     Reinforced by sturdy rings of iron,
     It is not damaged by rolling around.
     The soldier decides to see what will come,
     Testing with flames if the barrel is sound.
     Cast into the fire, wood crackles and snaps:
     Blood and wine pour out from a hundred taps.

57   Udito avrai dal Tauro d'Agrigento,
Quando dal rame suo concavo e pregno,
Ne' mugiti non suoi sparse il lamento
Del fiero suo fabricatore ingegno.
Così ne l'apprensibile elemento,
Alimento infondendo il cavo legno,
Impinguava la fiamma e fore intanto
N'uscia fra duo licor confuso il pianto.

58   E presente a tal vista e tanta rabbia
Nel petto allor la genitrice aduna,
Che sembra orrida tigre a cui tolt' abbia
Il cacciator d'Armenia i parti in cuna,
Quando con lieve piè l'ircana sabbia
Trascorre, in vista minacciosa e bruna,
E fa, sospinta da crudel pietate,
Tutto d'urli sonar l'alto Nifate.

59   Tosto a tor l'altro infante il passo gira
E 'l conduce fra noi quella infelice,
Che de l'orrenda e dispietata pira,
Onde 'l primo è fatt'esca, è spettatrice.
In pari incendio di pietate e d'ira,
Tra sdegnosa e dolente, avampa e dice:
—Per farlo, o crudi, incenerire a pieno,
Vi bastava riporlo in questo seno,

60   Là dove, quasi in immortal fornace,
Sue faville ognor vive Amor mantiene;
Ma se lo strazio altrui tanto vi piace,
E perduto una parte ho del mio bene,
Rifiuto l'altra, a voi la dono in pace,
Ben ne l'avanzo incrudelir conviene.
Prendetel dunque, ond'io d'entrambo priva
Resti e se morto è l'un, l'altro non viva—.

57   "The tyrant Phalaris once built a bull,
       Which would send forth from its hollow insides
       The terror within it, which made it full:
       Anguished cries of captives burning alive.
       In this way, the blazing element pulled
       Forth more and more fuel to feed its fire:
       The temperature mounted as the flames roared.
       As two liquids mixed, out the screams poured.

58   "Witnessing such a sight, the woman feels
       The fierce rage grow in her breast, then and there
       —Like a mother tiger, when hunters steal
       The newborn cubs yet unweaned from her lair,
       The great beast runs through the desert and hills
       Baring fangs and casting menacing glares;
       And all the while, her mournful howls resound,
       Sad echoes that fill the air all around.

59   "Having caught sight of the impious pyre
       That was cooking and boiling her son,
       She made a dash with the quickness of fire
       To take up in her arms the other one.
       Flaming with hatred and seething in ire,
       She mocked what Malachi had done:
       'To burn him completely—leave nothing left—
       You need only stuff him into my chest!

60   "'There, in an oven of undying heat,
       Most ardent love feeds the flames forever.
       But since you find that the pain is so sweet,
       Go ahead now and just take the other.
       My joy can never be full and complete,
       The very strings of my heart are severed.
       Let me lose both children. Take, I will give.
       If one be dead, the second should not live.'

61   Spada, a quel dir, di sangue ancor fumante,
Da cui non so, non men crudel che forte,
Vibrare io vidi e 'l rivelato infante
Mandar con cento e cento punte a morte:
Onde dubbiosa l'anima fra tante
Piaghe, ch'a la sua fuga aprian le porte,
Non sapendo per qual prender l'uscita
Su 'l morir lungo spazio il tenne in vita.

62   E la perfida allora:—Avrò pur io,
E de la patria mia dolce e diletta
Fatta in un punto sol—disse—e del mio
Sventurato figliuol degna vendetta.
O servi del tiranno iniquo e rio,
Or a voi sol di vendicar s'aspetta
Nel sangue reo de la fallace Albina
De la casa real l'alta ruina.

63   M'uccideste il mio cor; ma non andrete
Troppo lieti però di mia sventura.
L'ultimo, che nel sen morto m'avete
Figlio m'era d'amor, non di natura.
Riconoscere Albina omai devete,
Ch'ebbi Alessandro, il regio pegno in cura.
Quegli ch'or là nel suol palpita e more,
Quegli è del nostro re l'unico amore—.

64   Così diss'ella, e pien di mal talento
Per oltraggiarla il capitan si mosse.
Ma 'l pugnal, né so donde in un momento
Tratto o come da lei trattato fosse,
Ne la man feminil, senza spavento
Strinse con valor maschio, e lui percosse.
Io, io 'l vid'io del proprio sangue tinto,
Ed a pena il credei, cadere estinto.

61   "Then there flashed a blade still steaming with gore
       —I know not from where. Up and down it soared,
       Flying and waving around in the air.
       Thus the woman struck her child more and more
       With blows that the tiny body could not bear.
       She heaved and chopped until red blood poured:
       Vital sap gushed forth, stronger and stronger—
       In dying he lived still a bit longer.

62   "Thereupon, the disloyal woman yelled:
       'Now I have avengèd my belovèd land;
       I have avenged my ill-starred son, as well,
       My duty is done, and by my own hand.
       Servants of tyranny, sound the death knell.
       It is my own destruction I demand.
       Let the blood of faithless Albina pour,
       Soon the royal house will exist no more!

63   "'Monster, you killed the delight of my heart,
       Yet my misfortune should bring you no joy.
       The poor child from whom you have made me part,
       Was a son by love, but not my own boy.
       Recognizing me should not be so hard:
       As royal nurse I have long been employed:
       The limbs that are twitching there on the floor
       Belong to the child King Herod adored!'

64   "Thus did she speak, and our chief made a start.
       Meaning to strike the brazen woman dead.
       However—I do not know by what art—
       It was she who struck him, instead.
       With nary a trace of fear in her heart,
       She acted as if a man, born and bred.
       I saw him fall; stunned, he could not believe
       The strength of the wound that he had received.

65   S'al gran caso restò di nostra schiera
       Attonita ogni menta e sbigottita,
       Pensil ciascun, ch'aspra novella e fiera
       Inaspettatamente abbia sentita.
       Presa è l'iniqua balia, e prigioniera
       Già da' nostri si guarda e serba in vita,
       Però ch'una sol morte a tanto danno
       Parve piccola pena e breve affanno—.

66   Il fin non aspettò di questi accenti
       Il tiranno superbo e furibondo,
       E parve in atto il regnator de' venti
       Quand'apre l'uscio al carcer suo profondo
       E sferra a battagliar con gli elementi
       I guerrieri del mar, furie del mondo.
       Corre egli in sala, ed ecco a pena giunto
       Doride la reina arriva a punto.

67   A punto allor de la secreta soglia
       De la camera uscia la sventurata,
       Da lacrimoso coro e pien di doglia
       Di donzelle e di donne accompagnata,
       Che del fanciul la sanguinosa spoglia
       Su le braccia pur dianzi avean portata.
       Singhiozzando e gridando ella venia:
       —Dove, dov'è il mio ben? la vita mia?—

68   Qual, da poiché perduta aver s'accorse
       La bella figlia in su la spiaggia Etnea,
       Accese i pini infuriata e corse
       Già de le spiche l'inventrice dea,
       E co' rapidi draghi il ciel trascorse
       Stimulata dal duol che la traea,
       Cercando pur la vergine smarrita,
       Che fu in un punto sol vista e rapita;

65   "All the men in our crew were thunderstruck,
Utterly dumbfounded by what they saw.
An omen of the worst possible luck,
It seemed, had just appeared before us all.
The woman was promptly taken and stuck
In a prison to be judged by the law:
It is clear to me she cannot atone;
She must needs suffer more than death alone."

66   The arrogant tyrant, seething with rage,
Refused to wait for the report to end.
As when the Lord of Winds opens the gates
That are holding back his spirited friends,
And the elements rush forth in a wave,
Frenzied, the wild winds wind and then wend . . .
Like them, Herod was dashing back and forth
When his unlucky queen appeared in the court.

67   From far within, deep in the castle's halls,
The wretched queen rushes in sheer terror,
Followed by a chorus that sobs and bawls
—The women and the girls who attend her.
The remains of her child, horribly mauled,
Tell of the mistake, the gruesome error.
Seized by panic, the queen asks all around:
"Where is he? Tell me my child been found!"

68   The goddess who invented the harvest,
When her fair young daughter was stolen near
Mount Etna and whisked off into darkness,
Set torches aflame and by their light steered,
Drawn by two wingèd serpents in harness,
This way and that, through the heavenly spheres.
She searched everywhere for the sweet maiden
Who caught Pluto's eye, whom he had taken—

69   Tal ne venia l'addolorata: e, poscia
      Che vide il caro busto, al cor le nacque
      Tanta pietà, che, da soverchia angoscia
      Impedita, fermossi, afflitta tacque.
      Forato il ventre e l'una e l'altra coscia,
      Sdrucito il picciol corpo a piè le giacque.
      Tempestato di piaghe, era a vederlo
      Con cent' occhi sanguigni Argo novello.

70   O come allor de' duo vivi zaffiri
      Videsi oscuro il tremulo sereno,
      Come torcendo i languidetti giri
      Disciolse ai pianti, ai dolci accenti il freno!
      O Dio, di che dolcissimi sospiri
      Ferì le stelle e si percosse il seno,
      E svelse l'oro e lacerò le rose,
      Onde i crini e le guance Amor compose!

71   Al contrafatto volto il volto appressa,
      Lo stringe, il bacia, e sovra lui si getta:
      —Chi t'hà—dicea—sì concia, o di me stessa
      Sembianza estinta, imagine trafitta?
      Qual sì gran colpa ho contro 'l Ciel commessa,
      Ch'io deggia in cotal guisa esserne afflitta?
      Così, così ti dà d'oro e d'elettro
      Il tuo buon genitor corona e scettro?

72   O fera de le fere assai più fera,
      Amano i figli ancor le tigri ircane,
      E 'n quest'unico tuo, qual ria Megera,
      Ti mosse a incrudelir qual rabbia immane?
      Sfogasti pur la ferità severa
      De le rigide tue voglie inumane;
      Godi e sieno il suo sangue e i pianti miei,
      Vincitor trionfante, i tuoi trofei.

69 Like her did the sorrowing queen appear.
 Her son's remains gave her pain so acute,
 She felt such pity, was gripped by such fear,
 She simply stopped in her tracks and fell mute.
 The belly torn open, and his blood smeared
 Ev'rywhere, young life torn out at the root.
 Lacerated by wounds lay the carcass:
 Were cuts eyes, he'd be a new Argus.

70 How the queen's beautiful orbs of sapphire
 Filled with darkness as she shivered and quaked.
 Twisting and turning inside out their fires,
 They shed tears that yielded rivers and lakes.
 Sweet God, how her wails reached up to the sky,
 So even the stars did tremble and shake.
 She tore golden locks, she clawed at the rose
 Of pretty cheeks that once Love had composed—

71 She pressed parted lips to his bloodied face;
 Holding him close and kissing him, she groaned:
 "What has happened to your delicate traits,
 The features in which I once saw my own?
 Have I somehow brought the heavens disgrace,
 That into such grief I now should be thrown?
 Is this how your father, noble and true,
 Passes his scepter and crown on to you?

72 "Wilder beast than savage beasts of the wild—
 Hyrcanian tigers still love their young!
 That this fate should befall your only child—
 By what witchcraft or rage has it been done?
 Now you have satisfied your cruel desires,
 So the inhuman battle has been won.
 Rejoice! The blood and tears make a fitting trophy
 For a hero like you, for such a victory.

73   Dimmi spirto di serpe, anima d'orso
Dimmi cor di diaspro e di metallo,
In che poté con pueril discorso
Fallir giamai chi non connobbe il fallo?
Com'esser può che de l'età precorso
Abbia l'arbitrio il debito intervallo,
Sì che devesse in sua stagion non piena
L'error futuro anticipar la pena?

74   Uom te non già, né d'uman seme nato
Creder vogl'io: te la crudele e sorda
Sirte produsse, o l'Ellesponto irato,
O la Sfinge, di sangue immonda e lorda,
L'empia Chimera, o Cerbero spietato,
O l'infame Cariddi, o Scilla ingorda;
E ti nodrì, là fra lo stuol vorace
De' dragon di Cirene, Arpia rapace.

75   E tu tel vedi e tu tel soffri, o Cielo?
Figlio, ed io vivo? E con la destra ardita
Pur indugio a squarciar di questa il velo
Che sol per te mi piacque, afflitta vita?
No no, che se di morte orrido gelo
Preme la guancia tua fresca e fiorita,
Non convien, che la mia, languida e priva
D'ornamento e splendor, rimanga viva.

76   E se teco troncando ogni mia speme,
Chi già l'esser di dié, l'esser t'ha tolto,
Non mi torrà, ch'almen ne l'ore estreme,
Con lo spirto io ti segua errante sciolto.
La spoglia mia col tuo feretro insieme
N'andrà, né senza il ramo il fior fia colto.
Così lo struggitor de' miei conforti
Autor fia d'una strage e di più morti.

73   "Tell, venomous spirit with a bear's soul,
         Speak, you whose heart is made of cold steel,
         What wrong could a babbling babe ever do?
         How can there fault in the faultless be?
         How might his young mind, in so little time,
         Conceive plans of the slightest treachery?
         Why should he pay, at such a tender age,
         For crimes recorded on unwritten page?

74   "You are no man, not born of human seed,
         I believe. You were coughed up by a swamp
         Or else were vomited forth by the sea;
         You were suckled at the teat of the Sphinx,
         The Chimera, or Cerberus. Indeed,
         Scylla or Charybdis once made you strong,
         Feeding you among the ravenous worms,
         Harpies, and all else their intestines churn.

75   "Heavens above, is this hell to be borne?
         My son is dead, yet I live. Why, oh why
         Not put an end to a life that I scorned
         But for the one who was the light of my eyes?
         No, no, if chill, frozen death must deform
         This rosy cheek and snatch away warm sighs,
         Nothing more has meaning. He was priceless.
         I should die—I am already lifeless.

76   "The one who once gave you your breath now takes
         It from you. With it, he takes hope from me.
         But he will not stop the exit I make.
         Just wait, my soul will join you presently.
         If the flower is cut, let the stem break
         Too. May your coffin receive my body.
         In this way, the man who tore your life's thread
         Seeking one death has left many more dead.

77   Deh quanto era il miglior, se 'l dì ch'apristi,
      O pargoletta mia tenera prole,
      Al pianto i lumi dolorosi e tristi,
      Chiusi gli avessi eternamente al Sole;
      Deh quanto era il miglior, se, quando uscisti
      A trar vagiti in cambio di parole,
      Dato, pria che l'umor di questo seno,
      T'avessi di mia man mortal veneno.

78   Ma questo sen, di se medesmo avaro
      Troppo a torto ti fu, stolta ch'io fui,
      Che darti non devea, se già sì caro
      Gli era il tuo peso, ad allattare altrui.
      Ora al tuo vel, non men ch' amato amaro,
      Scarso non fia de' ministerii sui.
      Vo' che con larga usura al figlio essangue
      Quanto negò di latte or dia di sangue—.

79   A queste note intenerissi alquanto
      Di quel rigido cor l'asprezza alpina.
      Pietate il punse, e se ne trasse il pianto,
      Affetto novo a l'anima ferina.
      Snudato ella un coltel che sotto il manto
      Vestiva, al cinto appesa, aurea guaina,
      Ferì se stessa, e cadde in su la porta
      Smorta in un punto e tramortita e morta.

80   Non ebbe allor la feminil famiglia
      Tempo da ritener l'irata mano.
      Erode stesso con bagnate ciglia
      Ratto vi corse e la soccorse in vano.
      Di dolor, di stupor, di meraviglia
      Tremò, gelò, quasi insensato, insano.
      Al rigore, al pallor statua rassembra:
      Già di sasso ebbe il core, or n'ha le membra.

77   "Woe! It were better, little son of mine,
If—the day you first opened your sad eyes,
Filled with pain—you had then, and for all time,
Closed them again to the heavens' bright light.
Woe! When you first made weak and halting signs
Of speech—not yet true words, but only cries—
Instead of giving you milk from my breast
I should have fed poison to make you rest.

78   "But no, my breasts were too tight and too mean,
I was wrong and a fool beyond compare.
Even though you were yet unweaned,
I placed you in another's care.
My breast will not stint, nor will it be seen
To refuse my dear child his due share.
Now, let it pay, with the interest accrued,
In blood all the milk it denied to you."

79   At these words, the tyrant's cold heart of stone
Melted somewhat. For the first time ever,
Mercy moved in him—a feeling unknown.
He shed a tear! Before, there was never
Even a sign pity dwelt in his bones.
It was too little too late, however;
His wife drew a knife from under her gown,
Thrust it in her heart, and fell dead to the ground.

80   The other women had no time to forbid
The motion she made with her enraged fist.
Indeed, Herod himself, with dew-soaked lids
Rushed over to grab the queen by the wrist.
The attempt was in vain; no good it did.
On both royal faces, the sharp pain twists
Its blade, and the cold dwelling in his breast
Spreads its chill over the body at rest.

81   Barbaro re, re folle, or che diresti?
Vedi quanto è fallace uman consiglio.
Trovi a punto colà, dove credesti
Trovar lo scampo, il tuo mortal periglio.
Il figlio e 'l regno assicurar volesti,
Ecco perdi in un punto il regno, e 'l figlio:
Tua sentenza in te cade, e da te stesso
Fu punito l'error pria che commesso.

82   Come membro talor tronco repente
O da ferro crudel trafitto al vivo,
Non già subito fuor manda corrente
Il sangue ancor smarrito e fuggitivo;
Ma tosto poi che si risente, e sente
L'offesa e 'l duol, versa vermiglio un rivo,
E, quasi onda da fonte, apre la vena
Fuor per la piaga a la sanguigna piena;

83   Così, tardi riscosso il rio tiranno,
Cui l'improviso duol la lingua strinse,
Poi che diè loco al dilatato affanno
Ruppe i silenzii e i gemiti distinse;
E, da gli occhi rivolti al proprio danno,
Quasi sangue de l'alma, il pianto spinse,
E cadde là dove la moglie e 'l figlio
Parean scogli di marmo in mar vermiglio.

84   —Ecco a che fiera vista, occhi dolenti
(Che più state a serrarvi?), il Ciel vi serba;
Per dare il varco a i tepidi torrenti,
Forse aperti vi tien la doglia acerba.
Alessandro, Alessandro, ohimè, non senti,
Fior de l'anima mia reciso in erba?
Dori, Dori, non odi, e non rispondi?
Deh perché de' begli occhi il sol m'ascondi?

81   Barbarous king, madman, what can you say?
    See the deceit in the declarations
    Of your counselors. You have fallen prey
    To their false promises of salvation.
    You sought to make both your son and reign safe.
    Now all succumbs to disintegration.
    Your decree has come back to punish you
    Even before it has been carried through.

82   As an arm or leg, when struck by a blade,
    Even though it has been cut to the quick,
    Need not bring forth blood right away,
    For humors can run slow and stick:
    But after a moment, one feels the pain,
    And ruddy torrents gush fast and thick.
    Like a fountain that shoots waters in jets,
    The veins pump; ever fuller the wound gets—

83   Then it bursts. So was the king affected.
    In unforeseen grief he opens his mouth,
    Admitting feelings he has rejected,
    Breaking the anguished silence, he screams out;
    Seeing the ills that he has inflicted
    On those nearest, dearest to his own soul,
    He falls down where his wife and son lie dead
    Like two marble cliffs in a sea of red.

84   "Look upon the cruel scene, my blighted eyes,
    That the skies above have reserved for you.
    The bitter tears that are clouding my sight
    Now hold you open so that you may view
    My son, Alexander, whose corpse there lies.
    Woe is me, his limbs are scattered and strewn.
    Doris, dear spouse, won't you speak, make a sound?
    Why hide your gaze in the dirt on the ground?

85   Misero, quale in prima e qual dapoi
Pianger degg'io? Te figlio, o te consorte?
Te spenta in sul fervor de gli anni tuoi?
O te, morto al natal, nato a la morte?
Piangerò, lasso me, me stesso in voi,
Piangerò 'l proprio mal ne l'altrui sorte.
Dunque del mio diadema il lucid'ostro
Sarà, figlio e consorte, il sangue vostro?

86   O, di quanto crudel, misero e mesto
Padre, mal nato figlio e sotto avara
Stella concetto, è questo il trono? è questo
Lo scettro imperial, ch'ei ti prepara?
O che apparecchio tragico e funesto:
Il letto marital cangiato in bara,
Le faci, ond'onorar, dopo qualch'anno,
Le tue nozze sperai, l'essequie avranno.

87   Forsennato mio senno, e qual ciò volse
O tuo fallo, o mio fato? E come avenne?
Sconsigliato consiglio; e chi mi tolse
La mente e come cieca ella divenne,
Sì che te sol, quando l'editto sciolse,
Al gran rischio sottrar non le sovenne:
Ma fu vostro tenor, luci rubelle,
Fiamme inique del Ciel, perfide stelle.

88   Anzi fu pur vostr'opra, empie, infernali
Furie stimulatrici; anzi commisi
Sol io l'alto misfatto, io de' miei mali
Fui sol fabro nocente; ed io l'uccisi.
Da me l'onor de' fregi miei reali,
La mia vita di vita, ohimè, divisi,
Che dovea meco e dopo me del regno
E de la regia stirpe esser sostegno.

85   "Wretch that I am, I do not know which one
      I should mourn first. Is it you, my heir,
      Or you, my wife? My poor spouse undone
      In the best years of her life—lies there
      With her son who never saw the Sun!
      You show me my ills beyond compare:
      All that is left to me of kingdom and crown
      Are your bloody remains down on the ground!

86   "Unlucky child of cruel and sad father,
      Under ill-omened star were you conceived!
      Is this the throne and is this the scepter
      That I once prepared for you to receive?
      What a tragic scene here now is offered:
      The nuptial bed turned funeral bier,
      Torches meant to light your way as a groom
      One day, accompany you to the tomb.

87   "Insane mind of mine, how did it occur—
      Was it your fault? Was it simply my fate?
      True, bad advice acted as a spur,
      And I should not have taken the bait,
      Yet how could it be that I failed to make sure
      That my own child was resting somewhere safe?
      It was you that did it, treacherous lights,
      —Deceitful stars, unjust flames of the night!

88   "Wicked and infernal goads, it was you.
      You did it—yet I performed the crime;
      But was it I alone who saw it through?
      No, yes—either way, the killer am I.
      The royal trunk can never be renewed;
      Woe, I have cut my own life from the vine.
      My son was supposed to rule at my side,
      Inherit the crown, continue the line.

89   Or qual vendetta e qual, figlio infelice,
      Figlio infelice d'infelice madre,
      Che basti ad appagar sua rabbia ultrice,
      Ti pagherà lo sventurato padre?
      Non la maligna e perfida nodrice,
      Non de' miei danni le ministre squadre,
      Non, s'anco a l'ombra tua mi sia concesso
      Col regno mio sacrificar me stesso.

90   Re più dirmi non vo', padre non deggio,
      Padre e re, se non fui, m'appello a torto.
      Fui mostro infame, infernal furia e peggio;
      Indegno er'io di te poi che t'ho morto.
      Ahi quanto, or che del mal tardi m'aveggio,
      A gli uccisi fanciulli invidia porto!
      E ben oggi dovrebbe in me fornita
      Esser, come la gioia anco la vita.

91   Potessi almen quell'animette ignude
      Ch'io spogliai dianzi, or rivestir di velo
      Per di novo spogliarle: ed a le crude
      Fere espor le lor membra, al vento, al gelo.
      E se pietoso il Ciel l'accoglie e chiude,
      Per sempre essiliarle anco dal Cielo,
      Che poco fora al mio dolor profondo;
      E chiamassemi poi crudele il mondo.

92   Ahi chi mi reca in man la fiera spada,
      Che troncò le mie gioie, accioché sotto
      L'armi, onde cadde il figlio, il padre cada,
      Né resti intero un fil, se l'altro è rotto?—
      Così doleasi e 'ntanto ogni contrada
      Piangea l'alto esterminio al fin condotto.
      Ma già i felici spiriti immortali
      Ver l'Elisia magion spiegavon l'ali.

89   "How to avenge you, my poor boy, my poor son,
       Child of a most unfortunate mother?
       Can your father atone? What he has done
       Is a crime that no one else can pay for.
       Your murd'rous nurse is not the guilty one,
       Nor even those who performed my orders.
       It is not enough if, besides my land,
       I sacrifice my life with my own hand!

90   "The title of king I do not deserve,
       Nor is 'father' an appropriate name.
       Foul monster, fury of Hell, and still worse
       Am I, for I alone merit all blame.
       How much envy my soul, cruel and perverse,
       Harbors for all the children I have slain.
       Today, I have lost all joy forever,
       And so, let joy and life leave me together.

91   "If only I could clothe once more with life
       The tiny souls I did shear and despoil,
       And strip them once again with the knife,
       Hang out their limbs to twist and coil!
       Though Heaven already clasps them tight,
       Yet I'd wrest them from their gentle folds . . .
       It means nothing at all in my great pain,
       Nothing! Let me not be called cruel in vain!

92   "Woe, who will place the proud sword in my hand,
       Which has cut short my joy? Where the son fell,
       Let the father fall, too. Torn is the band
       Of the one; let the other's tear, as well."
       Thus he lamented, as over the land,
       The air filled with wails, shrieks, and yells
       The blessèd spirits take wing amidst the roar:
       To Elysian mansions the Innocents soar.

93 Sì come là per entro i folti orrori
  De' boschi ombrosi in su sereni estivi,
  Vacillando con tremoli splendori
  Volanti animaletti e fuggitivi
  Sembrano, a' peregrini ed a' pastori,
  Animate faville, atomi vivi,
  Onde dal lume mobile e mentito
  Il seguace fanciul spesso è schernito;

94 O com' api sollecite ed industri
  Per l'odorate d'Ibla aure novelle
  Nel vago April, fra rose e fra ligustri,
  Vanno a libar queste dolcezze e quelle,
  Onde fan poscia, architetrici illustri,
  Nobil lavor di ben composte celle,
  Moli ingegnosi e fabriche soavi
  Di bianche cere e di odorati favi:

95 Così da' veli lor, tutte contente,
  Sen gian quelle beate anime sciolte,
  E fu chi le mirò visibilmente,
  In un bel nembo di fiammelle avolte,
  Incoronate di diadema ardente,
  In lieto groppo, in vaga schiera accolte,
  Fatto di se medesme un cerchio grande,
  Agitar balli ed intrecciar ghirlande.

96 Sparver turbini e nubi e il Ciel sereno
  Con chiare stelle a i lor trionfi arrise;
  Austro e seco Aquilon, con l'ali a freno,
  Sì vaghe danze a vagheggiar s'assise;
  Con festevoli plausi, a l'aria in seno,
  Scherzar l'aure e gli augelli in mille guise;
  Colse l'Aurora le sanguigne brine
  E ne fe' gemme al seno e rose al crine.

93   As in the darkness, leafy and dense,
Of a shadowy grove on summer's eve,
There are sparkling, slight, and tremulous
Little creatures that float on the breeze,
Which seem, to the shepherd's untutored sense,
To be flames that live and fires that breathe.
One sees the wandering light dart and flit
And often children try, in vain, to grab it—

94   Or as the busy and dutiful bees
In Hybla fly through the perfumed air
In warm April, among roses and trees,
Gathering sweet nectar here and there,
Which their artisans make by degrees
Into complex cells deep in their lair—
A structure of ingenious design
Worked in fine wax and honeycombed lines—

95   Thus, happy in their garb airy and light
The blessèd souls now took flight heavenward.
They seemed a cloud of flames on that night
As they steered their course upward and soared;
Crowned in diadems fiery and bright,
And gathered in cheerful accord,
They performed dances in vast circling rings,
Weaving great garlands of stars with their wings.

96   The clouds and mist vanished. The serene sky
Twinkled and smiled at the procession.
The winds halted their gusts, stood to the side,
And paid the gay dance full attention.
The breezes and birds expressed their delight
By playfully flying among them.
When bathed in the dawn's luminous pools,
Stains of blood changed to roses and jewels.

97 Riser gl'abissi e la prigion di Morte,
  Che de gli antichi eroi l'ombre chiudea.
  Le tenebrose sue serrate porte
  Indorate a quei lampi intanto avea.
  Quivi il real poeta, il pastor forte,
  Che fanciul rintuzzò l'ira Getea,
  Posata allor di Lete in su la sponda
  Con la cetra e lo scettro avea la fionda,

98 E i negri prati de l'opaca riva,
  Ne' cui sterili rami i mesti augelli
  Ammutiscon mai sempre, impoveriva,
  Per trecciarsene il crin, di fior novelli;
  Quando per l'aria, d'ogni lume priva,
  Gli ferir gli occhi i lucidi drappelli,
  Prese egli il plettro, indi 'l furor concetto
  Con sì fatta canzon versò dal petto:

99 —Liete, liete novelle, ecco i messaggi
  De la celeste a noi luce promessa:
  Vedete i puri e i vermiglietti raggi
  Precursori del dì ch'a noi s'appressa;
  Tosto termine avran gli antichi oltraggi,
  Tosto ne fia la libertà concessa.
  Già spunta il Sol, che le nostr' ombre indora;
  Chinianci tutti a salutar l'aurora.

100 Pace a voi, gloria a voi, voi pur giungeste
  De la sperata al fin cara salute,
  Sospirati corrier. Ma che son queste?
  Queste che son sì strane aspre ferute?
  E chi segò le gole e chi le teste,
  Ohimè, trafisse di punture acute?
  Ahi qual petto, ahi qual cor fu duro al pianto!
  Ahi qual mano, ahi qual ferro ardí cotanto!

97   The Abyss itself laughed, the house of the dead,
Where dwell the shades of ancient heroes.
Its iron gates, which inspire such dread,
Now darted with light's golden arrows.
Here, the poet-king, the mighty shepherd,
Who, still a lad, struck down the overbold
Giant, had laid his harp, his staff, and his sling
By the stream which quiet oblivion brings.

98   On the black fields by the cloudy river,
The sad birds roost on boughs of sterile gloom,
Never singing. Here King David gathered
Flowers, to fashion a wreath of their bloom,
When, in the air, a spiraling ladder
—A bright chain of light—came into his view.
He takes his ancient harp from where it rests
And pours a new song out from his breast:

99   "Happy and gladsome tidings, hark the word!
Into the soft celestial light, go
Forth; for now is fulfilled what once I heard:
The promise made long, long ago.
Justice no longer will be deferred,
Soon, for us, gentle freedom will grow.
Already, the Sun has gilded our shadows
Let us kneel before the dawn so hallowed.

100   "Peace unto you, and glory be,
You have found salvation.
But little couriers, what do I see?
Whence your sore laceration?
Who is it that inflicted wounds so deep,
Caused your poor desecration?
Tiny bodies mutilated and maimed
—Who or what did this, and in whose name?

101   E voi, chi tenne voi dentro voi stesse,
Rovinose procelle, allor ristrette?
Venti, chi v'affrenò? Chi vi ripresse
Da l'usato rigor, nembi e saette?
Sì ch'impunita l'opra ir ne devesse
Dal giustissimo Dio de le vendette?
L'opra, da far, tra l'ira e l'odio eterno,
Stupir le Furie e vergognar l'Inferno.

102   O sacri, o santi, o cari, o benedetti
Martiri trionfanti, invitti eroi,
Invitti eroi, dal sommo duce eletti,
A morir pria per lui ch'egli per voi;
Colti da dura men pomi acerbetti,
Imtempestivi fior de gli orti suoi,
Del proprio sangue ruggiadose e nate
Tra le spine del duol, rose odorate.

103   Teneri gigli e gelsomini intatti,
E di purpureo nettare conditi
A i giardini di Dio serbati, e fatti
Per arrichir gli eterni alti conviti;
Rami a forza schiantati, a forza tratti
Dal tronco genital che v'ha nodriti;
Piccioli e rotti sassi, ove la santa
Chiesa novella i fondamenti pianta.

104   Verginelli che 'n fronte, a noi dolenti,
Il nome Redentor scritto portate,
Semplici pecorelle ed innocenti,
Candidette colombe immaculate,
Olocausti purgati, ostie lucenti,
Nel proprio sangue e de l'Agnel lavate,
Vittime prime e da rio ferro aperte,
Al Re de' Santi in sacrificio offerte.

101   "Gusting winds, why do you hold yourselves back,
        Why do you now rein in your gales?
        What makes you stand so still and so slack?
        Why do thunder and lightning not assail
        The blackguard who performed these acts?
        Should, then, no punishment avail?
        God of retribution, vengeance, and flame,
        Such outrage makes Hell itself blush in shame.

102   "O sacred, holy, dear, blessèd martyrs,
        Unconquered heroes and chosen few,
        Ones elected by the highest leader
        To die even before he dies for you.
        You were harvested by a cruel reaper,
        Who are innocent, unripened fruit;
        Made crimson by your own blood, you were born
        Like fragrant roses between piercing thorns.

103   "You tender lilies, O jasmines perfect,
        Vessels carrying bright nectar of red,
        For God's garden you are selected—
        To join the table and sit at the head;
        Boughs and branches disconnected,
        Grow strong again from the rich soil's bed.
        Now, in you, a new Church takes root
        It rises and sends forth blossoms and shoots.

104   "Tiny innocents, who bear the name
        Of our Redeemer inscribed on your brow,
        Gentle lambs, doves without blame,
        Immaculate victims—you, who now
        Shine bright in your own blood's flame,
        Washed by angels who kneel and bow,
        Pure offerings from a guilty blade,
        Holiest sacrifice to Heaven made,

105   Venite, illustri spirti, anime belle,
Venite, felicissimi bambini,
Fresche a recarne omai certe novelle
De gli aspettati giubili vicini.
O stille, o sangue: o stille no, ma stelle;
O sangue no, ma porpore e rubini,
Gemme degne di far ricca e pomposa
La corona di Cristo e de la Sposa.

106   Piaghe felici, anzi sugelli e segni
Del sofferto martir vivi e veraci,
E di gloria e d'onor securi pegni,
E di grazia e d'amor lingue loquaci,
Or chi sarà, che voi ricusi e sdegni
Lavar co' pianti ed asciugar co' baci?
E chi fia che non bea sì dolci umori
In coppa di pietà smembrati Amori?

107   De gli spruzzi desia del sangue vostro,
In vece de' suoi lumi, il Ciel fregiarsi.
Torrebbe volontier, di sì fin ostro,
La Luna il volto candido macchiarsi.
In sì chiaro ruscel, nel sommo chiostro,
Braman le stelle e gli Angeli specchiarsi.
In sì bel mare ambizioso vole
Imporporarsi ed attuffarsi il Sole.

108   O carissimi gemiti e sospiri,
Lacrimette soavi e lusinghere,
Dal cui stridor, de' lor canori giri
L'alto concento imparano le sfere;
O dolcissimo duol, da' cui martiri
Tutte le gioie sue tragge il piacere;
O bellissima morte e ben gradita,
Cui di pregio e d'onor cede la vita!

105   "Come, illustrious spirits, beautiful souls,
        Come, you most fortunate children,
        And bring us, from the heavenly scrolls,
        News for rejoicing and jubilation.
        What wounds and what blood is it I see—no,
        Stars and rubies are your decorations!
        Treasures more splend'rous than those of the Earth,
        Fit to crown Christ—and his bride, the Church.

106   "Happy injuries, like signets and seals
        Of martyrdom suffered; living and true,
        You guarantee honor and glory,
        As tongues speaking of love and grace, too.
        Who, who would not wash you with tears,
        And then with his kisses dry you?
        Who is there who would not drink the sweet nectar up
        If your cherubic wounds were poured into a cup?

107   "The sky above would fain illustrate
        Itself with your blood instead of its lights;
        Gladly the Moon would stain its pale face
        With the darkness of your red so bright.
        Its pure stream, in Heaven's highest place,
        The stars and angels behold in delight.
        Even the Sun rushes in a hurried motion
        To draw its deepest blush from your ocean.

108   "O you who are the dearest sobs and sighs,
        You smooth tears, graceful threnody,
        From whose sound, far up in the skies,
        The spheres have learned their harmony!
        O sweetest of pains, there on high,
        From you joy derives its ecstasy!
        O death light and beautiful, to whom
        Life itself cedes honor and room!

109 Deh quanti in Ciel v'ha preparati e quali,
   Spiritelli amorosi, alme leggiadre,
   Nel campidoglio empireo archi immortali,
   Chiare palme e corone il sommo Padre!
   E qual gloria magior? Forze infernali
   Domar, vincer re forte e armate squadre,
   Disarmati campion, nudi guerrieri
   Fatti del Figlio in un scudi e scudieri.

110 Tosto colà ne la stellata corte,
   Dove chi vi mandò trionfa e regna,
   Ciascun di voi, de gli Angeli consorte,
   Spoglia di sua vittoria avrà ben degna.
   Quivi de l'Innocenza e de la Morte
   Spiegar la bianca e la purpurea insegna
   Vedrenvi, e, per trofeo, fra quelle schiere
   Far de le rotte fascie alte bandiere.

111 O ne' tormenti ancor felice stuolo,
   Che più che sangue assai latte spargesti,
   Ti fu principio e fine un giorno solo,
   Nel primo dì l'ultima notte avesti.
   Ti convenne provar la morte e 'l duolo
   Quando la morte e 'l duol non conoscesti;
   E con lacere vele il legno assorto
   A pena entrato in mar, portasti in porto.

112 Noi, noi, dir poi potrete, atleti inermi
   Caduti in lutta, in grembo a Dio n'alzammo;
   Noi, de la Lattea Via lattanti germi,
   D'orme sanguigne il bel candor segnammo;
   Noi co' piedi, beati anzi che fermi,
   Anzi le sfere che 'l terren calcammo;
   Noi del tenero sciolto e picciol velo
   Abbiam prima che 'l Sol veduto il Cielo—.

109   "Lovely souls, spirits ethereal,
      How many arches of triumph and crowns
      Has our great Father imperial
      Made for you on high Empyrean ground!
      You recall glory immemorial:
      Hell and its legions are beaten down:
      Its haughty king and his minions must all yield
      To unarmed babes bearing the Son as their shield.

110   "High above, in the celestial court,
      Where Victory has brought you and rules,
      Each of you, from the angelic cohort,
      Will, in turn, receive triumph's due.
      There, in white and in red, to escort
      The innocent dead, will be viewed,
      As a trophy won in the battle below
      A banner made out of swaddling clothes.

111   "Happy throng, even in torment,
      Who spilled more blood than milk was nursed,
      One day, for you, was beginning and end;
      Your last night was also your first.
      Death and pain you experienced
      Before you knew either one's curse.
      And even though your journey was cut short,
      Still it is true that your ship reached the port.

112   "'Unarmed champions,' you can say, 'are we,
      Who are risen again in God's bosom.
      High above in the Milky Way, indeed
      Upon the skies themselves we have written
      Red signs by the step of our tender feet
      (Which yet we could barely stand on).
      We were taken ere our lives had begun
      And saw Heaven before we saw the Sun.'"

113   Così cantava, e da le candide alme
Fur le sue voci e l'ombre a un punto rotte.
Levaro i vecchi padri al Ciel le palme
Sperando il fin di così lunga notte;
E de' cari bambin le lievi salme
Gian per l'orror di quell'ombrose grotte
Portando in braccio, e ne' lor volti santi
Iteravano a prova i baci e i pianti.

113   Thus did he sing until his voice ran dry,
When the souls shone forth, full and bright.
The patriarchs raised their hands to the sky
Awaiting the end of the endless night;
Their arms held the babes' frail remains inside,
As they walked in the dark caverns that sighed.
They wept with visages holy and worn,
Kissing the dear dead, they sobbed and they mourned.

Erik Butler has written widely on the archeology of modernity and translated numerous works of philosophy and literary criticism. His books include two cultural histories of the undead—most recently, *The Rise of the Vampire* (2013).

Wakefield Subverse